BARCODE TWO

D0357887

2 0 FEB 2013

C00 12235334

EDINBURGH CITY LIBRARIES

2 0 FEB 2013 6/3

ONE DAY AS A TIGER

Clever young historian Martin Hawkins throws over his promising career at Trinity and returns to the family sheep-farm in Tipperary to brood on his own past instead. Hostile to the people around him, at odds with his conscientious brother Pierce and furtively in love with Pierce's restive wife, Etti, he harbours strange convictions about the lamb he calls Missy.

Missy is one of a flock that has been 'improved' with human genes. Pitiful, infinitely touching, and surely unsheep-like, with eyes that seem to ask very human questions about love and loyalty, Missy figures significantly in Martin's imagination. When Etti too comes to regard Missy with the same tenderness and empathy, she and Martin embark on a reckless and terrible adventure.

Anne Haverty's first novel is a tour-de-force. A brilliant evocation of rural life, with its moments of beauty and passages of despair, *One Day as a Tiger* is a tragicomedy about the mistakes we make, the damage we bring about unknowingly, and the dangers of ennui and pity. Beautifully written, with a subtle humour that cuts through the tragic pull of the story, this novel heralds the arrival of a very important new voice in fiction.

ANNE HAVERTY was born in Tipperary and now lives in Dublin. She has published a biography of Constance Markievicz and also writes poetry and film.

BY THE SAME AUTHOR

Constance Markievicz

The author wishes to acknowledge the financial assistance of the Arts Council of Ireland in the completion of this book.

ONE DAY AS A TIGER

Anne Haverty

HW

Chatto & Windus
LONDON

First published in 1997

1 3 5 7 9 10 8 6 4 2
Copyright © Anne Haverty 1997

Anne Haverty has asserted her right under the Copyright,
Designs and Patents Act, 1988 to be identified as the author
of this work

First published in Great Britain in 1997 by
Chatto & Windus Limited
Random House, 20 Vauxhall Bridge Road,
London SW1V 2SA

Random House Australia (Pty) Limited
20 Alfred Street, Milsons Point, Sydney
New South Wales 2061, Australia

Random House New Zealand Limited
18 Poland Road, Glenfield
Auckland 10, New Zealand

Random House South Africa (Pty) Limited
Endulini, 5A Jubilee Road, Parktown 2193, South Africa

Random House UK Limited Reg. No. 954009

All rights reserved. No part of this publication may be
reproduced, stored in a retrieval system, or transmitted in
any form, or by any means, electronic, mechanical,
photocopying, recording or otherwise, without the prior
permission of the publisher.

Papers used by Random House UK Limited are natural, recyclable
products made from wood grown in sustainable forests. The
manufacturing processes conform to the environmental
regulations of the country of origin

A CIP catalogue record for this book
is available from the British Library

ISBN 0 7011 6628 2

Printed in Great Britain by
Mackays of Chatham, PLC, Chatham, Kent

EDIN. | AC C0012235336 | CL F LIT
HW — GIFT

For A

It is better to have lived one day as a tiger
than a thousand years as a sheep.

Tibetan proverb

1

I USED TO BE quite a normal fellow. I was never a chap who needed much explaining. And yet the most crucial acts of my life defy any reasonable explanation – defy it, yet cry out for it. After all, you cannot ruin people's lives without attempting to explain why and how you did.

A couple of years ago everyone in Fansha knew all there was to know about me. I was Pierce Hawkins's younger brother, the smart fellow who was going on to be a professor up in Trinity College, Dublin. In the history department in Trinity they might not have put it quite like that but the gist would have been the same. I was Dr Williams's – Harvey's – favourite, a young historian who had shown signs of brilliance and, if he played his cards right, had a brilliant career ahead of him.

Then there set in what you could call my madness – or maybe the word 'folly' is more accurate since I had my own excuses, inadequate though they may have been. Anyway, it was when the white candles on the blooming chestnut trees in Front Square were pristine and upright that I found I could not endure my life any longer and came back to Fansha once and for all. When I could not bear anymore the thought of the flowering chestnut in the middle of the long field, and the pink hawthorn and the white hawthorn of Fansha and the green fields carpeted with buttercups an incredible yellow; the pomp of a summer to come going on without me.

1

Up at Trinity they were appalled, and strident in the expression of their appalledness.

'I am appalled,' Harvey declared, 'at this decision. Mr Hawkins, I must tell you plainly, I am appalled.'

The 'Mr Hawkins' unnerved me. To Harvey, for several years past – how many? – three or four anyway – I had been Martin. After those first undergraduate years of mutual familiarisation, getting the measure of each other, I was no longer, with professorial condescension, Mr Hawkins, but Martin. The bright amenable student with just the right mix of originality and cynicism. His right-hand man, selected after long observation and groomed from then on to assist him in his research into nineteenth-century agrarian policy, in line for a graduate post and in due course a Fellowship. Harvey was ambitious for me. Or at least in his ambitions for himself I was included; even, with time and as our work enmeshed, essential.

Harvey's reversion to 'Mr Hawkins' in this exchange expressed of course his outrage; but also, I knew, with a new sensation of delinquent independence, his recognition of me as an adult, a newly formidable fellow with a mind of his own. His 'Mr Hawkins' was a gesture of respect, of appeal man to man.

And yet, no longer Martin, I felt a great loneliness descend upon me as I cast off from our coolly uncommunicative but implicitly intimate circle. The circle in which I knew who I was and where I stood and who Harvey was and how we all fitted in together, himself and myself and the others, students and staff, friendly satellites by and large in orbit around us. The classical walls of Trinity encircling our world within, our charmed lives of complacency; the city and its people outside a picturesque and remote backdrop, their minds unilluminated with radical perceptions on Victorian agriculture and so of no possible interest.

2

As far as Harvey could see, I was electing to join them in their darkness. Adult I may well have been. But a pitiable one who had made a foolhardy, not to say insane, decision. Sure, I was the first to see that, from any point of view apart from my own, my decision was insane.

His appeal, however, cut no ice with my resolve. As a recognition of our new relationship, I heard myself call him Dr Williams in our few remaining exchanges on the couple of afternoons that I went in to clear out my desk. There was an awful lot of paper. This was what my life amounted to in the end – a great heap of paper. I dumped it in a corner in boxes labelled 'Research Notes H. Williams'. I don't suppose he ever gave me any credit; I never saw his book. I did leave him in the lurch, right in the middle of things. Apart from the events of the last year, I have been ever since a solitary individual. Marty Hawkins, the unfrocked eremite of Fansha.

Pierce was sorry. He expressed his sorrow for me, he told me how sorry he was that I was unhappy up at Trinity. He had no wish to be at Trinity himself, but he liked having me there, he liked being proud of me. He liked the appropriateness of our futures, he a flourishing farmer, me his successful younger brother in the groves of academe, adding in future years some modest illustriousness to the name he would carry on. He liked things to be safe and categorised. Foilmore would be his and my fine career would be mine.

I know he regretted my failed career. Deeply. But I also know he used to say to relations or to anyone around who enquired – 'Martin? Oh, he went up to Trinity. But he came down out of it again.'

Dismissively. Implying with this country locution that the place wasn't good enough for me. This illustrates Pierce's sense of loyalty, though I can claim in my arrogant fashion that it was in a way true. It wasn't good enough. But Pierce

3

couldn't be expected to see that. He didn't see it. He took it on trust however or pretended to, stoutly. This was typical of Pierce. He always let on to understand me, to accept my own proud estimate of myself. Sometimes I think that I existed purely for this one malicious purpose, to test Pierce. To test the grandeur and nobility of his character, to allow him to emerge from the crucible of the consequences of my failure and my inadequacies finer than ever.

'There are no flies on Pierce.'

That was what they used to say about Pierce, respectfully, the people around. This astonished me, when I could see that my brother was riddled with flies. Where I was concerned, anyway.

I am a flawed character. Riddled with flaws. One small virtue in my favour however may be that I do not regard my own self with any more importance than I regard others. Except for those who are dead. The dead have earned their self-importance, it seems to me, and an infinite pathos, and a life of form and brilliance even if there was nothing of apparent brilliance about their earthly life. This might be one of the emotive reasons why I abandoned history and threw up my university career. Who was I, living and deficient in sympathy and understanding, to rake through the bones of the dead?

This reaction in me is not fully consistent. It's not one I am always able to sustain either in principle or in practice. I am not, even if I give that impression, quite inhuman. There have been a few among the living to whom I have granted inordinate significance. But terrible things resulted from that.

2

O N A W A R M day last spring I was seated here in the middle
of the field under my chestnut, in the shade of its young
translucent leaves, observing my princedom. The fiercely
known panorama of Foilmore, our Hawkins fields, foamy
with the fine Hawkins flocks at their spring fattening,
replete with Pierce's husbandry and care. The scraggier
patches of the Delaney and Kilbride fiefdoms intruding here
and there with their sparser herds of cattle. My own little
glade, my own fair flocks – for Pierce was always generous
to me in his proprietorship – at their grazing.

Below, gleaming in the new light, the bright silvery roofs
of their winter quarters that I helped Pierce put up around
the time I came down. A fit of energy then, making myself
useful. The sagging mossy roofs of the older outhouses in the
farther distance. Raffles' shouts travelling across the fields
from the dosing shed. Pierce's jeep buzzing along the tarred
winding road, into town again for more supplements or medications or whatever they were dosing them with that week.
Prosperous, oddly arcadian, the smell of its diesel scenting the
air.

I was watching for Etti to come out into the yard. I knew
that the following day I would be close by her in the jeep all
the way up to Dublin and back. But this wasn't enough for
me, no siree.

I was waiting obstinately for her to come out squinting into
the light, unused to it. She might emerge to give the dogs their

5

dinner or the cats some milk. When at last she did come out she was empty-handed and the dogs jumped up and ran around her with already disappointed expectation and then lay down again, their heads between their paws. When she glanced up in my direction, I knew she had seen me because she quickly turned away. When she looked again, I waved and she returned my wave, too fervently, and went back inside. I could sense her irritation, her shyness about being observed.

Sometimes I would pull my cap down over my eyes, pretending to be heedless of her or maybe asleep, and I would watch her secretly and not wave at all. Then she might sit in contented mindlessness on the wall, a leg drawn up under her chin, in a pose of contemplation. Sometimes she would set off down towards Clegg and the river and until she disappeared between the clump of trees in the hollow, I watched her, her straight white legs moving without haste down the stony boreen into the shadows.

What a snug little world I had made. Love and deceit still wrapped in innocence, in safe uncertainty, suspended in our mild dispassionate midland sunlight.

That day it was sultry and close. The Kilbrides' chainsaw was purring in the distance, a drowsy summer sound. No two days ever quite the same of course, on the land. A little breeze maybe, blowing this way one day, the other way another, or a wind now from the north, then from the south. Any little shift can give a different look to a tree or a bush. Very little rain that month. It's the rainy days that are most the same, the most monotonous, the eyes tending downwards out of the wet, blinkered, so you have nothing to see.

That day, I observed Young Delaney coming across the fields to me. Young Delaney. This was Robert's name for Augie Delaney, that became a half-joke and settled on us.

6

Robert – have I mentioned Robert? Robert was my father. Anyway, Augie we call him to his face, Young Delaney.

To me, Young Delaney was as old as Fansha. Together, we walked home from Fansha National School every evening, wrestling and kicking each other at intervals. Except when it was cold or wet and my mother, Nancy, sent Robert down in the red Peugeot to convey us home and Young Delaney would sit up in the front seat making farmer's talk with our father. When that long child-time came to an end, Pierce and I went off as boarders to Rockwell while Young Delaney travelled in every day on the bus to the Brothers in town with the rest of them. And in due course I went farther still, up to Dublin and Trinity.

Young Delaney and Pierce were by nature closer. They spoke in the same Tipperary way, the long sonorous Rs, the slow but explosive delivery of some Tipperary-style quip. In Pierce's case, of course, a protective colouration, though put on with zest all the same.

'I do be often thinking . . .' Pierce would tell Young Delaney seriously in some discussion about grass-seed or fertiliser. He would never use such a quaint locution with me. And at Rockwell if he tried it on, he would be met with a supercilious raising of an eyebrow that would make him blush in his Piercey boyish way and there could be no question of a repeat attempt.

Pierce carried the manners of the locality, effortlessly and credibly, as a badge of identification with his milieu. Young Delaney and himself, they understood each other, born farmers the two of them. When I tried to assume the mantle, it didn't come off and the lads looked at me sideways as if to say, would you ever give over, Marty. A ham actor, not to be believed. But there was something I shared with Young Delaney. His brand of shiftiness wasn't mine but they were related.

7

I watched him now throw his long sturdy legs with agility over the final fence and walk up the field towards me, his hands in his pockets, his face screwed up in the sun, the lambs dancing and shying away from him and the ewes imperiously calling out megamegamega in alarm.

Still some way off, he called out, 'How'ya doin', Marty?'

Heartily, as a statement, not an interrogation. I made no response.

'Queer aul weather,' he said as he came up. 'I don't like it. Unseasonal.'

'I like it,' I said.

This kind of statement marks me out as an outsider, a dilettante. Personal likes and dislikes should not come into one's reactions, as a farmer, to such an important matter as the weather. A farmer approves of weather because it's seasonal, not because it's a thing of cheer or of solace.

'We can't complain I suppose,' he agreed, but grudgingly.

'Isn't it grand to see the lambs,' he went on, resuming his matey heartiness. 'How many of them have you now? Would you have the thousand?'

He can't resist that kind of enquiry though if I told him the exact number he'd only have contempt for me.

'Ah, we wouldn't,' I said. 'But thereabouts.'

Now if it were Pierce, with his candour of a baby, he'd tell him precisely how many, down to the last little fellow disporting himself in Clegg beyond the river. Young Delaney would nod grave and respectful assent and then in his own mind add on a few hundred more. Young Delaney would never reveal the real number of his stock and neither, he'd be sure, would Pierce. The real farmer is cute about these matters.

I stood up and offered him a cigarette and he took a deep appreciative pull out of it and the two of us exhaled in silence as we gazed over the sunlit pastoral scene. I waited for Young Delaney to speak. When he strolled over here, as he did on

8

occasion, it was not to talk to me about farming. Anything he wanted to know about farming, he would ask Pierce. Whatever interest I had for him was based on the fact that he couldn't fathom out what I was up to. I'm a Hawkins after all. Must be up to something. Something to do with Dublin and the books, he'd be convinced, something I'd be working away at on the quiet while I let on to be only putting down time.

He considered his cigarette nestled in the cup of his hand, taking deep significant drags, as if nursing some profundity in his head. Slowly, he unbuttoned his winter jacket, displaying his grey winter pullover inside it, so thick and matted that it had an invincible antique look to it, like armour. His thick red hair was matted too and dark with sweat.

'It's fierce warm all right,' he said.

Settling himself into the shade of my horse chestnut, he was able to rest his elbow in the fork of the lowest branch. I could not do that with comfort. He's a big fellow, Young Delaney.

'Did you hear the news?' he enquired.

'What news is that?'

My tone was neutral but I was on my guard. Whatever the news was, coming from Young Delaney who had traversed the fields to tell me, it was something to do with me and unlikely to be good.

'I thought you'd have heard. Caroline Quinlan.'

My chest lurched, but slightly only and briefly. To hear Caroline's name spoken could still have that effect. I recognised this, however, as a reflex action to a familiar stimulus rather than a response to overwrought feelings, the delusion of sensation an amputee feels, they say, in a long-severed limb. Indeed I was even aware of a vague sense of relief that the news was merely of Caroline.

'I hear she's engaged.'

I have enough country cuteness in me not to please Young

9

Delaney by refraining from expressing interest beyond a restrained 'Is that so?' in the Fansha mode. I stole a look at him all the same, willing him to say more. He took another smoke. He was developing, I noticed, an incipient manly stoutness.

'Who's the lucky fellow?' I was obliged to ask.

He was forthcoming enough.

'A dentist, I hear. From Dublin . . . We won't be seeing too much of her around here anymore I suppose.'

His tone as he said this was heavy and declamatory with a sighing note on the end of it. As if he was putting it up to me. As if one of the damsels of the tribe was being carried off by a hostile foreigner into a strange country and it was up to someone, preferably me, to bear her back into the lush bosom of her townland.

'We haven't seen too much of her of late,' I said. A disengaged and limp response, Young Delaney would find it.

Caroline always was one of those girls who was going to marry young. Could you still call her young? She's a year or two younger than me anyway. But Caroline, restless and struggling with convention, might see herself as not young. That would explain the dentist. A dentist would not be my choice for her, nor hers for herself possibly. But she would give it her best shot. As for me, when Caroline was married, my former life would finally be over and done with.

With his boot, Young Delaney ground his cigarette butt into the clean dusty earth beneath the tree. The rural vista resolved itself into a blankness of peace and abnegation of action, what I had come back for. Fields breed fatalism.

'There's always money in teeth,' he said.

This is a very Fansha kind of statement and demanded no response. But Young Delaney seemed to be put out by my reticence. I felt an invidious pleasure at that. He turned to go.

'Well. Some of us have work to do,' he said.

Whether this was a dig at the dentist or at myself I couldn't be sure.

'We do, Augie. We do,' I agreed.

'Will we be seeing you in Toby's tonight? You'll want a jar or two after your heavy day.'

This was always his parting shot, his warped form of friendliness.

'Hardly not tonight, Augie. We're off to Dublin in the morning. You know how it is. Things to do.'

Already he was making away. But, arrested, pivoting on one foot, back he came.

'Is that so now? Up for a bit of shopping is it?'

His ears were pricked, you could nearly say, like a gun-dog scenting a prey. The naïvety of his alertness was touching. I had to give him some satisfaction.

'Shopping. I suppose that could be one way of putting it. We're going up to buy a few sheep. A special breed, from the Institute. Genetically engineered, if you ever heard of that. Pierce was reading something about them in the *Irish Times*.'

'Genetically engineered.'

Young Delaney enunciated the words with a rich and lip-smacking appreciation.

'Honest to God, Marty, there are no flies on Pierce. So he's getting into the genetically engineered stock, is he? A great man for the experiment. Always on to try something new. You have to hand it to him.'

You'd have to hand it too to Young Delaney. Though firmly rejecting the new-fangled for himself, he could wholeheartedly admire the inclination in Pierce. And the way nothing passed him by. Genetic engineering had been an innovation more or less unknown to me until a few days before when Pierce had announced his plans and their purport. The lambing was safely accomplished. He had earned a day out above in Dublin. That, as far as I was concerned, was the gist of it. Now here however was Young Delaney apparently well acquainted with the concept. With the ins and outs of it, indeed as he would say himself.

3

I DID NOT INFORM Young Delaney that Pierce was going to pay out to the Institute twice the price we had ever paid for a dozen lambs. That was my canniness and Pierce's business.

When it came to the columns of the *Irish Times*, Pierce's gullibility was rampant. He had enormous faith in the *Irish Times*. Rooted as solidly in Fansha as my tree in Shelley's field, he had at the same time the wistfulness for urbanity of a man remote from the centre. He would drive up for it every morning to the Cross, like Robert used to drive to the creamery. The *Irish Times* was his substitute for Robert's chat with the lads among the milk-churns. In the evenings, he read it cover to cover.

In the mornings on his return from the cross, Etti would take the newspaper from him and, settled comfortably on the couch, she would frown over the Simplex crossword after an ardent and grave perusal of the Death Notices. Etti took a special interest in sudden deaths. From her couch, she would comment with great feeling on the dramas that might lie behind them. Whether the deceased was young, old, happy or unhappy. In her conjectures, she could become unusually animated.

'Oh Marty,' she would exclaim. 'Only twenty-nine. An only son. What do you think it was? Heart? He wasn't married. Poor fellow.'

At this she would blush. Fearing the remark was a little

13

close to the bone. Pierce and Etti did not expect me to marry. She would change the subject.

'Is it still raining? The dogs will be soaked. Don't let them in, Marty. Please.'

Subsiding then into the task of filling in the little squares.

4

THE NEWS ABOUT Caroline brought to me by Young Delaney cast my outing to Dublin in a new light. My trips to Dublin, where everything had ended so badly, were troubling and therefore rare. I would be compelled, for example, to pay a visit to Trinity and have a solitary drink in the Buttery as a kind of gesture of repossession. Alone among the mill of startlingly childish anonymous faces, I would feel like a shade, my forlornness inhabited by ghosts.

One of these spectral figures was Harvey, glimpsed once or twice in the distance. I retreated further into my shadowy corner to avoid him. The hallowed place by his side destined for me, and that I had deserted, had been filled by a fellow from Cambridge. Said to be very keen, Fintan, who liked to keep me informed, reported.

A phantom half-desired of materialisation was Caroline. But she never showed. Maybe the dentist was already keeping her from her old haunts. Forgetful of the passage of time, I would imagine her wrapped in the green duvet in her Rathmines flat getting through a lesser-known Flaubert slowly in French. I might experience a rash inclination to go out there, to Rathmines. And then I would remember that she had moved on; a teacher of French now, living surely in an apartment somewhere, somewhere aspirant like Ballsbridge.

Anyway, even if I did find her by some chance still in Rathmines, what would we say or do? The wish to see her was a residue of my old self, nothing more. Like an old dog leaping a wall out of habit, without enthusiasm.

I might skulk towards a payphone then and ring Fintan, only to find him as often as not away at a conference or his presence required for an important faculty lunch.

Young Delaney's news freed me from my neurotic compulsion to make my aimless pilgrimage across the cobblestones. I could turn my back finally on the place. If I were the man I once thought I was shaping up to be, I'd have let Pierce go on his own to the Institute for his sheep while I searched the city for Caroline to wrest her from the dentist's arms. But I was not that man. I would pass the day with Pierce. And Etti. A shiftless brother who had deserted his own calling.

5

I SET THE ALARM and arrived up at the house in good time, as arranged, for the fried breakfast. This too had been Nancy and Robert's custom on a day out, the big breakfast. To sustain one for the arduous stresses ahead of being abroad in the world. They seemed to me to be sitting there at table with us, invisibly approving. They seemed to me to be often there. I used to wonder if Pierce sensed them there as well. I never got round to asking him.

Pierce was busy at the grill turning sausages, Etti ironing a smart yellow summery dress for her day in the city. The archetypal homey atmosphere of laundered clothes and fry, domestic harmony, a proper family again. To all appearances. But of the three of us, only Pierce fitted the bill. Husband, farmer, frater . . . He had picked the wrong brother, however, and the wrong girl for a wife. That was Pierce's flaw. In my case, at least, he had no choice. He was landed with me as a burden on his birthright. But he did pick out Etti, out of all the girls he could have picked. Maybe she represented the hidden wrong-headedness in him, an obscure tendency to self-destruction.

I was anxious for Etti. I feared she would be cold in her light butter-coloured dress. The wind had shifted to the north. With the icy glare of Arctic winds, it brought the harsh clarity of sunlight with it, refracted through scudding dusky clouds, revealing the coarse grain of the stone of the sheds, the life-

17

thrust of the weeds sprouting with their vulgar, random eagerness.

Pierce went out for a last-minute check-in with Raffles.

'You'll need a coat, Etti,' I suggested diffidently. It was not my place, to remind her of her coat. But I knew Etti could not be depended on to think of practical matters.

'I'm not an eejit, Marty,' she said.

I remember the smile she flashed me.

In the jeep, I sat in the back, watching the landscape I had thrown up my life for rush past. The Gillespies' new bungalow, McCarthy's neo-Edwardian monstrosity that's the envy of the neighbours. Luttrell's, falling in. No change there, at least. It's always changing, this place. Even since I first went up to Trinity with Robert at the wheel, old landmarks have gone, new ones sprung up. Old Mick Allen who still drove the horse and cart then replaced by a goer of a nephew who came back from the States and drives two tractors. Allen's sheep were munching turnips in a few acres of brown field.

I was born into change. Old houses falling down beside new ones, brash concrete structures rising up in farmyards, new machines appearing daily on the roads. Loads of money one year, little of it the next. In the country, nothing stays the same.

I sat in the back, keeping an eye on the trailer careering along behind. Even with a trailer, Pierce wouldn't modify his violent style of driving one bit. With his slow movements and his size 38 waist, you might not think it; but Pierce was a man of action. And his shyness, the way he would blink shyly behind the golden lock that hung over his left eye. The lock creeping seductively down his forehead that Nancy was so fond of. But it was his stature Etti fell for, his country stature, not his yellow ringlet. She's a town girl, from the wrongish

18

side of town. Pierce must have seemed so solid to Etti, so comfortable and safe.

His posture in the front, heavy and slack but attentive; hers upright and slight but dreamy. They might have been Nancy and Robert and I their boy. I had after all delivered myself into their hands.

When I travelled with Etti and Pierce, there was not the same conjugal murmur of voices from the front as from Ma and Da. They did not talk much, as far as I could see, Etti and Pierce. I took a furtive satisfaction in that. But Nancy and Robert were of a generation that talked incessantly. Or they just had more to say to each other, those two. Choosing the soothing out-of-time hours in the car to talk about the past, they discussed friends and relations. Whose son had got the good Leaving; would Paddy or Mick ever marry now; whose hair was turning grey.

'Philly has got very grey,' Nancy would remark. Complacently, because her own hair was fair and lustrous as always. Who was expecting their seventh . . . 'Hmm, a bit Catholic of them,' Nancy would say, ironically, and Robert would look sideways at her appreciatively and laugh. Who had taken to the drink, whose face had a strong tint of red, showing the signs . . . Mythical figures to me, people they knew long before they knew me, whom I had never met or had met once and forgotten.

Robert drove the red Peugeot then. The farmer's car, that, disconcertingly for the kind of boy I was, showed up its patina of farmyard muck in the city and reeked humbly of cows. Their voices drifting in and out of our consciousnesses, my brother's and mine. Older I see us then, oddly, looking back, and more competent, than we were later as adults and orphans, noting with the luxurious look of inheritors without responsibilities the movement of clouds across the sky, the stout brown cows of the midlands, the familiar names of

19

the villages we passed through in our stately way. Robert, unlike his elder son, was a cautious driver. Easily shaken by men working on the road, any unexpected hazard, a woman on a bicycle tending to veer into his path . . . The slightest element of the unexpected would bring us to an abrupt halt and drivers hooting angrily behind.

All those lost conversations, those lost people. All gone now if I were to count them up. The Hawkinses are a short-lived family.

The customary stop at Kildare for us all to pee. The woman-figure, Etti-Nancy, returning from the ladies' room wearing fresh lipstick and a look of renewed comfort and composure . . .

Etti and Pierce and I, we resorted to talk about money. There were so many subjects we preferred to avoid. It's a safe subject, money. Of course we spend more money than Nancy and Robert did and we put down more time spending it so maybe it's normal to talk about it more. Nancy and Robert now would not have gone to the Clarence for lunch. To Robert, restaurants were daylight robbery and Nancy went cheerfully along with this economy as she went along with all his little foibles. No, the picnic was Robert's choice of repast when abroad in the world. On windy beaches, on chilly benches in Stephen's Green, on a dusty roadside where the grass margin was perilously accommodating, we were given sweet stewed tea from flasks and damp tomato sandwiches out of fading biscuit-tins kept from some old Christmas. I remember the scalding taste of the tea and the grit in my apple. And my child's shame as strangers looked at us, I was certain, with pity and condescension.

That day, we went, Pierce and Etti and myself, to the smart dining-room in the Clarence for our lunch. Like Robert, Pierce had an essentially frugal nature but he was happy to bow to Etti's wishes and try the Clarence. U2's place, I told them.

20

They were impressed. 'Bono will get the price of a haircut anyway out of that,' remarked Pierce with a hearty laugh when he was paying the bill.

We drove down Dame Street with Trinity standing up at the end of it, its reproach somehow agreeably muted. At College Green, a short stroll from Grafton Street, Etti left us. Etti liked shopping and trying on clothes and planning outfits for the Races. That day she was sure she wanted to go to race-meetings all summer, and she crossed at the lights with a jaunty step without looking back for a final wave, her long afternoon of browsing and decision ahead.

As she walked away from us, I already felt some of the light go out of the day and a vague anxiety. I was liable to worry that she would turn up early at the Clarence and panic because we weren't there. She was a country girl, after all. Or late so I would be convinced she was lost. Or be unable to find the Clarence or forget it was there we were meant to meet up. I was liable in my obsession to worry like this once she was out of my sight. I was not yet fully admitting it to myself at this time but already I missed her. I suppose all I really wanted by then was to be by her side.

We left the granite bulk of Trinity on our right, more or less unaffecting as a bad tooth when the nerve is dead, heading northside up the brash length of O'Connell Street, over-bright in the hard new light. White-complexioned women struggled with over-laden carriers and buggies, young chaps were loafing and old characters with eyes screwed up against the fitful sun were ambling up and down the promenade under the grimy burgeoning trees.

It was as it always was, but I had a sensation of remoteness, of the freedom from attachment I have had in foreign cities. And also, I knew briefly, coolly, before I put it out of my mind, that I had chosen illusion in place of reality. Fansha,

21

Etti, the sheep; they were Pierce's reality, not mine. Mine was here but I had discarded it.

The Institute was well known to Pierce. An industrial-looking place, but neat and peaceful, out on the County Louth border. In the foreground, a small Georgian farmhouse used for administration standing with an unconvincing serenity, dwarfed as it was by the high flat-roofed constructions around it of corrugated iron in harsh Arctic colours, magenta, mauve, petrol-green. These housed the animals reared with intensive and experimental methods. Beyond them there was what looked like a mile of hi-tech pens, some containing mêlées of species, emitting the odd subdued bleat or bellow or moo; others empty with hosed-down concrete steaming faintly in the afternoon sun.

This was Missy's birthplace. Progressive, tidy, scientific, more attractive to humans than to animals. Devoted to life certainly, rather than death, in the short term at least, still it reminded me of a progressive concentration camp in some pastoral spot, like Poland. The only honest-to-God agricultural thing about it was the smell of silage.

We did not meet any of the scientists whom you could call, in a sense, her progenitors. They were, I suppose, busy in the Lab working out the recipe for some other scientific freak. It was a hearty good-looking farmhand who led us out to the covered pens where the new breed of lamb was kept.

I had had no particular expectations but all the same I was vaguely disappointed. They were the usual woolly little beasts I knew so well. Though with a fine conformation certainly, well shaped, well grown for their age, healthy as snipes. Pierce was impressed. I could tell when Pierce was impressed. Hands in his pockets, head cocked critically for the assistant's benefit, he strolled up and down, looking them over with a barely controlled admiration. Deferentially, I kept my distance.

'Explain to me,' he said at last to our host, his survey

22

completed, and flattering the man in his inimitable manner, 'what's so different about these little fellas. Genetically engineered. Is that it?'

Pronouncing 'genetically engineered' with a halting deliberation as if it was a foreign notion to himself as an amateur but which the Institute man, as an expert, could be relied upon to explicate. The fact was that Pierce needed little about the concept explained to him. He would have read it all up beforehand and been on the phone several times to the Lab. It was just Pierce's way of making friends with the chap.

Drawing himself up to his full height, the chap explained.

'You have it there, Mr Hawkins. Genetically engineered is right. You see, what we're at here is experimenting with the genetic makeup . . .'

There followed then a longish discourse on the genes as the building-blocks of life and DNA and all the rest of it. And about the radical developments in the science, where the genes of one species were being incorporated into another at an early stage of foetal growth. This far, I was listening only with half an ear because I was always a bit of a duffer at science and anyway the fellow wasn't especially erudite on the subject. But the next thing I heard him say gave me a bit of a shock.

'They're very troublesome to manage, sheep are, Mr Hawkins, as you know yourself. But these human genes make them resistant to a lot of the usual ovine infections. Make them that bit less sheeplike, if you follow me. These little fellas here now are a fantastic improvement. They're close enough to what you could nearly call a trouble-free sheep, Mr Hawkins.'

'Very nice,' Pierce was saying, squatting on his hunkers in the pen. 'Very nice,' running his hands expertly over their small compact bodies, in his blinkered farmer's way. I stared around me at the milling flock, meeting their stupid ovine gaze. Sheep that were not sheep. Human sheep. But they did not look any different.

The Institute chap's genuine pride in them was mixed with the professional fondness of the good husbandman.

'You know, I'm sorry to see them go,' he said. 'I get attached to them. I reared a few of them myself on the bottle. And I'll tell you, there's some of them would nearly talk to you.'

'The mothers died?' Pierce jerked his head up in enquiry.

'Not that. No. They were just young ewes who couldn't be bothered. Two-year-olds. That young, they're inclined to reject them. Don't know what they're meant to be doing with them. Only young ones themselves.'

He laughed. Uncomfortably, I thought later, looking back.

Pierce noticed nothing. He made one of his culchie remarks, that the sheepman would expect, about the steep price the Institute was charging. Your man countered that with one of those 'they're-well-worth-it-believe-me' protests. The honest salesman.

He gave us our pick of the flock. This I left to Pierce. They were his, after all. What was I but the kid brother, the ne'er-do-well, there on sufferance, brought along for the outing? He burrowed among them, examining them with his firm, experienced, gentle hand, and making frequent murmured noises of appreciation.

It was then, waiting for Pierce to make his selection, staring about me with a new alertness, that my eye caught Missy's. She was not yet Missy to me but it was very soon after that I gave her that name, inspired by some absurd but touching quality of pride and hauteur in her bearing.

She was standing at a distance of a few yards from me, slightly apart from the rest of the flock. Her eyes were fixed on me, glittering and unfathomable, but with a look full of hope and pathos. It was a look I had seen in no lamb's eyes before. Certainly, she was as mean a specimen of a lamb as

24

you could find. Scrawny, as if her mother had been dry as a bone, one ear floppy, and a freakish bluish tinge in those eyes of her. But almost at once, I knew I had to have her. Not for any farmer's purpose, not for meat or to breed from, but to watch and understand. Impulsively, I called out to Pierce.

'I want this one, Pierce.'

Over he came, glad doubtless of my fit of interest. After a cursory glance at my chosen lamb, he stared at me in disbelief.

'Marty. You know as well as I do she's a dud. All you have to do is give her the once-over.'

'I don't care. I want her.'

'Will you look at her, man. The legs on her. And she's sickly. A sure sign of a bad suck. Sure she's not fit to be in with this lot at all.'

At this juncture, the Institute man interjected apologetically.

'You're right there, Mr Hawkins. She's not up to standard at all. The trouble with this one now is that she was rejected by the mother. It was touch and go for a few days. But once she got the hang of the bottle she was grand. She'd come running up to me and look into my eyes all the time I was feeding her, like a baby. I only put her in with the rest of them to see how she'd get on.'

I could see he thought I was an eejit. Any fellow who knew anything about sheep would see this one was a dud. He had quickly sized up Pierce and treated him with the respect he always commanded. Myself he treated as a child, that is, he ignored me. I didn't care. I was determined to stick to my guns. I was taking the dud home.

Pierce tried to distract me, to draw my attention to a sturdy blunt-nosed specimen with fine-boned legs and a stupid eye. As if I were a sulky kid that you could wheedle with a compensatory lollipop.

'What about that fella, Marty? If you want a lamb, now he's the lad for you.'

25

'It's this one I want.'

As always in his dealings with me, Pierce relented. But as a gesture of his disapproval, he made her an extra, going for thirteen instead of the twelve he had intended. Making a joke about a baker's dozen, the Institute man threw her in for half-price. I knew he was glad to be rid of her, this embarrassment to the Institute's husbandry, the runt of the flock. He tried to cover up his relief with optimistic chat.

'Ah, she'll thrive all right. All she wants is a bit of time. The breeding will stand to her. She has the personality anyway, I'll tell you that.'

Whatever affection he had conceived for her personality he had overcome. When we were loading the lambs into the trailer, she was last to go in. Pierce would have nothing to do with her and sat into the driver's seat, revving the engine to express his impatience. Struggling in my arms, she made heart-rending panic-stricken little cries, twisting her head around to catch what I could tell was a last glimpse of her mother-figure. The same man had bid a heartily false farewell to me, as if I was a girl who had to be humoured, and was already walking off towards the house. My lamb's cries took on a falsetto note. He did not turn around. By the time I had fastened the hasp on the trailer, they had subsided to a despairing whimper. Then she was quiet.

In the Clarence, we found Etti sipping a vodka, several glossy carrier-bags heaped on chairs around her. She was bright-eyed and happy. Her enquiries about the new lambs were transparently disengaged. When Pierce slagged me off about the freakish specimen I had set my heart on, she laughed without quite knowing why. We had a quick pint. The lambs were packed tight in the small trailer and Pierce wanted to get them settled.

All the way home to Fansha, my brother, conscientious about the welfare of our cargo, went at a slow and careful

26

pace so that the trailer rolled in our wake like a boat on a tranquil tide. Near Kildare, Etti dropped her head on to his hefty shoulder and drew her legs up under her in a curve on the seat. She was soon asleep.

The light was still holding as we drove west with a metallic glow in the sky above the grey. There was a storm forecast. I forced my gaze away from Etti's dark head and watched the strange light fade into night. It had an unnerving lurid look to it as it died, like in some baroque painting depicting the day of the Apocalypse.

6

IT WAS AFTER my parents' funeral that I began to go down-hill. In those months after Nancy and Robert died, I acquired the worst qualities of a troublesome adolescent.

At first I appeared, most of all to myself, the same old Marty. Left Pierce to his newly solitary life in Fansha as soon as decency allowed and returned to Trinity. Performed in seminars with my usual keenness, read widely in the Library and with the acuteness that gave my keenness such an impressive edge. In the Buttery with the chaps, discoursed with an appropriately wry and donnish cynicism on the temperaments of professors, girls, and sundry politicians.

Little by little, I changed. Disclosed to my colleagues my opinion that they were pompous and boring. Strode later and later into my classes. Conveyed to my students with a perverse enjoyment that I had little interest in whatever subject was under discussion. Let them make all the running and then scotched their efforts with rash and ill-founded arguments. Arrogantly denounced the professors.

Then I took to not turning up at all, left no excuses with the Secretary and went off to see a movie instead. This form of anarchy, unknown in my experience in the Department, caused consternation. They held secret meetings to discuss me and my difficulties. Really, in the circumstances, my colleagues showed remarkable forbearance and understanding, displaying their concern only by enquiring with a discreet solicitude about my state of well-being.

After all, I had suffered a terrible trauma. Helena – what was this her name was? – Gough, Helena Gough – Clever, industrious, plain Helena Gough invited me for coffee to her rooms, no doubt at Harvey's request, and tried to get me to talk about it. I would not. Our evening ran into the sands with Helena knocking back the whiskey she had taken out in a vain attempt to disarm me while she wept copious tears over the death of her sister when they were both children.

'Have you not cried, Martin?' she pleaded. 'Have you cried properly? But you must cry.'

I could not cry. I mopped up the whiskey Helena had spilled on the rug, patted her shoulder and left. No one's loss seemed as great as mine, so unamenable to expression.

My best pal Fintan was deeply concerned. Then I had to contend with his barely hidden sense of outrage at my rash and irresponsible carry-on. He was ringing me up at all times of the day and night, trying to arrange rendezvous at which he could counsel and advise me. After a while, I left the phone off the hook. I always had to be on the watch crossing Front Square in case he would appear suddenly at my side or pop out from some nook to waylay me.

At nights, my sleep was short, intense. Yet I was never tired. In fact, I was excessively energetic. I took to walking. Far too early on cold bright mornings, I would stride out to Rathmines to Caroline's flat and drink long draughts of tea while she sat sleepy and irritable on the floor wrapped in her duvet beside the heater. I used to insist on turning it off. I was always warm, fired with some sort of fever.

The fever was a passion. Not for Caroline, and she knew it. No, for my dead parents, who had become abstractions, cyphers.

My corporeal warmth was like a compensation for what was going on upstairs. Fresh icy winds were blowing through my skull, cleansing, bleaching, down to the bones. The shelter

29

of my complacency, the invisible glass dome comprising College, society, family, that I had lived inside without being aware of it, had shattered. Leaving me prey to the elements, alone, and free. It was a freedom I did not want and didn't know what to do with.

I had rationalisations for my behaviour and my conceit. The brand of historicism they were pushing in universities at that time suddenly, I found, repelled me. The revisionist stuff where old heroes become villains and old villains heroes and the pain of the conqueror is opposed to the pain of the conquered, the old broken altar raised up again for their sanctification. Inevitable, I suppose. The wheel has to keep on turning, throwing up some new silt for us rakers of the past to forage in.

In our Department, the greater your taste for revision, the better your chances of publication, a lectureship, success. I had gone along with it, compliantly, without thought. I just thought I wanted that success. As much as the next man anyway. And I was complacent. I had a better chance of it because I was keener and cleverer and knew how to handle Harvey.

In my altered state, my fever, it was the thought of Nancy and Robert's confusion at this reversal of their past that fired my scepticism. It would grieve them, it was a betrayal of them and of the generations behind them. They would be obscurely estranged from the son who was betraying the dead. Attempting to understand me, and failing, their convictions, their world, would emerge blurred and pallid.

An uncritical devotion to one's forebears' untutored beliefs is not, I know, correct, historian-wise. I remained historian enough not to seek to defend myself. And my irrepressible outbursts were countered with mild accusations of emotionalism, lack of objectivity.

Perfectly natural, Harvey assured me, seeing as I was in the grip of an emotional crisis. Absolutely to be expected, in view of the great misfortune that had overtaken my family earlier in the year.

Harvey was deeply sympathetic. 'I sympathise deeply with you, Marty,' he told me. Would I not consider taking a holiday? The west of Ireland, he suggested, was the place for me. Harvey was a great believer in the recuperative powers of the west of Ireland. I declined, and with bad grace.

My fierce scepticism was one of the more explicit reasons for returning to Fansha. But I don't care about any of that now, the historiography. I have to concentrate to reassemble my arguments and remember how I felt. The one thing I am still convinced of is that I had to come home.

Another reason, secret and more pressing, was that I missed Fansha, I yearned to possess it as I never had. Suddenly, it was plain to me that it was the one place in the world I loved. Its fields, the house, the dogs, the neighbours, the Delaneys and the Dwyers, the Kilbrides and the Phelans. As I tramped the cobblestones of Trinity, fevered, contrary, they appeared to me, ridiculously, in the guise of innocents before the Fall. The birds singing in the blossoming trees of the College squares I heard with an anguished sense of deprivation and betrayal, reminding me of the songbirds of Fansha who were not singing for me.

I awoke to my love for them. I awoke to Fansha. I returned to my house and lands of Foilmore in the townland of Fansha, my half of them. And was hardly there but I gave them up. Handed them over.

7

ROBERT'S WILL, MADE years ago, he must have intended to change. He made it when Pierce and myself were boys, before my academic abilities made it plain I could run a profitable career of my own elsewhere. His instincts would have told him it was madness to divide up the place between the two of us, that neither of us would be able to make a go independently of our halves.

Probably he was pandering to Nancy's softness for me, and her sentimental attachment to the family unit they had created. To the idea of it remaining intact, as united as we had been at the start, fixed and unchanged in the charmed circle of Foilmore. He would in time certainly have changed the will. But he did not foresee that he and Nancy would be separated from us so prematurely. Whipped away forever from Fansha and from consultations in Philly Garnett's solicitor's office by the whim of a blown-out tyre at Toomlally Bridge. They were on their way to Dublin to pay me a birthday visit. Robert had been waiting for me to grow up, to prove I was in no need of Foilmore, so that Pierce could take his rightful place as heir, with me, the younger, established in my own chosen domain of life.

Philly Garnett came out from town to the burial in his capacity both as professional and as family friend. It was Philly who, as the mourners turned away from the graveside, moved courteously among them with a bottle of whiskey, his apprentice a step behind him bearing the glasses on a silver tray. A sharp wintry wind had made the mourners shiver with cold and they were glad of Philly's thoughtfulness. I was grateful to Philly; and to the girls that there was a bite back at the house in Foilmore for them to eat.

The female element in the area saw, as Philly had seen, that we, being only young men in the throes of shock and grief, would be useless at organising the refreshments it is customary to provide at a funeral. In the morning, they came to us, their normally cheerful faces respectful and solemn: Eimear Moore, Tina Kilbride, Siobhan Phelan, brisk young mothers whose new names in marriage I did not know. Lipsticked, with new hard helmet-like hairdos and too-tight black skirts, their funeral uniform, they carried boxes and great platters covered in Clingfilm from their cars into the house and took over our kitchen. Arranged sandwiches on plates, sliced ham off the joint, mixed salads, checked our supplies of tea and sugar, placed apple tarts and chunks of iced Christmas cake left over from the season in readiness on the sideboard.

They pressed our suits for us, advised us on what shirts to wear. Produced a selection of black ties belonging to their husbands or fathers, that had seen many a man through many a funeral, and gave us our pick. Made discreet enquiries as to whether we had enough in to drink. Audited the number of crates Toby Dwyer had sent up unasked and assured us we had plenty.

'Watch out for Laddy Minch,' Tina counselled. 'Laddy is a terror for the whiskey at funerals.'

They rummaged in cupboards for table-cloths, washed the good china, gathered chairs from rooms upstairs and lined them up against the walls in the parlour.

They were subdued in the face of our loss, kind, capable, with the quiet but irrepressible cheerfulness of the uninvolved, the unbereaved. When I was in my room getting ready, their teasing voices and laughter rose from below, as if they were

33

preparing for a party. I felt sustained and, briefly, safe. For a moment or two I pretended to myself that Nancy was down there with them, overseeing the arrangements in her accustomed place.

That day, not even Pierce was good for anything. We sat, numb and stiff on either side of the hearth in the parlour, under the framed pictures on the mantelpiece. Our brash boys' faces; Nancy's and Robert's younger selves playing tennis; in a laughing group at a dance; standing on a cliff beside a Morris Minor. This had been taken at the Cliffs of Moher, on their honeymoon when they toured Ireland. Pierce, with his unaccustomed pallor, was surprisingly elegant in the old dark suit of Robert's that may have been his wedding-suit. I was suitably attired in the suit Nancy and I had selected together in Switzers for my Commencement ceremony.

I remember a succession of faces hovering, eyes wide with compassion, pressing words of sympathy, a sandwich, a glass, upon us. Faces at once both known and unknown since many of them I had not seen since boyhood and time had taken its toll on the colour and quality of hair and complexions. Once I almost laughed hysterically, almost declared aloud to my brother, 'What would you say, Pierce. Hasn't Jim got very grey . . .'

I remember how after a while the particularity of their features seemed to be washed away, giving them the look of an archetypal chorus in a tragedy in which we were the lead players though with mercifully few lines expected of us to say. When, for a moment, we were left untended, I would hear a heavy involuntary sigh of sorrow from Pierce and I would be aware of a nervous tic that had come on me since the news, a nerve going ping ping over the eye in my left temple.

The shrill voices of children playing, the children of mourners, came in from the yard along with the excited yapping of the dogs. Once, we were those children, blithe in the face of the tears of others, playful observers of the pageant of death. That was the day we took our places on the other side. That day, we were the men in the dark newly-pressed suits with the strange haunted look in the eyes.

So long removed as I had been from the culture of the country funeral, it was a revelation to me, the gathering of the tribe. The three boys of the Ffrenches were there, grave and silent in black suits that were verdant with age and still bore the outlines of larger Ffrench ancestors. They were steadily making their way through Toby's beer, while managing to give their thirst the appearance of a homage to the hospitality of the house. Laddy Minch stood with them in a stiff new peach-coloured shirt, drinking but decorous, attempting to engage them one after the other in converse and red-faced from the exertions of the hopeless endeavour. Young Delaney was looking after the crowd in the kitchen, playing host, ourselves being incapable. His mother, wearing a faded black straw hat, was making tearful woman-talk on the window-seat with Mrs Kilbride, pressing tissues extracted from her handbag to her weeping eyes.

The arrival of the Minister and a Dail deputy at some point impressed the assembly hugely. From opposing parties, I had to be reminded, Fianna Fail and Fine Gael, since I had little interest in local politics. Two bulky men, they were received with reverence and intense murmurings confided to the ear as they gently worked the room. Veiled promises perhaps of a pension, a grant, a planning permission . . . I have learned the form all too well now since I came home.

Caroline did not come to the funeral. She telephoned to say how deeply sorry she was; but she was taking an exam and couldn't make it. However, Cissy Quinlan, her mother, was there, her soft face pink and creased with emotion, moving round from group to group haplessly with a large

35

teapot and pressing my shoulder in wordless sympathy at intervals. And of course, JJ Quinlan, her father. Andrea, I suppose too, though I did not know her then, was there somewhere in the crowd. Andrea always hangs out in back halls or wherever the men are, at funerals.

Harvey drove down, with Fintan. Stood around awkwardly in a crumpled overcoat and told me several times to take it easy. Assured me I need be in no hurry back. But that I might remember all the same that it was only work that could put grief to flight. When all was said and done. Fintan embraced me, clumsily and mutely, but with a genuine sympathy I was grateful for. It wasn't his fault that I turned my back on him and his sympathy in the months to come.

It was that day, the day of the funeral, that I first laid eyes on Etti. She came late, and only to the house in the evening, because she had to wait for her brother, who was on the day-shift at the factory in Thurles, to arrive home and give her a lift out. At the sight of her, Pierce's mood lifted remarkably, if briefly. I felt it in him, I felt him start and looked at him and then followed his gaze. I saw a thin, dark-haired striking-looking girl hovering uneasily in the doorway. Her brother, a youthful grumpy individual, must have made straight for the kitchen or the back hall where the men were. I was made aware of her importance by Pierce's rising from his place to greet her, his pallor lit with a sudden blush. I saw at once she was his girl. I saw how, when she laid a hand feelingly on his arm, he let out a deep sob in a release of emotion. He led her over then to meet me.

'This is Goretti Hanna,' he told me.

This is the one, I knew he was telling me. This is the one.

'Goretti, my brother. Martin.'

'Etti,' she corrected him, with a slight impatience. 'And you're Marty.'

She did not mumble 'sorry for your trouble', which it is

customary to say in condolence. Etti has an instinctive inca-
pacity for convention. I could see it then in her clothes. A
black outfit certainly, but stylishly put together so it looked
more festive than funereal, suggesting a funeral costume for
the stage or maybe a slightly rakish cocktail party.

Instead, her eyes met mine with a tortuous expression of
empathic sorrow. There was the pink inflamed mark on her
forehead that I now know blooms when she is unsure of
herself or upset. Also the dark glossy hair that she piles
severely on top of her head. She was upset for Pierce.

The way she was self-consciously biting her lip, a long thin
lip, with her delicate white childish teeth suggested to me a
faulty character, amoral somehow. Her looks would have been
striking to anyone with half an eye; but to me she was deeply
interesting because of that mysterious flawed character she
projected. As if, behind her schoolgirl's face, she had an inner
life or a past that was knowing and complex and guarded. I
don't believe Pierce ever saw it. I suppose, since I saw it, I was
doomed to discover it, like lands glimpsed on a clear day
across the horizon.

I should not have seen Etti for the first time in those circumstances. My nerves that day were both ice-cold and fiercely
heightened. I should have met her in some urbane situation
that would diminish her and where I was safe in my own
world and my detachment. Pierce could have brought her up
to Dublin to meet me. He might have come bashfully along
the path by the cricket pitch with her on a sunny day in May
when Fintan and I were lying languid on the grass with a beer
from the Pavilion. Or he could have brought her along to the
Bailey where myself and Fintan were in our urban groove.
Fintan would have made some supercilious remark about her
name; Goretti, the martyr-girl who died for her virtue. I would
have topped it with another. I should have had Fintan's urbane
protection.

37

There indeed Fintan was, sure; in a corner, chatting with Harvey and a couple of the Ffrenches. He was available, at my disposal. But he meant nothing to me just then. Already, though I didn't know it, Fansha had claimed me. But I should have had some support.

The mourners were drifting off, down to Toby's. Philly Garnett made his way over to us. In the country way of denoting a business intention, he nodded significantly and extended his neck in the direction of the small room we call the office.

'Pierce, and ah, yourself Martin, would you step inside with me for a minute?'

Closing the door with a firm click behind us, he ushered us to the couch and picked his briefcase up from behind it where he must have discreetly placed it on his arrival. He sat on an upright chair at the desk and opened the briefcase.

As Philly read out the contents of the will to us, I felt nothing. To the life I imagined I was impatient to return to, it seemed to have no relevance. But it must have caused enormous shock and disturbance to Pierce. He was already serious then, about Etti. However, if it did, he made no sign. For a long time afterwards, I, for my part, continued to feel nothing, unconscious of Foilmore and any interest in staking my claim to it.

Philly's tone, when he read the will, was heavy, his dismay at Robert's dilatoriness in updating it almost tangible.

'In the event of my wife's death, to my two beloved sons, Pierce and Martin . . .' It was plainly stated. We were both to inherit the place in equal shares. I looked stonily at Robert's account books, lined up tidily on their shelf behind Philly Garnett's head. It will be Pierce writing in them now, I was thinking.

8

IT WAS A SHORT, and as far as I was concerned, an insignificant interview. The three of us rejoined the assembly, now
greatly diminished. The mourners had repaired to Toby's. Old
Mrs Kilbride accepted a glass of sherry. 'Lord have mercy
on the dead,' she proclaimed loudly in the archaic mode of
salutation, holding out the glass at arm's length before she
put it formally to her lips. A chill invaded my bones and
maybe everyone's bones, because there was a sudden mut-
edness in the buzz of talk. Then Philly consented to another
glass, and Pierce and myself, as we were at it, filled the glasses
of our remaining guests and made our noises of assent as they
marvelled once more at the death-trap that was Toomlally
Bridge and the good price for cattle.

The weeks passed. I found myself again in the subterranean
light of airless seminar-rooms, my students mouthing deriva-
tive analyses for my approval. As they droned on, I would
find myself falling into a dream. The fields of Fansha rose up
in my mind, my delayed love for them discovered with a
fierceness that appalled me. I would tap my Biro absently on
my desk and the students' voices would grow hesitant and
drop away into silence.

Impatient to reinhabit my fields, to indulge my dreams, I
would tell them, brazenly, dishonestly, 'You haven't read
enough to discuss the topic. You'd be better off spending your
time in the library instead of wasting mine.'

Out they would file, leaving me at last in peace. The timid

39

ones awed by my high standards, the braver ones muttering treason. Other times, to get rid of them, I might claim a headache.

I fought that growth of love as if it were unnatural. And it was, it was perverse. Opportunistic, primitive, greedy, everything my education was meant to breed out of me. It was a betrayal of Pierce. Brothers have killed each other for less. The glass dome was shattered and I was to take the sword and flail at the last jagged shards that stood up still out of the ground until they were fragments and dust.

In that time, I received two letters from Pierce. He was not in the habit of writing letters. But I suppose what he had to relate was of such importance that a statement of intent and then of its achievement had to be given concrete form.

In the first, he stated that he had asked Etti to be his wife and she had accepted the proposal. Reading it, I was uncomfortably aware of a stab of jealousy that I decided was natural in a newly bereaved and therefore lonely younger brother. In the circumstances – I assumed that what he meant by this was his recent bereavement – Pierce wrote, they had arranged for the marriage ceremony to take place in Rome. To be married in Rome is the traditional recourse of those who want to avoid fuss and expense but who have all the same a sense of style to keep up. An easy way of imparting a veneer of glamour and sophistication to the occasion. I hardly knew Etti but decided a Rome wedding suited my reading of her character.

The second letter, some weeks later, was to tell me that the event had taken place.

'We were lucky enough to get an audience with His Holiness the Pope,' Pierce wrote, 'in the company of a few dozen other couples. We found it surprisingly moving.' He described the hotel they stayed in, or at least gave its name and situation – Pierce was not what you would call a descriptive writer. He assured me of his and Etti's happiness and hoped I would pay them a visit at Foilmore before too long. Finishing up with 'Hope your studies are going well. As ever, love, Pierce.'

His handwriting was still that of the conscientious schoolboy. He would have repaired to the office with the air of a man with some serious task to do, and written slowly and steadily until it was done. Maybe it was the lack of the customary wedding with its assembly of relations and friends that impelled him to vouch this gesture of documentation.

So, Etti was installed in Foilmore. I refused to admit it, but this knowledge must have been working at a subterranean level, increasing my impatience to return. The more I fought it, the more inexorably Foilmore crowded into my head. Shelley's field with its thistles and the big chestnut in the centre of it. The tousled hedge with its pink hawthorn and its white, below. A little clump of birch that before I wouldn't have given tuppence for rose up like the forests of myth, drew me like a mystic grove, its leaves waving in a gentle dreamlike breeze. All fenced and barred from me.

Often I had to fight the impulse to get up from my corral in the library, leaving my notes and my books behind, and head for Fansha. Straight to that grove, to lay my head on the soft grass under the birch trees and be cooled by its divine winds. I gave in to it in the end. You always have to give in to love.

41

9

When I rang Pierce up from the station to ask him to come in and pick me up, I detected nothing in his voice but pleasure at my arrival. He had no inkling of course just then of my intentions, since I didn't tell him. When, after a while, I did tell him, of my decision to break with Trinity and to stay on with himself and Etti for good, he revealed none of the animosity or outrage he must reasonably have felt. A practical man, he went a bit quiet. Probably trying to work out in his head some way it could be viable.

He made no attempt to dissuade me. Gave me to understand he knew how I was motivated by love. I would have the lodge, he said, seeing as I was on my own. Raffles had moved out of it into a new bungalow, now he was married. Better than let it fall anyway, he said.

The same day, I went into town to Philly Garnett's office and signed over my half of Fansha to my brother. I was condemning myself to being little more than a pot-boy around the place; but I was building up our dome again.

That is one way of looking at it. In reality, I think I was bad and more than a little mad. Locking Pierce and myself into a relationship in which the burden of goodness lay on him, I might as well have challenged him to a duel, a fight to a spiritual death. In handing him the freedom to cast out without hindrance his brother from his inheritance, I gave him the freedom to despise me and his children to despise me. Making myself dependent, an object of charity, I forced

42

him to be the good, the charitable, the noble day after day, season after season. This I put up to him.

Enough, as Nancy would say, to try the forbearance of a saint. Making myself powerless, I had become the all-powerful, the passive instrument of his fall or his salvation. I made him the repository of virtue, the inheritor of the virtues of the Hawkinses. As long as I chose to stay at Foilmore, I would test him, my noble, my loyal brother, to keep the Hawkins standard.

He never faltered, Pierce didn't, on the path I had dug for him. Every month he paid a generous amount, set by himself, into my bank account. 'Your salary,' he called it. I called it my allowance. I had little use for it. Not until France. It came in very handy in France.

It was my noble brother too who presented me with the Norton. At seventeen, I developed a craze for motor-bikes and roared around on Robert's old Norton all summer. Then one day it seized up, as they do, and I threw it into the old piggery and forgot about it. But Pierce remembered. Soon after my return he pulled the bike out of the back of a shed and brought it into town on the trailer to Teddy Millea, the bike-man. Wheeled it into the yard of the lodge one evening, and presented it to me, refurbished, resprayed, going again. A little surprise for me.

'Seeing as you're gone all sentimental,' he said, 'I thought you'd like it.'

10

At the start, to see how Missy would get on, I put her out with the others in the field, making my getaway without a backward look, my fingers pressed in my ears to deaden her anguished cries. That strange strangled cry so different from the imperious bleats of Pierce's healthy young sheep. Creeping back later by another route for a covert look, I found her lying awkwardly against the gate through which I had disappeared, her head, as if it was too heavy to hold upright, between her limp outstretched forelegs like a dog. Gazing in an attitude of forlorn hope in the direction of the house. Whatever attempts she had made to eat, she had abandoned. I took her into the lodge then to try her on the bottle.

Pierce was a farmer, he took pride in being an able and ambitious farmer. Why should he care whether Missy lived or died? An animal that has no hope of thriving could hold no interest for him. He could see nothing in her. I understood that.

But he was patient with me. When he wandered down to the lodge for a visit and found me trying to feed her from a bottle while she slithered around unwillingly from my grasp, he leaned against the dresser and laughed.

'Would that bottle be too hot, Marty? You wouldn't want to burn the little tongue.'

Then he took her from me and got her to take the milk. His authority even Missy recognised. Appealing to me, she appealed to the wrong man.

44

I used to suspect in those frustrating feeding-sessions that she knew exactly what to do to draw out the milk but had made a decision not to. Then it came to me that she was pining to the point of despair for the fellow at the Institute. Once I saw that, I resolved to make myself his substitute and win her love.

Pierce was patient because my obsession with Missy he regarded as a nostalgic attempt to recreate the past. He imagined I was reliving the old days when we were children and Nancy would sit in the same armchair covered in faded cretonne that I now sat in, with a couple of lambs who had lost their mothers butting at her for their bottles. He was good enough to let me at it, with brotherly indulgence to encourage me.

He always did indulge my little oddnesses. Maybe he was calculating that after a plunge into nostalgia, I might come to my senses with the passing of time and return to my proper billet in Trinity. I don't know. I'm not sure that Pierce was capable even of such rudimentary calculations where I was concerned.

My awareness of Missy's despair made me anxious in the early days that she might have died in the night. In the mornings I went out first thing to her pen which I had made for her after she cowered with such distaste or fear when I put her in with the others. As I approached among the deep morning shadows, I would see hers, humped, still, her short stubby legs elongated comically. She would be waiting for me, her nose pressed between the boards, as if she had been alerted by the creak of the bed as I climbed out or the click of the door-latch when I lifted it. I would carry her in to the warmth of the house then for her breakfast.

The memory of those warm, unguilty mornings of early summer are very painful to me. Still only half-dressed and half-asleep, not being constitutionally an early riser, I

45

stumbled, Missy under my arm, from the cooker to the table preparing her bottle. Collapsing into the armchair as she scrabbled for a footing on my lap, half in fright, half eagerness.

The kitchen would be glowing in the mellow post-dawn when I came downstairs, the oblique beam of the sun shining through the south-facing window. By the time I had coaxed her through her bottle, the full blare of its light would be streaming whitely in, showing up the cracks and burnmarks in the old appliances and the dust on the empty shelves and the shoddiness of Raffles' makeshift arrangements that I had never bothered to improve.

Pierce's exasperation with me was understandable. Missy was too mature for a bottle. Lambs her age were long out on pasture, tugging keenly at the fresh grass like their mothers. Missy wouldn't touch a blade of grass. She had no knack of eating it. When I attempted to feed her some, her nose wrinkled up and she let it hang loosely out of her mouth like an idiot.

However, on the bottle her body was losing the pitiable limpness of the half-starved and was achieving something of the solidity of the well-fed lamb. Soon she learned to trust me, to depend on me. When I put her down after a reasonably successful feed, hungry myself and wanting my own breakfast, she no longer shambled from corner to corner of the room in search of the Institute man or perhaps something unnameable to solace her yearning, but nestled against my knee companionably as I ate my cornflakes or stood at the cooker frying a couple of rashers.

All the time I talked to her, as you would talk to a young child. My favourite refrain then, and you would have had to agree it was hers too if you saw us together, was the nursery rhyme 'Mary Had a Little Lamb'. I changed it to 'Martin Had a Little Lamb', and would be composing new verses suitable to our situation as I walked about the kitchen or smoked a cigarette with my final cup of tea. She would follow me or stand at my knee, her head cocked and her glistening eyes gazing into mine, their look not anguished then but considering, alight, the look of an intelligent child.

It was not only grass, however lush and sweet, that she refused to eat. When I tempted her with mangels, nicely wilted cabbage, delicacies her kind eagerly laid into, I was convinced I heard her sigh as she wanly pecked and nibbled at them, to please me.

With the good secateurs I went out very early and cut fresh leafy branches from the young elm sapling springing up by the avenue, fresh elm being counselled in an old book on sheep-management that I found, as a food for a convalescent or finicky sheep. This act Pierce would have regarded as vandalism. He was delighted with the resurgence of an elm at last after the blight of Dutch elm disease. Missy welcomed this wantonly hacked offering no more than she welcomed the hoariest mangel with the pocks of the spade in it.

It nearly makes me laugh now. When I think of those efforts I made in my persistent attempts to induce in Missy a credible sheepiness. The misery I put her through. To prove to myself something I knew very well to be false.

At last one morning on a whim and out of desperation at her half-starved appearance, I placed in front of her my bowl of half-eaten porridge, drenched in sugar and milk, still warm. Voraciously she lapped it up and then looked at me beseechingly for more. With the look I interpreted as beseeching, the look she fixed on me when I approached her pen during the day and passed by, steeling my heart. I prepared another cupful, Missy warm at my knee as I stirred the pot. She lapped it up. This was her first decent meal. Human-food. Baby-food, even puppy-food. But not sheep-food.

11

On those mornings when I rose early, I had Foilmore
to myself. The lambing was over for another year and
Pierce, if he was up, would still be going around in the red
dressing-gown I gave him one Christmas, brewing tea to bring
up to Etti in bed. Nancy and Robert would have been astonished if they could have seen our lackadaisical way of getting
up and into the day.

In their time, there was the big herd of cows to be milked
and the churns to be got to the creamery by ten. There were
all the different species to be fed, the cattle and the calves,
the hens and turkeys and geese, the two pigs they always
kept. For a short while, as an experiment, they had half a
dozen goats in the paddock. All these animals had their uses.
But when you could buy battery eggs and meat and bacon in
the supermarket, they no longer paid their way. In the space
of a few years, the cackle of hens and the grunting of pigs
died out across the townland.

These animals were not in my care. I had little feeling for
them. Mute, despite all their bawling and mooing, sometimes
a nuisance, sometimes objects of curiosity, but rarely of my
affection, a backdrop to my life. My life was school, football,
watching television with Young Delaney, reading comics at a
good distance from them in the orchard or under my tree in
Shelley's field. Maybe I was distancing myself from the pitiful-
ness of their destinies.

A motley collection of dun-coloured beasts, that's how I

remember them. Standing forlornly by gates, slurping foul-smelling mixes from troughs and buckets, carried away to the fair or mart one day and replaced by smaller versions of themselves the next. My heart was a small hard boy's heart, free of the burden of compassion and care. This burden Nancy and Robert carried for me.

All that busyness and activity. Ma and Da rising in the dark, pulling on their wellingtons that from year to year cracked and were replaced. Going from cow to cow under the dreary light of the bare electric bulbs in the milking-parlour, ferrying buckets hither and yon, mucking out, their hands like hams from the cold. Calling us to get up only when the kitchen was warm and the sky was whitening and our breakfast under way.

All gone now, those mornings and they with them, and the generations of animals, as many as the years I am old. All the work of all those creatures, for us. For what else? For the fulfilment of the moment maybe, as the philosophic mind claims. But all those moments end in the present moment and my present is not worthy of that past.

Pierce's was. They could have approved of Pierce. Even though he got into the sheep and had few of the cares that got them up. His were of a more abstract kind. Accounts, meetings with banks, interest rates.

But Young Delaney they would understand. Young Delaney keeps up the old ways. Gaggles of this fowl and that running around the muddy yard. The manure heap beyond the out-houses giving off a reliable agricultural aroma. Two pigs fattening in the lean-to by the cow-byre, snuffling and squealing. The long low modest farmhouse that nearly everyone else has replaced with a white hacienda, its lichened roof sagging inwards in the middle and forks lined up against the wall. It's a place that is, as we say, very shook. But holding. In winter, when I crossed the fields with a Christmas bottle of whiskey, like a set, with its mucky, cacophanous autonomy, for a nostalgic film about rural wretchedness.

Young Delaney could be like the rest of them and go to work in the factory in Thurles, leaving his farm to be a tidy little park with a few cattle to keep the grass down. But young Delaney is not ambitious, not in the way ambition is expressed down here. He understands ambition, he's deeply interested in it. But not for himself. Lesser men, like myself, should have it. But for himself it's the hard road. No bank-loans for Young Delaney, no fancy machines or fripperies. He may be poor, but he's independent. King of his kine and of his acres and witness to the past that stirs in its dreaming sleep behind the white walls and sparkling silvery roofs of his neighbours.

But he's no naïf, Young Delaney. He's one of the cutest fellows you could meet. And he's not idle, no sir. He's slow, slow in his movements and in his walk, and as the years go by, he'll go slower still and develop a limp or a bad back like the men before him. He will attract some disability or other from all the hard work. His independence demands constant toil. In fact, the air of neglect around the Delaneys' displays his industry. All those animals have to be foddered. Housed and watered. Dosed and dipped. Milked and sheared and slaughtered. All this he does himself.

The lined-up forks are taken into the fields to dig the turnips and mangels everyone else has abandoned for nuts and mixes we buy in town. He doesn't have the money for such bought-in fripperies as feed. He stays outside the cash economy.

His bending and lifting will twist him into a hoop in time. Young Delaney, I used to think, was shaping up to be one of those thin wistful old bachelor farmers who drink up in Toby's at the Cross, who develop a tremble in the hand that holds the pint and have a patina of grime around the neckline. Young Delaney gives them a hearty thump on the shoulder when he arrives in Toby's.

50

'How ya doin, Harry?' he says. 'A bad day, Pat. What?'

'Those aul fellas,' he would say to me, 'they were never able to farm.'

I used to wonder why Young Delaney wouldn't find himself a girl. What would he do when his mother was gone? But the way he saw it, it wasn't his destiny at all to join the geriatrics at the Cross. That destiny was mine if I didn't buck up. To win back Caroline from her dentist should be my play. Though he would have too much respect for Caroline Quinlan's native prudence to repose much hope in my success. Indeed, I should cut my losses and find any female at all willing to take me on. She might make a man of me yet and scour the notions out of my head and set me about some way of business. Get me to buy up a bit of land maybe that could give us a living. Or settle down to some sort of a career.

'Would you have any interest in the teaching at all, Marty?' he enquired more than once. He had the Christian Brothers in Thurles in mind.

As it was, I was clearly heading for early decrepitude. Scrounging the price of a few pints off Pierce, the loan of the jeep, the cast-off suit . . . That's how he saw me.

'Now, is that the way for Martin Hawkins to end up, Laddy? Would you ever have credited it?' I can hear him discourse on my sad decline up at the Cross.

I fear there are worse dangers ahead of me.

Young Delaney's destiny fits him. Rooted in tradition, though a dying one. And like all dying traditions, fast attaining the status of rural history, like rusty binders and plucking stools and warm milk squirting from the hand-milked udder on a winter's morning. In his declining years, Young Delaney might be able to rent himself out as an exhibit in a rural museum. But it was never a destiny intended for a Hawkins of Foilmore.

51

12

PIERCE DID NOT understand Missy, or me. He was not in sympathy with us. Pierce looked out, into the future. A technological man.

Often those days I noticed that he had a tendency to avoid my gaze, to turn away from me when he spoke. If he were Young Delaney he might say, 'Marty is going soft in the head.' But that would be too harsh a judgement for Pierce to express. His voice when he talked to me was often gruff and strangled. I suspect that he would have liked to say a lot of things to me which he could not bring himself to say. Maybe he hoped I still had the time and the wit to say them to myself.

I strolled over to the Delaneys' one day, across the fields. I had some notion in my head of ferreting out of Young Delaney's mother some insight about Missy. Young Delaney, I knew, would be out and about at his manly labours. I had a fondness for Mrs Delaney; and she always had a soft spot for me that I thought I might appeal to now. I was wondering if in her long experience she had ever come across a freakish little monster like mine. I wanted to elicit word of an antecedent for Missy and a happy end. Something to turn my absurd suspicions away.

Maybe Mrs Delaney might know of another lamb once as bereft as mine of any ovine instinct to follow her flock. One who would eat scrambled eggs and had a fondness for sweet biscuits soaked in hot tea. Who had an intelligence unnatural in her dull-brained species. Whose eyes could express joy one minute and a searing sadness to make your heart break the next. And who, if you caught her unawares, was looking in upon her own soul with a bewildered sorrow. Was there ever a lamb with genius before?

I needed the wisdom of generations, the folklore of the parish. Pierce was too new to the game.

It was our fields I crossed to see Mrs Delaney. Pierce in his goodness had the three fields between our place and theirs rented out to Young Delaney. Pierce had more than enough land for his stock; Young Delaney had too little for his. I suppose Pierce could make more than the rent he was getting by grazing them with flocks of his own. But renting them was his way of negotiating with the Delaney pride and his own delicacy in local matters. The rent he charged was rather less than the going rate, enough to let Young Delaney be glad of the bargain on the basis of the quasi-kinship of neighbours; but not so much as to hint of charity.

I walked knee-deep in yellow buttercups that day. At the close of the year, when the grass was bitten down to the root, I was thinking, Young Delaney would pay Pierce a visit. You would know at once he was making a business call. He would be wearing a tie done with a loose unpractised Windsor knot, his hair slicked back with an oil-dressed comb. He may not have much use for money but he always has enough of it for the uses he has.

The visitor seated as comfortably as his garb and purposes allowed, Pierce would produce the bottle of whiskey and Etti would bring out a cake bought from Keogh's up at the Cross and offer him a slice. He would refuse the cake and Etti would eat some, dreamily seated on the couch in an attitude of respect for the talk of the men. Rehearsing again the old topics. The summer gone by, the weather that was bad for one crop and good for another, the animal that paid its way and the one that didn't. Proceeding onwards to talk of the

53

future, the prospect for prices in the spring, the new EC proposals.

At some point, Young Delaney would extract a cheque from his inside pocket and lay it on the table.

'Thanks, Augie. The cash will come in handy,' Pierce would say.

Interjected into the middle of a conversation about the inadequacies in understanding of Mr. Yates, the Minister, vis-à-vis the farmer. The kind of remark Young Delaney understands and appreciates. Turning the deal into a fair exchange. Then Pierce would fill up the whiskey glasses, lavishly but unobtrusively as only Pierce knew how. You could not beat Pierce for manners. A real gentleman.

They're a lovely set of fields. Sloping down, lush and firm and broad to the grey huddle in the hollow of the Delaney outbuildings. Handy for the ewes in the hard months and the cows in calf. The Delaneys' own land beyond is rougher and stonier as if, back in the mists of time, they were pushed on to the margin, the bad land. Robert was aware with a measure of guilt of the superiority of his fine acres that was not entirely due to good husbandry. And at the same time you have to admire the herd of cattle Young Delaney keeps, their sturdy magnificence whether on rented or Delaney grass.

The Delaneys always had an eye for a beast. That's the Delaney talent. Young Delaney has inherited the gift. Enters the mart with the eye of a connoisseur. Not to buy, he buys rarely. But to watch, to judge, to keep up with the market. One day in six he might bid. And then comes home with the best.

He's devoted to quality, greedy for it, will bid for it with the same certainty and single-mindedness, as an art collector will bid for a picture in which the uninitiated see only a garish scrawl. When Augie Delaney arrives at the mart, the farmers huddled in chat around the rails, their breath steaming in the raw winter air, stand aside to make room for him. To ensure for him an uncluttered view.

When Augie Delaney bids, with that laconic jaw of his, the auctioneer's voice assumes an expectant gravity as if in the presence of a dignitary. And after the deal is done, the farmers make way in the pub for the fellow who has sold an animal to Augie Delaney. His father had the same talent and his father before him. But Young Delaney is turning out a better farmer than they were and maybe less liable to be ruined by drink. His mother's people were steady but reasonable drinkers, like Young Delaney himself. At the present time anyway. You can never depend on a propensity to relative sobriety, in the wrong circumstances or the long dark winter days in Fansha.

As I went down the daisied stony cow-path to the Delaneys' place the dogs came to meet me, their rusty hair greying and matted. Rose and Boyo, mother and son, bucking and barking in a simulated show of warning as if I were a stranger.

'What are ye barking at Marty for?' I wanted to know.

They fawned then, whimpering, curving the profile of their bodies, shy and blissful and pleading with their eyes and whimpers to be patted. Preceding me like scouts through the haggard to the house, running on, backing off, barking and whining in ecstasy. A visitor is rare enough at the Delaneys'.

The Delaneys' three-cornered patch of a haggard, resort of fowl, dogs and ourselves as boys. Strewn with the remains of industry and indecision. Rusted bits of old machinery, heaps of mouldy straw, withered stalks of cabbage from a year when some of it was tilled, the hulk of Young Delaney's first car, a yellow Mini, with hens roosting in it. The iron gate, listing and half-hidden under a growth of whitethorn and bramble, heavy to shift as it always was.

Mrs Delaney was in the yard, ineffectually pushing the yard-brush around with a great display of energy, raising dust

55

and strawy debris in clouds around her. She was wearing her faded navy-blue crossover apron with the sprigs of pink flowers on it. Her legs in thick support stockings were bulging in unlikely places.

She had always had veins. She was always the same. And there was the generic grey tea-cloth hanging out to air on the scrawny ornamental bush that sits outside the back window of the parlour to lend a genteel air and shade the view of the workaday yard. Implements lined up against the wall, the dusky-pink tea-roses in bloom around the peeling brown-painted door. The same dusty brown hens ambling around and pecking desultorily up at the far end of the yard by the barn, out of the way of the sweeping-brush.

As I came up, the dogs padding in front of me, she straightened up, raising her hand to her forehead to shield her eyes from the sun so she could distinguish who I was. This gesture of hers reminded me of Robert, waiting on the platform as the train from Dublin pulled into Thurles station late in an afternoon of early summer when I was arriving home for a well-deserved rest, or so I would be assured, after the triumph of my exams.

'Marty. Is it yourself?'

To display her welcome, she abandoned her sweeping and hurried to line up the yard-brush in its accustomed place beside the rake and the forks with their knobby tines and the plastic buckets. These humble articles in their habitual array I regarded with a nostalgic and painful affection. Rose, Boyo, Mrs Delaney; all of them greying and tiring but absurdly attempting to arrest the brutality of time moving on and on, unstoppable.

The dogs returned to their habitual posts, poor imitations of lions on either side of the door, content, their work of the day done. I followed Mrs Delaney into the kitchen, the screen of the television set glossy in the gloom, the fall of bright flowers of the table oil-cloth shining, but blurred and whitish on the table-top from too many wipes of the dish-cloth. A kitchen of odorous rather than visual quality. A temperate smell made up of frugal things. Brewed tea, souring milk, weeping stone, turf smoke, dog.

A lingering compound from the past but one that to Pierce was not pleasant. Sensitive to odours, Pierce was, sniffing interrogatively whenever we entered someone else's house. Kilbrides' he did not like for its sweet sickly jam-like smell. It was the faint but insistent whiff of sour milk that Pierce objected to in Delaneys'. Pierce liked clean worldly smells. Coffee, fragranced soap, diesel.

Mrs Delaney was hawking pots and kettles around the range, awkwardly because of her arthritis. She poured water from the big kettle into the smaller, swapped the positions of two blackened saucepans and carried the small kettle with a laboured step to the electric cooker.

'Now, Mrs Delaney, don't be making tea for me,' I pleaded.

The habitual protest of the country caller, a ritual not to be heeded. In my case, anyway. Mrs Delaney wouldn't dream of heeding me because of her pity for me as a man who had to fend for himself. Her own boy after all had his mother. I would always have to accept at least a boiled egg as if I were in urgent need of nourishment. She peered shortsightedly into the kettle and lifted it on to the ring to boil. Then she peered across at me. She still had her soft white creased face.

'You look tired, Marty. Are you working too hard?'

My forehead reddened. I have not a great reputation for work. She must have heard, I thought, about my early mornings foolishly devoted to a sickly lamb.

'You're taken after your mother, Marty. The kind heart. You got that from her.'

I knew for sure then that she knew about the lamb. Young

57

Delaney had a way of knowing things that were no concern
of his.

'Your poor mother.'

Mrs Delaney's large delicate eyes were shining with unshed
tears as she stood in the light from the window with two
cracked cups held aloft. Tears came easily to her.

'And your father. What a terrible thing. I do miss them,
Marty.'

I sat receptively at the table as she placed a plate in front
of me and salt and a hunk of soda bread on its board.

'How is Pierce? And Etti?'

The latter name she pronounced hesitantly. She was
doubtful about Etti. Again my face reddened. Sometimes the
very name could throw me into confusion.

'Hasn't she settled down well in Fansha . . .'

This was the opposite of what Mrs Delaney really believed.
A girl who had settled down to country life would be rearing
fowl, not to speak of a child or two, and baking bread and
sweeping out the yard. None of this was Etti doing.

'A young girl like that from the town. But she doesn't seem
to miss it at all, does she, Marty . . .'

To Mrs Delaney a wife imported from town was one of the
worst fates to befall a man.

'Of course she had a lovely place to come to . . .'

Mrs Delaney would be well aware of the relative unloveli-
ness of the place Etti came from.

'Of course it's easier for a girl now. Etti doesn't have to
bother herself with the farm like the girls did in my time. All
the new machines and equipment and Pierce and yourself so
keen and willing . . .'

Her own man had been a drinker and a great sorrow to
his wife.

'She helps with the accounts,' I protested.

But Mrs Delaney could not relate to the comparatively

abstract pen and paper task of accounts. She moved gratefully on from the problematic subject of Etti.

'You have great comfort in your little place. There's no damp in it, Marty.'

The damp in her house was always a trouble to her. But she saw it as a visitation from God, not to be helped. Any alteration or disturbance in her domain would be a greater alarm to her. Like Young Delaney, she was anti-interventionist by instinct. If I suggested a solution, insulation maybe, damp-proofing, a damp course, it would fall on deaf ears.

'Although too warm an atmosphere can't be good you know, Marty... When you're not used to it,' she added hastily. In case I might take offence at any implied disparagement of the central heating and other modern comforts that Pierce and Etti indulge in. The Hawkinses always went in for comfort. Our reputation for comfort and progress goes back a long way.

She placed the blue, farm-sized enamel teapot on the hot ring where it set up a rhythmic babbling at once as it began to boil. She lifted the smaller kettle off the cooker, carried it back to the range and poured back the water remaining in it into the big kettle. Then she remembered my egg and filled a saucepan with the same water now well off the boil. Mrs Delaney has her own particular ways of domestic economy.

She brought the sugar-bowl and the milk in a large white jug from the dresser. She brought the garrulous teapot from the cooker and put it down on a yellow ceramic slab where it continued to gurgle away for a while. I recognised the yellow slab. It came from the rickety washstand that used to be in Young Delaney's room when he was a boy. More lately, this spent a year or two upended in the rank grass in the haggard. Now I guessed Augie had chopped it up for firewood. He always got round to these tasks in the end.

Returning to the range, she picked up two buckets that

59

were standing there and carried them out to the yard. I heard her call out to the hens. Chucky chuck, chucky chuck chuck. Ritualistically, pointlessly, since as far as I could see, the buckets were empty. Then she came back to me and brought me my boiled egg and sat down at the table and with a sigh poured herself a cup of tea.

I was wary of broaching the subject of Missy. I was wary of Mrs Delaney's pity.

'Poor Marty. He's losing the head,' Young Delaney would say.

She would defend me but be inclined to agree with him.

'It was the shock, Augie. The shock unsettled him.'

Tears might enter her eyes afresh on my behalf.

'He'll never make a farmer. He should have stuck to his studies. Sure what is he now only a stone around Pierce's neck?'

And they would be away on a hack, the familiar theme, given renewed substance now. Dissecting my failures, my oddity, my spoiled future. This is not vanity nor hubris. I know the coinage of conversation, domestic and commercial, new-minted and old, in Fansha.

She gave me more tea, an opaque brown bubbling liquid with a strong odour of decaying autumn leaves.

'Did I tell you, Marty? I've consented to it. In the heel of the hunt. What choice have I? I couldn't put down another winter like last year's.'

I was quick off the mark.

'You saw the doctor,' I said.

'I did. And between himself and Augie, they convinced me. I'm to go in on the twenty-first of August.'

'The right decision, Mrs Delaney. Aren't they all having it? Look at Willy Gillespie. He's a new man.'

'Willy Gillespie was confined to the bed before he went in.'

'And he's down at Toby's now every night of the week.'

'And in at the mart warm or cold, Augie tells me. Not a bother on him.'

'You'll be a new woman after it.'

She was getting the hip done at last. All the old lads were getting it done, bouncing around like colts when their fathers at their age were on the stick. I was surprised all the same at Young Delaney encouraging her. You never can predict what he will go for in the way of progress.

She gave a troubled sigh.

'I can't say I'm looking forward to it, Marty.'

'Who would look forward to it? But you'll be delighted with yourself afterwards.'

The table-cloth was giving off the faint stale smell of the dish-cloth. All this while, as I talked, I was thinking of my own purpose in being here. My head was feverish and my face flushed, exacerbated by the heat of the tea which I was downing in draughts like a hard-working farmer's boy. In the old days of my youth, I used to be confident and careless with Augie's mother. Now I was putty in her hands.

A dark shape passed the window. Through the open door we heard muttered exclamations as Young Delaney removed his boots. Then a squeal as a boot thrown in Young Delaneyish good humour hit one of the dogs a belt.

He had finished early in field or bog. A sense of relief calmed me. It was his mother's brains I had wanted to pick. Better maybe now not to bring up the subject. Better postpone it anyway. It was too outlandish for everyday discussion.

'Marty Hawkins. Yourself it is.'

Big, hearty, sunburned, he slouched across the kitchen in his stockinged feet. He pulled out a chair and sat across from me. His mother made her laborious way to the dresser, fetching a mug for his tea.

'All we want now is for the weather to hold up,' he said. 'Would you say it'll hold up, Marty?'

61

He brought the aroma of the bog with him, the damp sweet smell of freshly-cut turf and the sweaty man-smell of himself.

'Will you be on for the bog, Marty?' he asked.

'I will,' I said.

'It's lovely, a day in the bog,' said Mrs Delaney approvingly, conveying her insistent impression of me as a city boy, a visitor merely to Fansha.

'There's nothing like it.'

A country truism. That the bog on a summer's day is the only place to be. At the National School we wrote compositions extolling the joys of a day at the bog, with sub-lyrical descriptions of the camaraderie and the peewit's cry and the boggy thirst slaked with bog-brewed tea.

'Did Pierce send you over about the draw-bar?' asked Young Delaney.

'He didn't,' I said.

'Tell him I have it for him if he wants it.'

He looked keenly at me then, as if to discern my mysterious purposes.

'Did he ever get the loader back off the Ffrenches?'

'I haven't a clue,' I said.

He took a slug of his tea and looked me full in the eye.

'You're up early these mornings, Marty.'

There was a distinct enquiry in that remark.

'A touch of insomnia,' I said.

He guffawed. 'Marty Hawkins with insomnia. That's a good one.'

'Now, Augie. After all Marty went through,' murmured Mrs Delaney reproachfully.

'Tell me something, Marty. Is it this little pet lamb you have that's getting you up?'

Young Delaney tilted backwards in his chair, rocking on its two back legs. He was swinging one arm idly to and fro behind him and his leering smile was malicious and knowing.

62

I made no reply and took a slice of bread and buttered it with slow deliberation. But I felt the heat rise in my neck and suffuse my face.

'Marty has a little lamb. Did you hear about that, Mammy? Is she weaned yet, Marty? Or is she still on the bottle?'

He was rocking idly on his chair and looking at me with his teasing grin of malice and contempt.

'She won't do any good now, what would you say, Mammy? A bit long in the tooth now for the bottle.'

'She's off the bottle,' I said, too stiffly to disguise my anger.

'Fit for the factory, so, is she?' crowed Young Delaney, triumphant at my disclosing that much. 'If they'd take her.'

'Now, Augie. Marty is fond of the lamb, maybe,' said Mrs Delaney with a warning note in her voice.

''Twould take Marty,' said Young Delaney with his manic laugh, 'to be fond of an aul sheep.'

'A dog can be great company,' said his mother. 'Would you get a dog, Marty?'

Young Delaney levelled up his chair and leaned across the table so his grinning sweaty face was close up to mine.

'Wouldn't you think he'd go the whole hog when he was at it, and get a woman for himself?'

I pushed back my chair and stood up.

'Thanks for the tea,' I said.

He was shouting after me as I made it into the yard.

'Slaughter her. That's my advice. Sure you'd get a dinner or two anyway out of her if the factory wouldn't have her.'

His manic chortle, the dogs barking in tune with him and his mother calling out to me, troubled and upset, as I reached the byre. She had hobbled out painfully in my wake.

'He was only teasing you, Marty. You know Augie . . .' Her voice trailing off.

To assure her that I bore her at least no ill-will, I gave her a wave. Her hand shading her eyes, she stood in the yard, a broad dark figure in her pinafore, watching me shift the heavy gate. To annoy Delaney I left it ajar after me. I went on up the haggard with murder in my heart. Kicking at the cabbage-stalks, suffused with a savage wish to see that grinning skull of his thrown among them and the detritus of his life.

That was getting to be the way it was now between myself and Young Delaney.

13

MOST OF THE sheep were sheared and their lambs on the gambol in plush new pastures. Raffles was finishing off the job. I left him to it. He's a good sheepman and he was managing fine long before I turned up. He's happier anyway working away on his own. Or at least without any bother from the likes of me. Pierce now, that was a different story. His deference to Pierce was ready and genuine.

Raffles used to be a wild man – 'like us all, like us all, Marty', as Young Delaney would say. Until, I suppose when he was ripe for retirement, he ran into Fran with her nurse's salary and firmly domestic aspirations and settled down to the family-making business. He was renting the lodge from Pierce until they had the new bungalow built and a splendid and fancy-looking structure it is.

After Raffles, a young pair from Thurles took it for a few months. They were happy for a while growing a few rows of onions and courgettes and drinking pints in Toby's on dole-day. But that soon palled and they moved on. Now I keep my odds and ends on Raffles' makeshift shelves and occasionally come across, like a fossil, an emaciated onion in the patch of wilderness encroaching the lodge. Left to me, the lodge could fall in. Pierce used to hint as much.

'No fear,' I would assure him. 'Look at those walls. A couple of foot thick.'

'The roof, Marty,' he would murmur. 'The roof.'

'Dry as a bone,' I would tell him. 'Dry as a bone. No call

to go to bed under an umbrella. So far anyway.' Then I might give a gleeful cackle, sounding even to my own ears like Young Delaney. And Pierce would turn aside with that worried look on his face. I was cause for worry.

In the days of our youth, Raffles was long and lithe and alert with the heady satisfaction of his desires in the drinking, carousing and women line. His hair was sleek and black, his eyes luminous with rapture, calling for black pints and downing them in sensuous gulps, jingling his car-keys with the ceaseless activity of a youth on the go, itching to be off to some disco in a far-off town where there would be more girls for him to try.

The hair is greying now and the eyes are dry and shrewd. His body is solid and his pace measured as if all that energy that drove him and that he used to discharge like electricity is tunnelling inward and concentrating itself in matter around his midriff. He will soon be what you would call stout. He has grown into a man. A countryman. This was always what he was going to be. I would never have seen it. I saw nothing before. Now I see Raffles and everyone grow into themselves year by year. But I shouldn't be referring to him as Raffles. He doesn't any more, though once he revelled in it, like that name. He likes to be called his real name, Ralph. I forget, too often for his comfort or mine.

Funny. Pierce was manly, there was no one more manly. But somehow also boyish; as if the boy and the man were all of a piece. The man harmoniously and gracefully nascent in the boy. There are few, apart from Pierce, whose grown selves are not a surprise, not to say a shock.

Raffles does not take me seriously. He made a play of deferring to me in my supervisory capacity that came with my status as the bossman's brother. But with an over-stated courteous manner as if I were a bit of a half-wit or a child to be humoured. I was not at my proper work, his manner implied. I was playing at a farmer, dogging the heels of serious men like himself and Pierce. A nuisance.

I sought a means sometimes of imposing my will on him. Like reminding him one day when we were dosing the lambs that we were to use the Ivomec, when he was going for the other stuff that we gave them the last time. They could be in danger of developing an immunity to that, I pointed out. He didn't like it.

'You're picking up the jargon, Marty,' he said. 'You're learning.'

As if that were all I was picking up. As if I could make it with the theory but he was the man for the practice.

I left Raffles to his shearing. Came back up to the lodge and made a pot of tea and put some black pudding on the pan for a snack. Missy was lying morosely in a patch of sun in the doorway. Her fleece looked dingy and sparse and as I stood at the cooker I could see her thin, almost transparent skin shining pinkly through it in spots as if she had the mange. Its curl was limp, a hirsute growth more than wool.

I ate in quick bites, stabbing my fork into the thick coins of pudding, cropping them briskly but with appetite and supping mugs of hot tea as I observed her coldly. It was not long after my botched visit to the Delaneys'. Augie's words were still rankling with me though I was aware of that only obscurely. Anyway, I was determined not to dwell on anything that fellow might say. I was aware however of a cold wave of callousness rising in me, as they say can happen when one is presented with a victim nature. He to whom evil is done . . . Maybe I wanted to prove him wrong, that I could be as tough as himself or Raffles any day.

I brought the plate to the sink and then I took the Ivomec that happened to be lying on the dresser and I picked Missy up, roughly, so that she made a sharp squeal of protest. With her head clenched firmly between my knees as if she were any old lamb out in the field, I sat on the couch and dosed her.

She would not consent to it. She scrabbled with her small misshapen hooves on the floor, stuck her teeth fast together and glared at me more in anger than in terror. It was her sense of outrage that made me determined to beat her. I prised her mouth open, stuck the tube in and shot the stuff into her. This is how you deal with a stupid sheep that won't take its medicine.

Naturally, stronger than she was, I easily got the better of her. Her body jerked with horror and distaste as the stuff flooded down her throat. Then I pushed her aside and poured myself another cup of tea and drank it off though it was cold and sour.

What was I up to? What was the good of dosing Missy? She was not out feeding on pasture where she could pick up disease, not in contact with the flock, infected or no. She was hardly a lamb at all. I was treacherous and cruel and weak in attempting to force compliance on her, to impose meek ovineness on a creature bent on rejecting her sheep's costume, steadfast as a dissident bent on martyrdom.

Upstairs, I pulled off my boots and lay down on the bed. With the curtains drawn, it was shady and dim. I willed the dreamy intimations of a drowsy summer afternoon to gather substance around me. The heavy scents of roses and manure and new-cut hay, the humming of wide-bodied insects and a woman baking . . . imagining the past into existence again. I dozed off for a while.

Waking, softened and remorseful, I went back down to the dusty kitchen and looked for her, calling Missy, Missy, with a cajoling note. I found her in the yard, exhausted, lying on her side, her head turned away, not quite successfully, from a pool of yellowy mess. She had puked the stuff up.

And still, I wanted to teach her some sort of lesson. I left her there in her wretchedness and went out to the shed with a rag and the can of oil and I wheeled out the Norton to give it a polish, a task that had been in my mind for some time. It came up a grand dully glittering green from its patina of dust. But my heart somehow wasn't in it. And when it was only half done, I threw my rags aside and went inside again to have a look at her.

Suddenly aware of me standing coolly in the door, watching her, she staggered to her feet and attempted to move off to the shelter of the lilac bush, cowering like a child who had been severely punished. I was filled with a surge of pity and regret. When I approached her, my hands raised in supplication, calling her name gently, sorrowfully, she made a high-pitched warning whine that I interpreted as a growl and the look in her eyes was angry and accusing.

She knew I had been unjust, that her Marty had betrayed her trust. Hurt, profoundly, as a child is by the beloved and benign guardian turning questionable and unreliable. Most of us have known that disillusion with some hero or other. Gazing into her hurt hostile face, I resolved never to give into that impulse to power again; but to be good, to be fair, to be superior to Raffles or Young Delaney. To be fine. Like Pierce. Pierce, in my condition of gullibility and conviction, would never have been brutal as I had been.

Stay away from me, do not touch me, Missy was telling me. And I obeyed her. Meekly, I went back in and filled a plate of cool milk for her from the fridge to ease the soreness in her mouth from the retching and placed it at a good distance from her and stood watching unseen by her at the window as she came up to it warily and then lapped at it slowly but gratefully.

Assured now of her willingness, however grudging, to accept consolation, I filled the big white sink in the pantry with warm water, testing the temperature with my elbow. A fragment of maternal craft that came to me from an old memory of some young mother, seen in a film maybe, I don't know. I went upstairs to the bathroom and selected a baby shampoo from the bottles I idly throw in my basket in the supermarket in town every month or two. And my favourite towel from when I was a kid, the orange one with Mickey Mouse in a furry relief on it. It wasn't fluffy anymore but it was a towel for a kid.

She was finishing up the last of the milk and I went out and, despite the way she cringed from my grasp, I gathered her up and carried her in to the bath I had prepared for her, talking softly to her, telling her of my remorse. She struggled at first, but once she accepted perhaps that I was unlikely to plunge her face in the water but was keeping her head suspended above it with my free hand, she relaxed a little and seemed even to enjoy a little her bath.

Careful with her eyes, I washed her weird unlamblike hair. Maybe she liked the smell of the shampoo. Or maybe she was just fatalistic. In any case she stood stiff and quiet for me, her watchful and still distrustful eyes fastened on me as I soaped her coat.

After carefully rubbing her dry so that she was scarcely damp when I had finished, I carried her to the yard where the evening sun was still shining, though with little enough heat in it, and placed her on the old brown Crombie coat that Nancy gave me when I went up first to Trinity, and which after this became Missy's security blanket. All the time I was murmuring words of cajolery to her to soothe her and convince her of my continuing affection despite my previous roughness. I thought she could lie there or walk about as she preferred and I suggested this to her, though naturally I knew it was doubtful she understood much of what I said.

Unresponsive during all my attentions she kept her face averted from me. All the same, she seemed revived and more receptive than she had been after the unfortunate episode with the dose. I was deeply sorry and ashamed of my behaviour and told her so again and again. Still she turned away her gaze from mine. However, I knew she would forgive me. I felt quite confident about that. After all, she had no one else, good or bad, to depend on, or to forgive.

14

M AYBE ON ACCOUNT of the little creature in the house and wanting to make it bright and cheerful for her, I took a fit of domesticity and set to work with the turquoise paint and the new paintbrush. Purchased last year in Roche's in Thurles, a big can of blue paint called Lagoon along with the brush, when I was expecting Fintan down on a visit. Fintan duly arrived sometime during August. But I never had got round to the decorating.

The work pleased me. Dipping the big flat brush in my blue Lagoon, its soft smooth slap on the rough plaster and the outrage of the colour against the shabby beige, cream in the freshness of its days. Probably a Raffles job. It pleased me to be painting out Raffles' handiwork. Orange, I was planning for the window-frames, and thinking I would go into Roche's the next day or the day after that to buy the paint. I was humming at my work. Tangerine Dream, it would say on the tin. Satsuma Splash. Or Sunset. The euphonious name of some lustrous Caribbean flower unknown to the average home decorator in the County Tipperary but in whose romantic imagination the inventor of titles at Dulux had naïve faith. Never something familiar and mundane, never Boiled Carrot.

Holiday imagery, that's the policy. The house as Hotel, the room as Paradise. I might slap up a palm tree across the wall, I was thinking. Give the ladies of Fansha with their browns and their pinks something to think about. What would Etti say? She wouldn't pretend. 'A bit gaudy, Marty?' A frown creasing her forehead. Or would she laugh? 'Bravo. Beautiful, Marty . . .'

I had no idea what she would make of it. But I wouldn't really care. I would be happy, I was thinking, just to have her here, considering . . . She could laugh at it as much as she wanted.

Just then, Pierce walked in.

'Evening, Marty,' he said.

I kept on slapping the paint up.

His face was ruddy already. Soon it would be tanned and his hair becomingly bleached with light. He always looked his best in the summer.

'You're keeping busy anyway,' he said approvingly.

That's what I'm best suited to, in Pierce's opinion. Indoor work.

'What do you think of it?'

'Of what?'

'The colour.'

'It'll be grand.'

'When it's finished.'

'When it's finished.'

But he wasn't very interested in my handiwork. He pulled out a chair and drummed absently on the table. He emitted a heavy sigh.

'Tired?' I asked.

'A bit.'

'You could put on the kettle,' I suggested. 'Make us a cup of tea.'

He made no move.

'Do you have nothing stronger?' he asked.

That surprised me. I turned to look at him. The suspended paintbrush dripped on to the floor.

'Watch it,' he said. 'It's dripping.'

'Sure. There's whiskey,' I said, balancing the brush on the tin. 'And a few beers.'

It was not Pierce's form to ask for a drink at this time of the day. Indeed, au contraire, as Fintan would say.

'We'll have the whiskey,' he said. With a few strides of his strong legs, he was rooting with alacrity in the press where I keep my tins of beans and soup and whatever bottles I happen to have in. Reluctantly, I wiped my hands and got down glasses off the shelf.

'There we are,' he said, pouring two good measures.

'Are we celebrating? Did you win the Lotto or what?' I asked, clinking his glass. I wouldn't have been surprised if he won the Lotto. I used to consider him a lucky bugger, the same Pierce.

'I did not.' He grimaced.

'And there's no sorrow you have to drown,' I stated, 'or I would surely have heard.'

'None I didn't have before anyway,' he said. That sigh again.

This, maybe, begged investigation. But I did not pursue it. I was shying away from intimacy with Pierce.

'How's Etti?' I asked after a while.

It was an effort to me to make that polite fraternal enquiry with the right degree of detachment.

'She's lying down. Headache.'

'Not sick?' Difficult not to make my quickening interest plain.

'No, no. Just the usual.'

He was looking into his glass and swirling it over and back as if it was some time-honoured taste-improvement ritual.

The usual. What Caroline and the Trinity girls referred to in more ghoulish terms. Funny. This aspect of girls the subject of black frightened jokes in our alarmed and wondering

74

youth. Now this mysterious female process vis-à-vis Etti a part of Pierce's everyday domestic life. I resented him for that.

He drank back his whiskey in one go and reached for the bottle again. This strange carry-on of his vaguely disturbed me.

'Twilight Peach,' I said, 'for the woodwork. What do you think?'

He raised his head absently from his glass.

'Peach? That'll be nice, Marty.'

That sigh again before he took another swallow.

I could tell there was something on his mind that day, something to do with Etti and her lying down. But I didn't want to know. Or I wanted to know, so intensely, that I wouldn't give either of us the satisfaction of discussing it. It was my meanness surfacing, my unwillingness to be brotherly, to meet him halfway, the hostility and jealousy, still half-formed and unrecognised but growing in me. I wanted him to slope off, as mute as he came, forlorn for a change. I didn't believe that whatever little trouble Pierce had could last for long. Comfort and strength seemed to me always to reside in Pierce's comely bulk, unassailable as a sun-baked Venetian fortress against the lowly barbarian.

'We'll be doing a cut tomorrow,' he said at last, breaking the silence. 'The lower fields. But sure you won't be needed for that.'

If he had reached for the Jameson again, it might have loosened his tongue. He might have unburdened his heart as I suspect was what he intended when he came to see me that day. But that strength of his came to his aid, for better or worse. He lost heart, I suppose. He saw I was the wrong man to confide in.

I noted with an obscure satisfaction how he was affected by his unaccustomed daytime indulgence in drink. His body

75

slack and over-plump, his fair hair damp and tousled, his features blurred.

Pushing his empty glass aside he stood up. I made no attempt to detain him. Though I could have displayed a modicum of friendship and poured us another glass and got him going.

'How's herself?' he asked, with a wry and weary smile.

'The finest. She's out taking the sun in the yard. Having a rest for herself.'

'Ah. She takes a siesta, does she?' Matching my irony.

He could have shown some interest in Missy, to please me. He could have gone out to have a look at her. But instead he went with a heavy step into the hall and looked distractedly out in the direction of the road, as if wondering whether somebody he was expecting would materialise. 'Well. I'll be off so, Marty.'

We were keeping our distance. Mutually ungenerous. That was what our conversations were beginning to reflect at this time.

Caesar was waiting for him in the porch. It was decent of Pierce, to leave the dog outside. He was thoughtful in these little ways, aware that a boisterous dog might scare Missy. Caesar bounded ahead of him to the gate. I watched Pierce carefully fasten the hasp and listened to the dog's high-pitched barks as they went on up the avenue.

He would be bounding into the bushes, sniffing and scenting and hurtling out again to reassure Pierce of his devotion. It gave me a lonely sensation, this canine form of protectiveness and camaraderie that Caesar marshalled for Pierce. Making simple, cheerful and noisy communication, valiantly trying to prove he had enough spirit for two. A dog can be a fine actor.

Somehow, I didn't feel like carrying on with the painting. The fit of simple optimism needed for decoration had gone. I banged the lid back on with the heel of my boot and pushed the tin out of sight under the dresser. I never got round to finishing it. The splash of blue on the wall has acquired an established look, like the jagged outline of a bit of ocean on a map. Greying sediments from the dripping paintbrush mark the flags as if they have been always there.

15

THE LODGE WAS filling with evening shadows. I went out to the yard and saw Missy huddled on the last patch by the wall to lose the glow of the day, her head raised to the embers of the sun in a posture of rapt and meditative solitude. She appeared to me as a mythic creature, wild, biblical, travelling in the desert under a white moon, into the cold black stretches of outer space, into seasons to come, following each other with inexorable bleakness.

I was suddenly tense and trembling with cold. I went upstairs and pulled on a jumper and straightened the bed. Glancing at my reflection in the mirror I saw my pallid face and shining eyes, a few resurgent freckles standing out like the pox. In the first heat of the sun, I turn white and my eyes glitter. The pallor of the mad or the drink-crazed. There was a time when I saw in it the pallor significant of mental brilliance.

It was a Friday. The night for Toby's. I took a couple of chops out of the freezer and grilled them for my supper. Watched the news on Raffles' old television while I ate.

What news were we given that day? No idea. We remember the tritest details of our lives. What we did on a certain evening, what we wore, what we ate, what we said, maybe even what somebody else said. And nothing of the ceaselessly recounted griefs of other people. Any little ebb or flow of our emotions more memorable to us than the traumas and crises of the rest. The deaths of hundreds or thousands by famine, or murder or war, the numbers or the means being equally unimportant.

A terrible thing, we might say. Some phrase to exercise the conversational muscles in Toby's, to prove we are not entirely parochial. An implied complacency certainly that it's happened to someone else, and no funeral to demand attendance. This is normal. It's the way we are in Fansha anyway. Marty Hawkins isn't the only one. To go too far the other way would be the abnormal thing.

No, Missy's small bewildered sufferings would never make the news, nor the ache of mine and Pierce's fraternal relationship. Only the crude and brutal makes the news, the bit of havoc worked by simple gross emotions like greed and power-hunger. At best, television would indulge my fancifulness, append it as an amusing little soundbite to the menu of more everyday horrors.

I was mad of course, the nation would be implicitly told. By someone rooting for a farming story. Yep, go for it, an editor would agree. We haven't had the rustics on for a while. A bit of human interest... Hey, that's good. Put that up as the catchline. It'll make a change from the dip in prices anyway...

'There are many instances of the freakish in sheep,' a pert, hard, monotone voice would declare.

'Yes. Yes indeed.' The measured fruity voice of an expert from the Institute wheeled on to confirm this observation. The lamb born with eight legs, the lamb naked and pink as a bonham...

'That was back in, what, let me see, 1973, well-documented...'

I could write the script for them myself.

'Mr Hawkins however remains unconvinced...'

Footage of me looking my craziest. An implicit titter from the reporter, Ms Reasonable, sharing the joke with the nation.

79

Her hair miraculously stiff and unassailed despite the strong breeze blowing from the Galtees. Missy cowering in front of the camera, clearly a mere retard, the unfortunate gobbet of the flock.

It would impress them all the same, around Fansha. Anyone who makes an appearance on television, even if only to make a fool out of himself, is a bit of a wonder. A one-day wonder anyway. And they'd be delighted to have it announced once and for all on the television no less that I'm a can or two short of the six-pack.

'He's to be pitied. A burden though on poor oul Pierce. Pierce is grand.' The old refrain ever since I turned up here again, out of place, like a lost wandering swallow in winter, given new life.

This is how they talk now about Etti. She has given them much food for talk. And they feed on it, constantly, voraciously, gnawing down to the bone. I know that for a fact. You wouldn't have to be a fly on the wall in Toby's to know that. No point in trying to tell her otherwise. She knows it too. I have locked her thoughts into the barren and bitter pattern of my own.

16

TWILIGHT WAS TAKING possession of the room. It was sombre, monochrome, the rapid lurid flickers of the television and the over-emphatic disputatious voices from some soap opera imparting to it an alien, vaguely nightmarish atmosphere.

I switched the thing off and went out to look for Missy. After the darkness inside, the yard was pale, restful and pastoral under the luminescent mauve sky, with an intimation of balminess in the air in spite of a thin cold breeze blowing this way and that. She was standing by the lilac bush, alert and watchful, her face turned to the rosy glow spread low across the western horizon. Not as if she was trying to figure it out; more in contemplation than calculation.

Squatting down beside her on my hunkers, my hand resting on the fragile curve of her spine, I talked to her like you would to a child suddenly enraptured by the unexpected rosiness above her head. I told her a story about a goblin and a fair princess and a magic horse and a girl-sheep who saved them all from the wicked wizard. Random personages from my old fairy-tale books assembled out of the past to people a wildly fantastical castle in the air fit for a two-year-old. I almost believed in it myself, the way the words came out soft and expressive and endlessly inventive, arriving inevitably at a happy ending for one and all.

Especially for the sheep, who, it transpired, was under an evil spell and was really a girl in sheep's clothing all along, and became famous throughout the land and in a great national fête married the prince's handsome brother.

Quiet, absorbed, she listened, her quaint floppy ears metaphorically pricked, gazing away into the sky beyond the familiar, troubling fields of Foilmore, its bright hue weakening little by little while I spoke as if my creatures, finding their resolution, were riding off into the hidden spaces of night to their ever-after happiness.

When the story came to its brilliant conclusion, she trembled. Perhaps, I allowed myself to think, in rapture. But thinking also of the chill eating into her thin bones, I bundled her up close to the heat of my sweater and brought her in to her bed, both of us consoled and momentarily contented.

Loth to leave her quite alone in the dark, I left lighting the old tasselled lamp in the corner that Pierce had brought down to me from the house. The subdued coral of its shade seemed appropriate that evening, a gesture towards the sublimeness of our interlude under the fading sky. Within easy reach I left her a plate of warmed milky porridge. She had a habit of finding an appetite once night was falling. Drew the green window-blind down to the full of its length to protect her from the eyes of anyone who happened to call, Pierce maybe, or Young Delaney on his way to Toby's.

I took my leather jacket from its hook and bid her gently goodnight. When she whimpered softly in reply, I was for a moment moved almost to tears. I knew she would miss me. Already, I could have a bad conscience about leaving her. But it was a Friday and I had to keep to my usual habits.

17

Even the Norton was light and frisky. I overtook Frankie Lawless chugging along in his battered Orion and pulled up outside the pub with my head cleansed of everything but the want of a drink. Taking heed only of Young Delaney's old Escort ditched at a crooked angle outside, nearly blocking the passage to the door. 'Work hard and play hard – that's my motto,' he was wont to declaim with an ironic glint in the eye and a toss of the head, daring one to take him seriously. He'd be into his third pint by now.

Sure enough there he was, Young Delaney, the big bulk of him leaning on the bar.

'Marty boy,' he called, raising his glass to me.

'Augie, it's yourself,' I answered with a put-on hearty grin. On my guard.

He called me a pint. Toby, noting my arrival with the suggestion of a sigh, nodded morosely from his position at the taps where he was fastidiously carving the head off a pint with his butter-knife. An implication that this new request might be more than he could cope with. The publican's life is a sad and a hard one, Toby's melancholy demeanour conveys.

Perched beside Young Delaney on a stool was old Laddy Minch, in his mid-week garb. Two halves of a suit, the coat blue and the trousers brown pinstripe, bony legs elegantly crossed, small feet in shiny cracked shoes. On Sundays, he dons a complete newer grey suit. To outward appearance a fine representative for Fansha of the old-style countryman.

But in his inner self he's more sophisticated maybe than the best of us.

The usual lads clustered in a straggle along the counter. Raffles and Willie Moloney. Andrea sidelined with her vodka and orange, waiting on the arrival of JJ Quinlan. Philly Comerford and the brother out from Thurles. Martina Lawless, dead keen, it was well known, on Philly and valiantly giggling at any stray witticism in her effort to stake out her rightful place in the company as one of the lads. Fran, Raffles' wife, in the middle of a bevy of young wives on the L-shaped banquette.

The lads were discoursing on our chances in the match on Sunday. In Toby's, our chances are after lengthy consideration inevitably deemed to be excellent.

Young Delaney turned aside from them to face me.

'How's herself?' He gave me a knowing wink.

My face stiffened and a blush of anger began its ascent up my neck.

'How would I know?' I countered stupidly.

Missy was not a topic I would ever consent to discuss in Toby's. The only viable mode of discourse in Toby's is one of extreme caginess.

'Who's this, Marty?' demanded Laddy, noticing my discomfiture and all alertness. Laddy is mad keen on gossip and the combinations and permutations in the couplings of the parish.

'How's the other lassie so?' queried Young Delaney with a laugh. Who did he mean? Immediately I knew it was Etti. How could he know? I had a sense of the whole locality knowing and of enemies waiting for a kill.

Baffled, Laddy was looking from one to the other of us for enlightenment. His native delicacy however impeded him from further enquiry. He contented himself with a playful slap on my knee.

'Marty's the lad for you,' he declared, dangling his pint in my face in salute.

Young Delaney, conciliatory, deciding to play it Laddy's way, leaned over the counter.

'Toby. What's keeping you? We have a man here who'd kill for a pint.'

Toby made funereal progress up the bar with my Guinness.

'Keep out of Marty's way now, Laddy, until he takes a few draughts,' said Young Delaney, with another of his winks. 'Marty can be a dangerous man when the thirst is on him.'

'I will, I will, bedad,' said Laddy, going along with the joke.

Young Delaney was toying with me, his big pink hands, formidable with the scratches and bruises of wrestling with briars and pitchforks on them, wrapped around his glass.

'That was a good day we had,' said Toby with a faint moan, laying down a stained coaster in front of me and placing my pint carefully on it.

'It was,' I agreed.

The pint was well drawn. That's Toby's talent, though he exercises it with maddening deliberation. They say we all have one. I took a gulp. It put me into better humour.

'Any sign of Pierce?' asked Young Delaney.

Was this somehow a loaded question? I decided to play it cool.

'They went into town. They're gone to the play.'

'To the play, is it?' echoed Laddy respectfully, a faraway look in his eyes.

'What play is that?' asked Marty.

'What's the name of it now?' I said. 'A Brian Friel, anyway. It's some crowd over from Galway.'

I knew well 'the crowd from Galway' was the Druid Theatre. It is the kind of information I effortlessly absorb. But it was wiser to stick to the in-speak, especially with Young

Delaney. To be a know-all, especially about the theatre, earns you no kudos in Toby's.

'Is it any good, I wonder?' asked Laddy wistfully.

'It's not bad,' I said. 'I saw it in Dublin. Different production, of course.'

Young Delaney was looking at me, as if speculating how he could get in a dig. He must have decided to change his tune.

'At the Abbey, was it?' he suggested with every appearance of gravity. You never could be up to him. He turned to Laddy.

'Would you like to see it, Laddy?'

'I would,' said Laddy, looking at Young Delaney with a boyish and grateful excitement.

'We'll go in some night so,' said Delaney stoutly. 'Yourself and myself. How long is it going to be on, Marty?'

'Till tomorrow night. That's the last night. As far as I know, anyway.'

'Would you be on for tomorrow, Laddy?'

'I would.'

'We'll go tomorrow night. Maybe the mother would come.'

'I'd say she might. I'd say she might,' said Laddy.

His eyes were shining with pleasure.

Laddy's mode of transport is his black bicycle. To be conveyed into town for a night out at the theatre in Marty's Escort would be a fine treat for him. He would wear his Sunday suit, his hair sleekly corrugated with Brylcreem. Walking into the Premier Hall from the car with Augie Delaney on one side of him and Augie's mother on the other, he would straighten himself up into the dignified figure of a cultivated young man.

I should have thought of it. I knew Laddy's fondness for an outing. I had an obscure feeling that I must seek allies, that I was engaged in some kind of contest with Young Delaney. He always managed to have the drop on me, Young Delaney.

The lads were nattering on about the long-range weather forecast and the possibilities the following week might throw up for hay-making. I examined the swollen umber patches of damp on the fuzzy wallpaper for patterns and could see none. The brown autumnal carpet installed in seventy-something, when I was ruthless and young in Fansha, containing the grime of all our years. The modest grey country plasterwork on the ceiling, weighty and bulging, looking as if it had absorbed the soft fall-out of countless downpours.

I banged my empty glass down on the counter and called up to Toby for another round.

The sour brackenish smell of ancient porter. Maybe it's hard to credit, but when I was absent from Fansha, a stray whiff of this smell in some city pub could provoke in me an absurd nostalgia and longing to return. Ridiculous, this trick the emotions play. They call it homesickness. Fraudulent, mocking, but unconquerable. Separated from them, platonic versions of Toby's, of Fansha and the fields of Foilmore would whirl seductively in my head. Returned to, as I have returned time and again like a fool with the springing heart of the lover, mockingly they assumed the familiar bleakness of unrequited reality, while I wandered around the place like a rueful ghost, tricked and cheated.

Only France was different. From France, with Etti, Fansha would assume, for that short time, only its actual importance, that is to say, none. But back I came, as I always have. This time as a man who has worn out, no question, his welcome. There's only so much a parish like Fansha can take.

Steadily filling up now on black stout, Toby's was entering into its final stage of our local version of bacchanalia. Young Delaney was gazing up at the distant television set, a fond smile suffusing his suddenly harmless features. From the far end of the lounge, the hum of talk had died down.

Laddy had turned his back to me and was twisted at an

87

awkward angle, his palm resting on his wrinkled neck, his stance suggesting a patient willingness to go along with the pervasive enthusiasm of the company more than a genuine interest.

A re-run of a match from a previous year's hurling championship, out of Toby's store of videos, was playing now on the television. Naturally, Tipperary had emerged the victor. Friday nights at the Cross were likely to end like this. The glorious triumphs of '89 and '91 played again, won again and cheered again with whoops of glee. Whatever year it was they were reliving now, I couldn't be bothered to make out. And it would invite derision to ask. Unless you were only a girl home for the weekend who could be excused on the grounds of feminine silliness or temporary enslavement to urban ways.

It was getting into its stride, the hurling season. The tempo would be quickening from now on, and when you saw a fellow with a grim and faraway look knitting his brows, you could tell with some certitude that he was going through Tipp's chances on Sunday and the crucial question of whether Miko's knee would be fit for the game. Friday nights, indeed any night into September, would be likely to end like this with rapt faces and loud hurrahs, the girding of the loins for the games ahead.

The women don't like it any more than Laddy does, but they endure it. They have won the right to drink in the pub but their tenure is too fragile still to allow them to call the shots. Drink up and put up, that's the women's attitude. As Andrea expressed it to me once, recognising in me a covert fellow dissident.

On public demand, Toby turned up the sound and O'Muircheartaigh's commentary reached its hysterical finale.

'Eighty-seven, Toby. Give us eighty-seven,' roared Young Delaney then. 'That was the best game of the lot.' He was banging his fist on the counter. We were in for a reprise.

The match won and the day saved. The annual ambition of the Tipperary collective, the games, victorious as they often are, dramatic arias in the operetta of the year. No harm in that, as Pierce would say.

I didn't mind the ritualistic replays of the videos. It gave me the opportunity to drink in peace in a reasonably amiable atmosphere of community and shared obsession. Kept Young Delaney entertained. Better anyway than to have him digging relentlessly into my soul.

Small white-limbed fellows were back-tracking fast down the field. Toby was doing a rewind. Wasp colours. Kilkenny's year to bite the dust. O'Muirceartaigh started up again, lulling the company into quiet expectancy. They knew to the second when to anticipate the first goal, when to set up a shout to see the ball safely into the net.

Robert brought me as a boy of five for the first time into Toby's, led me by the hand up to the immensely high, varnished counter, lifted me up on to a high stool, worn to a dull hollowed smoothness by big-buttocked men. I drank raspberry cordial, diluted with water to a cerise shade of pinkness, in a long glass with a fluted top. A suitably unique and eccentric drink I considered it. Toby's had a bare wood floor then with cigarette stubs lying in careless circles around the feet of the high round stools, and stark grey and brown painted walls. Into the golden porter-sour air seeped rich smells of intoxicating spiritous distillations. By my side my father stood, tall and glamorous and strong, his laugh ringing out as he and the group of men he drank with made men's talk; and Biddy Dwyer, Toby's mother, who was old but decorative and gold-coloured too, like the air, smiled demurely like a sphinx.

I tugged at Dada's sleeve. And young Toby, a pale thin silent boy in a white shirt open at the neck, was summoned, to take me out to the dingy lean-to in the back where the men went. I spent a long time in there examining the broken tiles and the makeshift paper-holder while I squeezed out some pee so as to justify the excursion.

Another memory I have of Toby's is a time when I was about fifteen. It was in its new incarnation as a lounge-bar and it seemed smaller and the air oddly greyer and Biddy was dead. I persuaded Toby to give me a pint and I swallowed it off fast, like a man, and smoked two Majors. And then I stumbled out to the Gents' and was sick as a goat.

I could be often contented enough in Toby's mulling over these memories.

'You're as bad as myself, Marty,' Andrea whispered loudly into my ear. She had come up the bar to join me.

'What?'

'You have no interest in the game. Any more than myself. Sit down and we'll have a chat,' she said. 'I'm sick of staring up at that yoke.'

'Quinn. You animal,' roared Young Delaney as your man swung his hurley and sent the ball into the blue yonder and high over the bar.

'And it's high over the bar,' roared O'Muirceartaigh. Delaney punched his fist in triumph into the air. A low murmur of appreciation travelled like a wave along the counter.

'If I've seen that once I've seen it ten times,' said Andrea. 'Honestly. Men. Are they children or what?'

She rearranged the silver chain around her soft plump neck and appraised me in a challenging manner.

'They are,' I said.

'Well. I suppose you should know,' she said with a laugh.

'There's a lot, Andrea, I don't know,' I said.

'And there's a lot you do,' she said archly.

This was Andrea being flirtatious. She was honing her art on me for want of some more responsive fellow. She settled herself comfortably into the banquette, crossing one round knee over the other.

'How's Etti?' she asked brightly.

'Fine,' I said. 'As far as I know.'

And again I felt a slow flush spread upwards from my neck. Convinced for a minute, like an adolescent, that Andrea could read my heart, and that by extension all the world, that is to say, everyone in Fansha could. Andrea is a nurse by profession. They have a knack, nurses, for divining things they have no business knowing. And she's a woman, an absolutely prime everyday specimen with all the intrusive intuitions of women. I took a long draught from my pint, using the glass to shield my face, hiding my disturbance.

'I don't see her riding much these days,' she observed. 'I used to see her a lot above at Grant's. But I haven't seen her lately.'

I knew nothing up to this about Etti riding out up at Grant's.

'Is she taking lessons?' I was incapable of quite masking my interest.

'Yep,' said Andrea. 'Though she doesn't need them. She's a fine horsewoman.'

A fine horsewoman. I was vouchsafed by these words, no doubt commonplace among the ladies up at Grant's for anyone who doesn't sit a horse like a sack of potatoes, a vision of Etti mounted. She looked glorious. My head felt feverish. The straight back, a tall chestnut between her long thighs, cantering across a field, her hair escaping in the wind from under a fetching cap pulled low over her forehead . . . She would be a good horsewoman. It would bring out the latent wildness in her that Pierce did not see and that I thought about furtively, in my solitude in the lodge.

Etti astride a horse. The picture formed in my head as a vision, a revelation. That's the febrile childish way I was

91

then. Childish stuff, banal, a cliché. But romantic, innocent, a version of Etti that reconciled her with the world, with the land, with the warm seasons and the cold seasons, with a more hopeful idea of myself, with her own troubled existence.

It made me stupidly happy. And it was mine, all mine. Choosing to forget that Pierce would know about Grant's, that for him the sight of his wife on a horse would be an everyday event, that they would be discussing casually at the tea-table the purchase of a suitable mare for her. Greedily I clung to that vision of Etti as my sole possession.

I was suffused with desire for Etti. It extended momentarily even to Andrea, who had been in fact a not unwilling recipient of my frustrated passion one drunken night around the New Year after Etti had gone off home with Pierce. Usually, this episode was not one I liked to dwell on. But now, sipping vodka and orange by my side, Andrea appeared as a conductor of life and munificence, a sweet archetypal presence. It was she who had granted me with an idle remark this burgeoning tenderness towards the everyday and all its unlikely creatures that love elicits.

Well disposed though I was, I was providing no entertainment for her. Andrea is a girl who likes to have a bit of sparkle and chat on the go.

'Andrea? Do you know what the word is? Young Delaney is mad about you.'

I lobbed that into the silence, a lame attempt at a bit of crack.

'He is in his arse,' she said.

Andrea's tongue is notorious. A nurse's tongue. Having to do with bodies and blood and birth and death on a daily basis.

'Are you having a drink?'

She stood up and pushed the low table out of her way almost toppling my glass, still half-full. Hers was empty. When

92

she was bored, she was a brisk imbiber. Contrite, I caught her arm and stood up.

'Let me, Andrea.'

Toby signalled to us with the sternness of a headmaster to be quiet and sit back in our seats. Toby likes to keep up the manners of the polite lounge-bar. The exchange of significant nods between himself and his customers. His emergence from behind the counter in due course reverently bearing his tray. Not for the few pennies extra he can charge for service but to maintain the appearance of gentility and modernity that the expensive refurbishment all those years ago in his youth was designed to nurture.

Andrea subsided on to the banquette. She crossed her legs, foraged in the bag. Lit a cigarette and stared into space. Her deportment expressed an almost insupportable tedium.

At the arrival in the door of JJ Quinlan, Andrea brightened up at once. She gesticulated energetically.

'Goodnight, Mr Quinlan,' I said, as he sat in beside her. I was still inclined to be deferential with Quinlan since the time when I was going out with Caroline and used to be a regular visitor at his house.

'Just in time, JJ,' she said. 'Toby is about to favour us with the tray.'

Toby, taking the situation in with a wearied glance, commenced the pouring of a pint for the new arrival.

'Good man, Toby,' called Quinlan, lustily rubbing his hands with anticipation.

A careful man, the same JJ. Likes his pint but makes sure to time his arrival into Toby's for when the night is more or less wrapping up. Little danger that way of imprudent expenditure or inebriation.

He was snuggling up now to Andrea as she giggled at some joke I didn't catch. Ever since he spent a few days in hospital with chest pains a year or two ago, he and Andrea have been,

93

as they say, the best of friends. Is there more to it than that? Fansha is surprisingly indulgent on this question. Successful and hard-working and careful and hail-fellow-well-met, Quinlan is above reproach. As with Father Murchess's soft spot for comely Martina Taylor, ferrying her hither and thither to matches and gymkhanas in his black Toyota.

JJ Quinlan's softness for Andrea is accepted with sympathy as the result of the inordinate gratitude a man feels for his nurses when he finds himself stretched out on a hospital bed at their mercy. Andrea by all accounts made a great fuss of JJ. In his dependency and gratitude, he was smitten.

'A great girl, Andrea. Lucky the man who'll get her. I'd snap her up myself this minute if I were a free man.'

For weeks after he came out, that's all we heard from him in Toby's. Andrea pooh-poohing but soaking it all in. The brush with mortality, an alarming thing for a robust unthinking man like JJ. The ward odorous with pungent medications, JJ trembling inwardly with the sense of what might have been – or not been. And Andrea's bright Fansha face going to and fro, a familiar face from home among all the alien possessors of the skill and knowledge to keep him tethered there. Her solid legs, her dimpled arms under her white starched sleeves . . . who wouldn't be happy to be confided to the care of Andrea?

That's what JJ used to tell us over and over again. Blindly he comes to her now, as to a lover. Arriving in to Toby's when the din at the end of the night is reassuringly loud and unheeding, he manages to separate her from the rest of us and they murmur away to each other in a corner like a pair of cooing-doves. His thirst for her company, satisfied in these brief gulps, seems to me to be raging.

What does Andrea feel? There's no future in JJ. After that episode in the winter I used to think she was fond of me. I was a challenge to her, I suspect. She wanted to see if she could knock me into shape. But she gave up on me before very long. With her shrewdness she would have known my thoughts were elsewhere, though I hope I gave her no clues as to where they lay, and she withdrew to the devoted JJ.

I take a keen interest in these matters. It's the only form of speculation that still interests me. What people are feeling. What carries them through the days. What they might say is of little account.

I thought it only polite to leave Andrea and her swain to their urgent excluding murmurings. Toby had pulled the plug on the video-show. With the idea of one for the road in my head, I joined the lads at the counter. One of the Ffrenches had come in. The Ffrenches are harmless, but Giles Ffrench was making a commendable fist of Toby-talk, better than I was capable of in my restless buoyancy. Ned Kilbride's car was at issue. Somebody's car generally is.

'I'd say the carburettor is faulty, Ned.'

'That's a costly item . . .'

'Did she buy the new Opel? Jaysus. She must have won the Lotto.'

Next, it was the list price of the Minister's car. Leading in to the Minister's appearance on your one's programme. A note of pride coming through in this discourse, that he acquitted himself well, the Minister, a pride more muted than in describing the arc of the deciding goal in the Semi-Final, but discernible all the same. You can say what you like about the Minister. But in the end isn't he one of our own . . .

I was inserting a remark here and there into the conversation to keep my end up with them. My thoughts were of Etti, outrageous thoughts, but soon they cooled and were succeeded by guilt and shame. As I stood there in gloomy silence, only half aware of the voices and guffaws around me, I found myself thinking of poor Missy and her misplaced trust in me. I was her only recourse in her world of shadows and confusion and it was to me that fitfully glimmering spark of comprehension, the cause of those strangled whimpers, made appeal.

They were having a great laugh now at the expense of the Fine Gael man, PB, who, Young Delaney claimed, would climb Slievenamon in a snowstorm in January if there was a vote lying on top of it. The idea of portly PB tackling the mountain gales for a vote afforded them no end of amusement.

'He's getting Laddy here a driving-licence,' I said.

Satisfactory guffaws all round.

'That's a good one,' chortled Young Delaney.

Laddy went along with it.

'That's what they'll be asking us to pay for next,' he said. 'A licence for the aul bicycle.'

'And they'll make non-payment a hanging offence,' said Young Delaney.

Home Boys Home, Toby was humming away under his breath, whipping himself into gear for the last lap and our-selves to face the road. I turned around and found myself facing Young Delaney. He was looking at me with that mocking smirk of his.

'Listen, lads. Did I tell you about Marty?' he said.

There was a lull in the conversation. His voice resounded like a roar in the silence.

'Marty had a little lamb,' he recited. 'Its fleece was white as snow. And everywhere that Marty went . . .'

I threw a punch, aimed at that big jaw of his. Just in time he ducked, staggered but steadied himself with the help of the counter. I saw caginess, even fear in his face. I was boiling with temper and put up my fists and punched the air as a challenge to him.

Raffles lunged in between us. 'Now, Augie, enough is enough . . .'

Laddy was at my side. 'What did he say? What did he say to you? Whatever he said, Marty, it was only a joke.'

'Easy now, easy,' Raffles was cautioning, standing in between Young Delaney and myself, his hands raised to ward off any blows. Young Delaney made no move.

'If you leave now, Marty,' murmured Laddy, 'you'll have got the better of him.'

I turned my back on them and walked to the door and out into the night.

18

In our way we were very happy, much of the time, the pair of us. She was the first living thing I loved, the first for whom my love was artless and compassionate and without egotism. And she was the first to allow me to love her, now that I was finally ready; and the first to return my love. Which she did more and more as the weeks went on, though dumbly, to most intents and purposes, and sadly, given her wretchedness, both bodily and psychically.

It suited me, at the time. She offered me a kind of practice run. It was like having a beloved, inexorably sickening child in the house whose days in this world, its kin are aware, are numbered. But who, coming from a fatalistic race, accept without protest such outrages and misfortunes as life flings at them.

When I use this word 'love', it was not of course the love which I was nurturing in the core of my secret being for my brother's wife and which was a mad and passionate but silent emotion. For Missy, my love was expressed as affection, simple, tender, paternal. My affection earned its return by her ardent and, I think, grateful acceptance of my ministrations and my concern with her well-being. Awakening in me a sense that I was not quite lost, that I could learn to love my fellows or at least recognise with compassion their need for love.

Did I not love her precisely because she was semi-human? No animal had ever elicited that feeling in me, none among the myriad species I grew up with, none of the dogs and certainly not any other lamb or indeed any other vulnerable young thing. Turning to me in her helplessness, she repaid my response by investing me with a faint gleam of hope in my ultimate return to a place in the human fold; or at least restored to me my sense of its loss. From that time with Missy I date the gradual soothing of the savagery that had sprung up in me out of my grief.

She had little choice, I admit, but to love me. Who has the prisoner to turn to in the end, only his keeper, or the prey to its hunter? But they turn not quite as she turned to me, not with the same trust nor the candour nor the optimistic expectant gaze. From me, she too was granted hope. Of release from her woolly cage and her wrong-shaped skull.

With every ounce of her puny little strength, she had forsaken sheep nature, she was appalled by the galère she had been cast among. It was me she identified with, me she wanted to be. A heavy burden for a man to carry. But it nourished a me in me that was of some benefit to me later, if not to her. Missy gave to me a great deal more than she ever got in return.

I have enough wit to recognise how naïve this may seem. How crazy to be honest. Cissy Quinlan, if she had got wind of it, would have been already crossing herself and thanking God for his gift of the dentist and the deliverance of poor Caroline from the clutches of a certifiable idiot. Above at the Cross, they'd be killed laughing. That's why I never told any of them.

'Pure harmless, God love him,' they'd say. 'Poor aul Marty.'

Weren't they saying it anyway? I knew I could give them no further cause for amusement at my expense. I was assiduous and I believe successful in that.

19

When I biked up to the Cross now for a few messages, as I did every couple of days, I would make sure to bring home a bar of chocolate, secreted in the pocket of my leather jacket, just as Robert used to in the old days when Pierce and myself were small. Listening out for the roar of the bike, Missy would have lurched up the hall to greet me on my return. I would crouch beside her on the floor and we would have our little game.

Scrabbling and snuffling at my jacket, she would discover her chocolate treat, just like myself and Pierce prodding Robert with our importunate little fingers. And she was every bit as efficient as we were in tracing its hiding-place, though her nose would nudge the flatter pocket first in a playful show of hunting for the treasure. Unable to keep up the pretence for too long she would dive in with the sureness of an arrow to where it lay and emerge with it gripped tight between her teeth and a look of triumph on her face.

Then I would have to take it from her, while she pretended to hold on to it in fury at being dispossessed, so that I could unwrap the skin of silver paper and feed it to her square by square. She savoured the taste like a gourmet. Turkish Delight was her favourite by far, I could tell, from her rapt look as she ate it delicately out of my hand.

After dealing out her portion of two squares, I would rewrap it and place it on the highest shelf of the dresser.

'That's for tomorrow,' I would tell her firmly. Arching her

head to one side, she would assail me with beseeching looks though she never made a fuss with whingeing or crying. She seemed to have an innate sense of justice and moderation. If she ate a half-decent supper, I would reward her with another square or two. She grasped this routine very quickly. After her treat, she would ramble off to the warm patch under the south-facing window where any stray rays of sun came in all afternoon and lie down peaceably, following my every movement with her eyes.

How easy it was, I now reflect wistfully, in these small ways to give her moments of happiness. Why did I not go up to the Cross for chocolate for her every day and let her have as much as she wanted? Twice a day. Ten times. Like a patriarch, I meagrely measured out the squares, for, as I informed her, 'your own good'. As if she had a long lifetime of chocolate and happiness ahead of her, and had to be taught the lesson that life was not a holiday or merely to be passed in self-indulgence.

As the summer came on, her appearance improved. She was achieving a look of plumpness and her hirsute coat, which I kept fluffy with the liberal use of an expensive shampoo – a brand that promised to 'maintain the balance of natural oils' – gave the impression at least of thickness. But her pathos, no longer painfully visible in her conformation, was evident more and more in her manner and that pitiful expression she wore at times. Perceptible perhaps only to an experienced eye like my own, I told myself. To outsiders, she might look merely peculiar, like some mongrel creature.

Sometimes now, too, when she nestled in my arms, or when I bent down close to her to tempt her with some snack, I noticed another phenomenon. She exuded a sweetish scent, bearing no relation to the oily brackish ovine smell, and quite different to the light flowery scent of the shampoo. After some thought, I decided it was evocative of the spicy odour of the

101

clouds of incense that the priest swings from his baroque silver censer over the altar and his congregation on solemn or festive liturgical occasions; or over the coffin at a requiem mass, the last ritual of ministration to the body.

A crazy notion flashed into my head when I first identified this holy exhalation from Missy as similar to incense. But the implications of this notion I would not allow myself to consider. It was nothing but the imaginative associations wrought by the circumstance of my experience of incense, I assured myself. The atmosphere of sanctity and other-worldly powers, the hush of reverence in the church, the haloes of lighted candles and the lowered eyes of the docile stricken statues. It could not possibly have any objective substance.

That notion I expelled from consideration. That notion had too much of the hint of madness. It was left to Etti to voice.

20

ETTI WALKED IN on me one evening. Cool, assured, as if
she was in the habit of dropping in of an evening for a
chat. Or as if she had the intention of making a habit of it.

I was slumped at the table with a can of beer. In a burst of
industry and fraternal assistance, I had put down a long day
at the silage. Missy had clearly missed me sorely during my
absence. She nuzzled me with half-whimpering, half-happy
mews of devotion while I pulled at her warm ears in the way
she liked. Coming back tired out like that, I could be quite
contented, with no energy left for thoughts that might unsettle
my mind. Maybe if I was like Young Delaney without a
moment to spare from one end of the day to the other, I'd
have been better off. All I was thinking when Etti landed in
was, would there be anything to eat in the fridge that I could
sling together in a hurry and whether I had any little treat for
Missy.

The door was on the latch as usual. I heard a step in the
hall and then the light ring of boots on the flags. Missy sat
up and watched the door as keenly as I did. We were united
in fear. I knew as certainly as if I had been expecting her that
it was Etti.

'It's well for some,' Etti, stepping into the room, declared
in her hearty country voice. A useful colouration she has
successfully acquired.

'Aw, give us a break,' I returned, on cue.

This was the kind of evasive, defensive banter we were still engaging in.

I stood up to express politeness. Scuttling across the floor, ears flattened, Missy launched herself under the couch, out of sight. I couldn't have given a damn, just then, if she stayed under it all night. With Etti standing there in the room, attempting to disguise her awkwardness with commonplace chat, I have to state, after all I've described, that it was true. Just then, I didn't give a damn about Missy. Without a qualm, I could have handed her over to the butcher to be slaughtered, if it would keep Etti here before me for a little while longer with her courageous provoking smile.

Mustering an attempted carelessness, I took a swig from my beer. My gaze was fixed on her, in a way that I knew must be disturbing, but I was unable to turn it away. She was wearing the stone-coloured pair of riding-breeches in which I had imagined her that time in Toby's when, thanks to Andrea, I was suffused with a sudden fever of desire. I struggled now for some banality to say.

Etti is not, strictly speaking, what you could call a looker. But she was somehow simply my ideal, girl-wise. Or there was something in me that insisted she was. I noticed now that the pallor she had anyway was especially marked. There was a small bright lozenge of pinkness on her forehead.

I must have looked odd, standing there staring at her. She went to the sink and poured a glass of water and drank it off thirstily.

'I fell off,' she said, with a rueful smile.

'The horse?' I responded hoarsely.

She nodded.

'Was that the first time?'

'Yep.'

'You weren't hurt, I see,' I offered with apparent callousness.

'A few bruises.' She reached up to touch her forehead. 'Here. And here.' Gingerly she patted the slope of her hip and made a small grimace. 'Nothing too serious.'

'Did you get up again?'

'I didn't. Couldn't face it.'

'You should.'

'I know I should. Jesus, Marty.'

The talk was settling me. I did not have enough callers, that was all that was wrong with me, I told myself wildly. That was the cause of my nerves. Not enough women. Andrea only a few times after Christmas. Ollie, the girl I met at the hunt dance who took to driving over from Kilkenny to visit me in the early part of the spring until, I suppose, she became discouraged.

Etti put her glass down and came into the middle of the room. The light was behind her. She stood looking restlessly about her, her hands buried in the pockets of her breeches, her face a pale moon and her features hidden inscrutably in shadow. I was desperate for her not to go.

'Sit down, will you,' I said, 'and have a sup of Jameson. You must have got a shock.'

'They gave me a brandy,' she said. 'A double. On Andrea's orders. I'm over the shock.'

She ran her fingers slowly along the pitted arm-rest of a chair. But she did not sit down. She was standing very near to me. I wanted only to pull her close to me and look into those dark unfathomable eyes until they might glisten with some sort of recognition.

'Marty,' she said at last, her voice newly shy but beguiling, 'Where's this funny lamb of yours?'

'You want to have a look at her, do you?' I said, mockingly.

'Pierce mentioned her.' She was choosing her words carefully, afraid I might take offence. A reputation for touchiness, has Marty.

The reminder of Pierce was an unwanted intrusion. But it brought me back to earth as they say, and a not unwelcome coolness to my head. Maybe that was her intention. I was suddenly forlorn but more comfortable.

'What did he say?'

'Nothing much. Just that you have some strange notions about him. Really, Marty.' She was wheedling. 'Please, Marty. I'm curious.'

'Sure you are,' I said. 'So you can have a laugh at her.'

But my prevarication was only a game I was playing. Wouldn't I have handed Missy over to the butcher that very minute if it would help my case with Etti?

'Here, Missy,' I called, slapping my thigh. 'Come out of there and say hello to Etti.'

Etti laughed. 'Is it a sheep or a sheepdog we're talking about, Marty?'

'So Pierce told you I was an eejit, did he,' I said.

'He did not,' she protested. But she bashfully looked away from me.

He thinks it's some kind of half-child he has on his hands ... Pierce's words were left unsaid. Etti would not throw them at me. Funny that. I wasn't bothered at all by the thought of Pierce and herself sharing a joke about Marty and his carry-on. One thing I was confident of even then was that Etti's attitude towards me was not patronising. Behind the banter, I could sense the interest in me that I so intensely had in her. Withheld, suspended, imperceptible to an observer but plain as a pikestaff to me. That complicitous thing. But I was still reluctant to reveal to her my convictions about Missy. Afraid still of her contempt.

'Missy. Hey. Come here, Missy.'

Etti, adopting my flippant matey tone, was looking imperiously towards the couch. In reply there was a faint protesting mewl of the kind that Missy made when she was especially alarmed. She was not accustomed to the presence of anyone but myself in the house, to anyone but me taking an interest in her.

Kneeling on the rug by the couch, Etti lifted the worn chintz and peered underneath. I let her be. There was no one else in the world I would have allowed to harass poor Missy. But I would let Etti do with her whatever she wanted. As she scrabbled under the couch for Missy, who I guessed was retreating to press herself against the wainscot, I watched, oblivious of the poor lamb's terror, the view of Etti's rear outlined so becomingly in her breeches. I say this without any ruefulness, but indeed with gratitude. For Etti, my brother's girl, his wife, I was able to accommodate romantic idealisation with a hot, adolescent lust, an unencumbered wholesomeness which in fact I do not remember ever fully knowing but in any case assumed I had lost.

Without a word of protest, I permitted Etti's probing fingers to besiege Missy's hiding-place and reach out peremptorily for her in the dark. Stood by as they clutched blindly, pro-prietorially at the weak despairing creature in my care, whose feet I heard scrape in terrified resistance on the stone flags of the floor, and dragged her out into the glare of day.

I could claim that this was not only callousness on my part. Maybe it was an obscure test I was setting the three of us.

Flushed and gleeful with triumph, Etti stood up, clasping the lamb insecurely in her arms.

'Gotcha,' she declared breathlessly.

She scrutinised Missy's face who, still battling miserably to escape, avoided her stare.

'Poor old thing,' she said. 'He's frightened.'

Purposeful suddenly, and assured, she took Missy on to her lap, and freely, with no sign of revulsion, caressed the poor freakish swollen head, arranging the thick struggling front legs across her shoulders as one might the sweet delicate paws

107

of a kitten, stroked the straggled hair and pulled gently at the naked ears.

'His ears are cold,' she said.

I had not swept for some time the place under the couch and Missy's coat was streaked with dust and grime. Etti's crisp white shirt too was badly smudged and there were cobwebs in her hair.

I would have liked to reach out and smooth the dust and cobwebs from her hair. Too huge and irrevocable a step to take, this seemed, however.

Bending her head, Etti rested it on Missy's and held the struggling flank firm against her chest. Over Etti's shoulder, Missy's eyes met mine. But I could see that she was too despairing, too distracted, to gain any reassurance from my face.

And Etti began then to croon the words of a song, a song with Irish words in it. Her voice was light but grave, the age-old voice of the nurse invoking the powers of light to soothe the terrors of the infant. With the second verse I was able to pick up the tune, returned to a schoolroom from long ago, smelling of chalk and ink and damp; and boys carried along with unexpected docility on a wave of reverence, standing straight and precariously on the seats of our desks that had been pushed together into lines. Our eyes fastened on the teacher, nice Miss Ryan, of the Ryan Jobs, waving her baton and showing her big pink gums as she mouthed the words to encourage us in our path of harmonies. The girls in the row in front coming in on cue, alert to the toss of her baton and that nod they were waiting on from Miss Ryan Job's prominent and dependable chin.

'Samhradh samhradh bainne na ngamhna, thugamar fein an samhradh linn, thugamar linne e is . . .'

Missy was calming down. Probably my joining Etti in the song had this effect on her. She was used to me singing and talking to her. Though this time it was not to Missy I was singing. Reaching the end, we began it again.

'You were one of those girls,' I murmured then, stupidly.

'What girls?' Raising her head absently from Missy's. And smiling then, as she understood.

'And you must have been one of those boys, Marty.'

'Well, learning to be one of them anyway.' And I grinned and took a drink out of the can to take the sting of the truth out of it.

'Cheers,' I said.

She was examining Missy's features with a critical and intense attention.

'How strange he is.' She spoke in a whisper, as if she saw that Missy might understand and be hurt.

'It's a she,' I said.

'The eyes. They have a really bright look, Marty. The shape of her head. And these funny ears.'

'You seem to have made a hit there,' I said.

Missy was calm now and submissive to Etti's caresses. This remark I threw out casually. But I was deeply moved. My hands were trembling and I knotted them behind my head out of sight.

'Oh, Marty,' she murmured, lifting her head again out of the lamb's coat. 'She smells so sweet. Like incense.'

'That's the shampoo,' I said.

'She smells like . . .' She hesitated. 'Like a saint.'

'A saint,' I echoed. Manufacturing an ironic smile to defuse my fervour.

'The lamb of God,' Etti announced, forgotten words from the schoolroom said in the rapt voice of a credulous child.

Yellow evening light, shadowy and dispersed through the young tender leaves of the sycamore that brushed the window, was falling on the pathetic little creature nestling on Etti's lap. She was dozing peacefully. Our eyes met with the same sense of playful but reverent comprehension. It was six o'clock. From the position of the sun, I was able to tell the precise time. My long watches in this room, observing, for want of anything better to do, its changing moods, have at least taught me to do that.

'What time is it?' Etti asked.

'The hour of the Angelus,' I intoned, in a sonorous monkish voice.

In retreat from our heightened mood, we laughed.

'Six? I have to go.'

She carried Missy to the couch and laid her gently down, carefully placed her head on a cushion. Missy stirred but did not waken.

Etti stretched her arms and stifled a yawn. Reverting to her habitual attitude of boredom barely held at bay.

'Pierce will be above waiting on his tea,' she said.

Pierce was perfectly capable of getting his own tea, she knew that as well as I did. But Etti liked to act the industrious little wife sometimes. That evening I saw that she wanted to effect a retreat from the bizarre and intimate road we had travelled. Now she was heading up the passage and away from me. Desperate to keep her, but unable to think of a ploy, I followed, downcast and inept as an old dog.

And just as she was going through the gate, she turned.

'Pierce might laugh,' she said. 'But I wouldn't. I would never laugh at her, Marty.'

21

While Missy slept on I drank my way steadily through several beers. The sun slid away out of sight to the west. Cold settled around me like a cloak. It was a long summer twilight, the sky fitful and whimsical in a brisk north breeze, glaring with an appearance of heat one minute, cold and moody the next. But I was too happy to bother about a fire or preparing a supper.

I was alone again after Etti left me. But with her had left too the extremity of my isolation. She had let me know that she understood. That she could rise above the indifference and scepticism of everyone else around me. I was mad for her return, would have given anything to hear the ring of her light step in the hall again. But my solitude was appeased by the promise and the warmth lent by an absence that is temporary only.

Alone, I became garrulous. I took to telling my thoughts aloud, on the subject of Etti, on the subject of her own existence, and mine, important matters of the soul, to Missy. Secrets released from the solitary heart, losing their bitterness. A trouble shared, a trouble halved, as they say. Sometimes, she looked at me with such a blaze of comprehension, I nearly expected her to talk back to me. But whatever her level of human intelligence, she had no verbal skills.

'I can't show you off as a prodigy anyway,' I would tell her. 'No show on the television, I'm afraid, for you, Missy.'

And she would cock her head to one side keenly as if to

hear better and bare her eight small crooked teeth in imitation of my laugh. I think looking back that she may have liked me best when I was making a bit of fun and not taking things too seriously.

22

WE WERE FAVOURED with a heatwave. It came up to us from the sandy plains of Africa and the air had a burning gritty thing in it of the desert and the heat of the noontime Continental sun. In the cooler fragrant evenings, I used to take Missy out to stroll in the fields, permitting her to wander among the fresh smells of honeysuckle and other flowers and the mown grass in the expanses of meadow drying into tawny hay. This I regarded in the light of a scientific mode of enquiry. A final opportunity for her to indulge her sheep nature, if she had it.

It was no surprise to me that she scorned all the edible stuff around her which would be sweet and appetising to any normal lamb. After an initial display of curiosity like a child in the brighter flowers and a roll or two in the wads of prickly grass, she ignored them. Gave the impression of enjoying the sensation of being out and about in the coloured balminess of the air only as I did myself.

Alarmed by the road, by distant voices or the noise of an engine, she would scramble briskly under the shade of a tree or a bush and huddle, feet gathered under her, head arched in watchfulness, in the straggle of uncut grass, aware of being tenuously hidden there from the prying eyes of strangers. I used to wonder if she had learned this instinct of self-concealment from me.

The cuckoo would be calling to us, her voice high and sweet and arrogantly pitched. Her two simple perfect notes proof of the triumph of beauty over duty, the savage beauty of egotism and treachery. And I used to wonder did Missy dream of Etti with anything of my constancy, did she remember the emphatic ebullience of her presence and would she single her out as an intimate of our house when she came again? Was she patiently biding her time, I wondered, to be held in her arms and caressed as Etti had held her that day? In this respect Missy was luckier than I could hope to be and I envied her.

When we came in happy and redolent of the fields, I would bake bread for our tea. For a while I kept up this fit of domesticity. Tall round loaves baked in a rusty cake-tin that Raffles or more probably the new-agers had left behind. The nostalgic smell of baking bread filling the house, mingling with the other smells of June. I wanted to create for Missy a sense of home, the warm sense of home that gives us comfort in our later forlorn lives.

While the bread was still hot and steaming, I would spread it with butter and break it into damp yellow pieces for her and moisten it with milk from the jug left to warm on the sill of the south-facing window. This was one of her favourite suppers, when the bread was warm and moist with butter. After that I would let her have some of the chocolate I had put by. She was eating well enough by this time, now that I had learned what she liked.

I had established a routine which, for as long as it lasted, she seemed to appreciate. She seemed even to enjoy her bath which took place an hour or so after her supper and would stand stoically, licking the back of my hand, in gratitude or perhaps forgiveness as I rubbed her down. I suppose you could argue that her relative contentment was too fragile and she too fearful and her origins too melancholy to enable her to engage in anything so forthright as rebellion. Anyway with hope and patience the days passed.

114

23

'THIS SUDDEN HEAT is not good at all,' declared Young Delaney darkly. 'The fields will be braised.'

He had called to ask that I give him a day at the bog. The heat did mean his turf was dry as a bone however and ready to be bagged. Young Delaney made his request with the diffidence he assumes with me when he is asking a favour.

'Of course, Augie,' I said, with the heartiness I in turn always graciously assume when I comply. 'Tomorrow will suit me fine.'

This was one of our annual ceremonies. Whatever was between us would come second to that.

There was no one else on the bog that morning. Only myself and himself and Laddy and two children in frocks skipping through the bog-cotton a long way off.

'The young ones of the Kennedys,' stated Young Delaney, after squinting into the distance and bending again to his task. 'Like two goats. Always together.'

'What Kennedys would they be?' I enquired stealthily of Laddy.

Sometimes, when I can forget my discord with Fansha, I get a notion to fill in the lacunae in my local knowledge.

'Kennedys of Reakle,' said Laddy.

'Cousins of the Quinlans, aren't they?' I was able to ask.

Laddy was surprised at my knowledge. This gratified me.

In silence we worked away, a silence cut with drily encouraging remarks from Young Delaney on the subject of our

115

industry as he moved rapidly away from us up the bank, leaving a lengthening line of teetering bags behind him. Once the gap between us had lengthened to the point of indiscretion, he would saunter back down and set to work on our rows, hopping nimbly up ahead of us across from Laddy's row to mine and vice versa. Equalising the rate of progress, as he put it.

By this means we all arrived companionably at the edge of the bank at the one time. It was Young Delaney's turf after all so he was naturally more inclined to work flat out.

'You're a great man to work, Augie,' called out Laddy, 'and that's a fact.'

And he flashed me a wink.

'Not like his father,' he muttered in a snide aside.

Old Delaney, though he had a great eye for an animal, none better, was famous for his idleness. Liable on a fine day to throw his spade in the ditch, extract the naggin of whiskey he always had secreted somewhere about his person, and stretch out in the shade to drowse the day away if he was let.

'Go up to the field and keep your father on his feet,' Mrs Delaney would instruct Young Delaney. It was a local joke. In the yard at school, the lads would repeat it to Augie for a jeer. And his face would redden and he would aim a kick and punch out wildly with his fists.

Resting for a moment, Laddy was standing up admiring the fine figure of Young Delaney, who always looked strong and tall and graceful and in his element out tearing with some heavy implement into a field. I stood too, observing his efficiency. His bare chest burnished to a ruddy gold from his days in the sun, his muscles glistening, his gingery hair streaked dark with sweat and with bog-mould, lost in the keen satisfaction his labours gave him, and oblivious of our gaze.

To me, he looked an archaic type; a man playing the part

116

of the archetypal countryman – one that had little use or necessity any longer – out of some obstinate inchoate sense of keeping faith with a worn-out tradition. But my scepticism was half envy. And half shame at whatever ruggedness was lacking in me and keeping me from engaging with Fansha like Young Delaney.

Beside me, Laddy sighed.

'He could beat the best of them yet.' Clearing the sweat wearily from his brow with the back of his hand as if dismissing a vision from his mind's eye.

'What do you mean, Laddy?'

'There'll always be a need for the small farmer,' he stated.

This is not the way things are going. The farmer, the small independent farmer anyway like Young Delaney, is an endangered species. An innocent, is Laddy. And at the same time, though I hated Young Delaney, for a moment I wanted to believe him. We bent to the sods again.

'Whoah, lads. We'll dine now,' announced Young Delaney, coming back down to us promptly about midday.

Laddy and myself filled another bag for the sake of decency and to display our keenness and then we left off and went to where we had thrown down our jackets side by side and spread them out on the springy heather.

'Ye're a great pair of men,' declared Young Delaney, uncapping the large bottles of stout which it is the custom for the proprietor of the bog to provide for his helpers. We swigged them thirstily and wiped the sweat from our foreheads and bit into the sandwiches prepared for us by Young Delaney's mother.

''Tis hungry work, the bog,' said Laddy, 'and no mistake.'

''Tis hungry work,' I echoed.

'You can't beat the ham sandwich,' remarked Laddy.

'You cannot,' said I.

This is bog-talk, ceremonial and inevitable.

117

'That's a grand breeze,' said Young Delaney. 'Only for it we'd be baked.'

With satisfaction he surveyed the coloured fertiliser bags we had swelled with his sods stretched out in tottering rows behind him.

The sky was a clean gay blue, the wind blowing briskly from the south. The turf was dry as tinder. I was thinking of how I had left the back hall open to the yard for Missy to go in and out as she pleased. And how I had scattered a few chunks of chocolate here and there under the shade of the bushes that she could forage for. To keep her spirits up, give a bit of purpose to her day. To remind her, if she felt abandoned, that I was thinking of her. Would Etti call, I wondered then, on her way back from Grant's? If we kept up the rate we were going, I could be home in time to receive her.

'You're looking very happy with yourself,' remarked Young Delaney.

'Is that so?' I said coolly.

He gave Laddy a dig. 'The chap is learning,' he said.

'Learning what?' I enquired.

'You're knuckling down. To real work,' sniggered Young Delaney.

I threw him a threatening look. But I said nothing.

'You can be a morose aul divil.' Young Delaney guffawed.

'Hasn't he cause?' protested Laddy. He stretched out and placed his cap over his face to shield him from the sun. 'Marty has had his troubles.'

'Everyone has their troubles,' I said sullenly.

'They have, they have,' mumbled Laddy from under the cap.

'The way we're going, another couple of hours will do it, lads,' said Young Delaney, jumping to his feet.

'Sit down, will you. What's all the hurry?' Laddy had no intention of forgoing his rightful period of repose.

I was as keen as Young Delaney to carry on and finish the job. But I wouldn't please him. Adopting Laddy's attitude, I stretched out too and let on to be settling down to a snooze.

Young Delaney gave in. I watched him out of my half-closed eyes cup his hands to light a cigarette and stroll off up the bank.

I forgot about him then. A lazy bee was droning near at hand, and far off a curlew called. The heather under my head was spiny and springy and arid as sun-bleached bones. Flowers dry and delicate as tissue paper clinging to the dust. This boggy wet, I drowsily reflected, the habitat of dry and papery things. And soft milky cacti the product of the thirsty desert.

Why? A schoolchild could tell you. If I ever could, I've forgotten. And it was unlikely that my companions could tell you either. We were shrouded in our ancient ignorance. I was happy with that. I am devoid of curiosity, I am no longer a researcher, it is only the appearance of things that interests me now. I will always now be a lily of the field.

A shower of brittle stuff was falling on my forehead. I opened my eyes and saw Young Delaney's big block of a head posed between me and the sun, his hair like a raggedy fiery halo around the dark obscurity of his features. He was on his hunkers and slowly dribbling turf-mould from his fingers on to my face. I had to shut my mouth tight to avoid swallowing the stuff.

'How's herself?' he said. His expression was meditative.

There he was, on at me about Missy again. I did not intend to make him any response.

'Etti I'm enquiring about,' he said. 'Etti Hanna.'

I lay there, slack and paying him no heed, but inside I began to seethe with hatred. What right had he to call her that? She was a Hawkins now.

119

'No sign of a son and heir,' he continued, with the same air of thoughtfulness. 'What's wrong there?'

I flung my head aside out of his aim and sat up.

'We're not the fucking house of Windsor,' I said.

'We use the royal "we" all the same, don't we?' He gave his insolent guffaw.

'It's a strange thing, isn't it,' he went on, 'the way that girl has managed to hook the lot of us.'

'What are you saying?' I demanded.

But he turned away from the murder in my stare. He stopped his pelting.

'Somebody should tell Laddy he shouldn't sleep with his mouth open,' he remarked.

And he jumped up and walked off, pulling his cigarettes and lighter out of the pocket of his grimy cord jeans. I watched him while he cupped his hand over the flame and the deep drags he took as he gazed out over the bog. His face was brick-red. I could tell from the set of him that he was heated and trembling with his unspoken passion. But he had said enough.

With intense effort I lay back and shut my eyes. I was burning with righteous anger. I was right to hate Young Delaney. I saw as clearly as the sky was blue that his passions were as strong as my own. Saw his contempt for me and his lust for Etti and maybe his contempt for my brother as well. I saw that maybe he had always despised the Hawkinses.

That was fair enough. He had as much right to misanthropy and disaffection as myself. A memory of a night up at the Cross some time last winter sprang into my mind. Young Delaney had been laying into the whiskey and had inveigled Etti away out of the company to a private corner. I had watched him thrust his boozy face into hers, and the way he caught her rudely by the arm when she drew back and made

120

to get away. I was watching that but it had meant nothing to me then.

The way he was always asking after her in that insolent manner of his. 'How's herself?' I could never talk to him but her name came up. Hers or Pierce's. He coveted Etti. Etti Hanna, he had called her. He would not allow us our possession of her. He had made his declaration of love.

I was suddenly cold. I almost trembled with cold. And even with sorrow for him and an odd fellow-feeling. But the chill that suffused me to my depths, to my very bones, had death in it. It was an oppressive and a malign love he had and all our loves could not abide together.

Nearby, Laddy stirred. 'Where's Augie?' he called out.

'Hup, lads,' called Young Delaney simultaneously behind us. 'Hup now and back to work. Think of the frothy pints I'll be buying the pair of you in Toby's when we finish up.'

I got on my feet and faced him. He was standing there, his stance strangely deferential, tall against the sun with a posy of bog-flowers clutched incongruously in his hammy fist. What was he thinking of, to have picked the flowers? Was it some kind of romantic impulse? Or even a peace-offering? He lifted them to his nose and sniffed them. He was wearing a self-conscious, even an apologetic smile, as he looked at me.

He let the flowers drop from his grasp. Wanly, they fell in a bunch, already wilted and lifeless from the sweaty clasp of his big hands, on to a sprig of heather. Idly he lifted his boot and kicked them and then they were scattered on the wind. We took up our places and bent over the sods again.

By late afternoon, we were done. The wind was still blowing and Laddy's yellowish complexion was flushed as a tea-rose.

'Well. That's it, boys, for another year,' said Young Delaney, gathering up the empty bottles.

'And where will we be, I wonder, next year?' asked Laddy wistfully. A youth still is Laddy at heart, always hopeful of some change to transform his circumstances. Whatever this might be, though, whether a Lotto win or what, I could not imagine, no more than I could for myself.

'In the same place, God willing,' said Young Delaney, slinging his jacket over his shoulder.

'Maybe you will. And maybe you won't,' I said to myself.

Tired, with no heart for chat, Laddy and myself traversed the bog in silence to the road, Young Delaney striding out ahead of us, whistling a tune with no air to it that I could tell. We came up to the Escort and Laddy sat into it. I revved up the Norton. After a few dying moans from the car, Young Delaney could get no gig out of it at all. I stayed on my seat, roaring my engine.

'Sounds like your starter-motor,' I shouted at last over the noise of the bike.

'It's only the battery,' he shouted back. Already he was in a temper.

I switched off and sauntered over to the Escort. Laddy was sitting bemused in the passenger seat, like a child waiting for the adult in charge to get his act together.

'Have you petrol in her?' I enquired sarcastically of Young Delaney.

He ignored that.

'You'll be all right, Augie,' Laddy said, trying to mollify him.

'What will you do?' I asked.

He didn't lift his head from where he was fiddling round with the ignition.

'I'll get her going,' he said.

'Hop up on the bike, Laddy, and I'll drop you home,' I said. 'I wouldn't like to think of you stuck out here all night.'

Tit for tat, that was the way we were, myself and Young Delaney.

Laddy looked from one to the other of us, unsure what to

122

do. He had had enough of the bog for one day. At the same time he didn't want to offend Augie.

'Go on, Laddy,' grunted Young Delaney.

Gratefully, Laddy searched for the door-handle and scrambled out.

'I'll call into Raffles if you want and see if he can get out to you with the jump leads,' I offered. For the sake of decency.

'No need for Raffles,' he said. 'I'll get her started.'

As we roared off, Young Delaney was buried under the bonnet. He could be there until nightfall tinkering away. It bucked me up, the thought of that.

24

WHEN I WAS absent on whatever business might make me stray from the lodge, Missy had few resources, such as at least I would have, to fill up the lonely hours. No words to enable meditation and reflection which are my principal occupation and solace. No rationale, however illusory, to soothe the surge of panic, no sense of the future to lull her into dreams of different and better times ahead . . . Born with none of these consolations, we learn them if we are lucky with age and experience. She was bereft of either.

At my appearance, she would scuttle out from beneath the couch. But as I stepped forward to greet her, she would turn her back on me and take up an unforgiving stance in a corner of the room. Whingeing, reproving, complaining. Telling me of her misery at having been left alone too long.

Letting her be, I would busy myself preparing our supper. Little by little, her emotional state subsiding, she would come to me, to be petted and reassured. It was this reassurance she always wanted first, before her supper. Adopting a playful attitude to distract her from her sulks, I would lift her on to my lap and gaze into her eyes, those light disconcerting, seeing eyes. With depths of sorrow and bewilderment in them that cut me to the bone.

What crazy parentage did she have, I would ask myself, speculating on the origin of the slice of human genius with which she had been wantonly infused. Knowing nothing of the means by which they procure the genetic material for their meddlesome experiments on animals like Missy, I imagined various melodramatic scenarios.

A sozzled poet type of which there are plenty wandering the streets of Dublin, indeed with a few of which I was once casually acquainted, selling a bit of his tissue to a laboratory for the price of a night's drinking. An accident victim, rifled for his genes while innocently stretched out under the knife having his fractured bones put together. In my mind, this unknown donor of Missy's human genes was always a man, whom I regarded, though technically speaking he had not engendered her, as her unknown father.

And for our mutual entertainment, I invented a tale, which she always loved to hear, I could tell, from the intent look in her eyes and the way she would hang her head to one side in concentration, about this father of hers. I made him a mythical black-bearded, blue-eyed adventurer, who travelled the seas in a sheepskin coat and a swashbuckling pair of leather boots, whose métier was the saving of a life or a heart at every port. I named him Harold.

Harold was a highly improbable hero, his adventures were the fantastical ones you would tell to a small child. But Missy was as innocent of the world of men outside Foilmore as an infant. And it allowed me endless scope for embellishments and for plots stolen from the half-remembered books of my own childhood. I reckon I got as much amusement out of it as she did.

I am convinced that Missy understood the words and their significance. And when I grew careless and absorbed in my own affairs and left her more and more alone, that she mulled over my tales and found joy and solace in dreams about Harold, her mythic father.

25

THE RAIN RETURNED, the mild warm rain of grey July. There was thin sunlight gleaming weakly on the bedroom ceiling in the early mornings, and sometimes the little musical creaks the ceiling makes when there's a wet west wind. A nostalgic sound, holding vague revenants of my youth in it that I reach out to try to grasp and put images to. More often than not, I fail.

And there would be a few gleams penetrating the low grey blanket overhead as the day pursued its course, low above the massed banks of the trees where the sheep shelter, monotonously dripping flurries of rain down on them like leaking umbrellas. The lilac blooms had died away but the resurrected flowery cones of the valerian were luminous in the dullness and drenched with moisture and the leafy trees weighted down with it. The air was close and leaden and sodden. It was a limbo season, neither here nor there, with confusing landmarks, vaguely disturbing, and little to feel safe by.

'We'll have a good crop of apples anyway,' I remarked, standing at the bar in Toby's. 'Great weather for apples.'

They looked at me sideways.

In the long lavender-coloured nights, they gathered on stools around the enormous video screen that Toby had installed for the season to watch the replays of the hurling matches. With colours still flying we had come through the Munster Final. Only Leinster to beat now and we'd be heading up to Croke Park in September. They were gearing themselves up for that. The competition would be routed, they were confident, outwardly anyway. The seating arrangements, sensibly retained from day to day by Toby who knows his best play is to cater for majority interests, gave to Dwyer's the appearance of a cinema for cowboys in some Tippified corner of the American Midwest.

With the closeness of the air and the slow drip of rain, the scents in the meadows and the hedges were released, secret and dilute. When I took Missy for a stroll in the fields in intervals between the showers, drops fell on my uncovered head from tall brambles and bushes that we had left uncut. Below me, Young Delaney's fields lay, trimmed and orderly. He must be out by night as well as by day cutting and hacking, I said to myself.

In the high tangle of hedge that borders the close-shaved meadow next to the lodge, a pheasant had taken up residence. In the evenings he came out to high-step delicately over the stubble like a bemused stray from another country. I remember the way Missy took a liking to that pheasant. In his company, there was no running off to cower, whining and mewling in panic behind me, like she did when she saw any strange thing at all and was afraid. She would move confidently ahead of me in her crooked little dance, keeping a safe enough distance as the pheasant stepped along in his watchful, gormless manner. And she would regard the big handsome innocent bird, her head hanging intently to one side, as she held it when she listened to my tales of adventure and heroism.

Missy was intrigued by birds, their cooings, their whimsical toing and froing. Perhaps because they were smaller than she was and bonily fragile and fluttered off in alarm at her approach. Just as she did when anything larger than herself hove into sight. Maybe she recognised in the pheasant one of the mythical creatures I had told her about who lived in the places her father journeyed to.

127

It moved me to think this. When I told Etti she laughed, that indulgent laughter she bestowed on the two of us last summer. Her laugh had scepticism in it, sure. But also warmth and the spirit of faith or at least of credulity.

26

'D O YOU EVER get fed-up with Fansha, Marty?' she demanded. Biting into the blue cheese sandwich I had prepared for her, she considered me speculatively. 'Do you have any plans?'

Her voice had a new note in it, as if the reckless thing that I had always seen in her but that she kept out of sight was coming to the surface.

Etti was calling often to see us in those weeks. I knew her habits as well as Pierce did, if not better. The days she went to town, to shop, to go to the gym or to visit her mother, the days she did nothing at all and the days she went riding. On town-days she was not back until tea-time and would go straight up to the house and Pierce. But from Grant's, it would be some time after four when I could begin to expect her. I made sure to be well prepared for her arrival.

She would arrive famished from her bout of exercise. I used to make sure to have a sandwich ready, filled with delicacies like smoked salmon or Camembert that I searched out in Crazy Prices or the L & N and put aside for her, arranged on my own-baked bread. My blatant wish to please her in these ways she accepted as her due. This had the effect of implying a complicity between us, and a mutually agreed role for me as suitor and provider. An implication that aroused such a tremor of emotion in me as she reached out to take what I was offering to her that my hand would shake.

'Do you think I should get out of Fansha?' I asked her.

'Is it Missy that's keeping you?' she countered with a smile. 'Or Pierce, or what?'

Lit by one of the regular shafts of thin citric light that escaped the sluggish movements of the lowering clouds, her dark hair glistened with moisture where she had been caught in a shower, and the soft damp complexion of her face, as she looked up at me after this suggestive but whimsical remark, had a faint pinkness.

'My wild rose,' I murmured impulsively, and raised my hand to her cheek. At my touch, she showed no surprise or disapproval, nor did she flinch or move away. As if this romantic form of homage too was her due.

The next time she came however we sat far apart in our respective chairs and she seemed remote and elsewhere as I, made desperate by her apathy, resorted to flippant stupid talk, Young Delaney talk. After she had left, my crudeness appalled me. I biked up to the Cross under a slow drizzle of rain and sat on a rickety stool in Toby's all night with my back to the wall, drinking heavily and malevolently through the glorious climaxes of several All-Ireland Finals, despising the white legs of the players and the broad behinds of the whooping fellows arrayed in front of me, their thick Aertex shirts stained with sweat in the stale and heavy air.

I had blown it. Etti would abandon us. Were the fellows around me as plain as they seemed, I wondered, or could any of them have any inkling at all of what I was going through? I knew enough of their secrets and particular tragedies, God knows. But not who it was they secretly loved, what bizarre and scandalous hopes they were nourishing inside their sturdy heads. But there was none among them, I was sure, as uniquely accursed as I was.

Later on in the night, Young Delaney came in and stood alone supping his pint up at the far end of the counter with a sardonic look on his face as he observed the familiar scene.

130

He, I suppose, in his own way was nearly as remote as I was from the lot of them. But that curious fellowship was only a deadly wedge between us.

Etti did not abandon us. A few days later, earlier than usual, she came.

'I'm not going riding. It's too wet,' she announced. 'But don't let on to Pierce.' She gave an embarrassed giggle then, as if unsure how I would take this, whether I would be willing to engage in subterfuge against my brother. The rain was still falling, on and off, with a regular rhythmic drumming on the coarsening leaves and the cobbles in the yard. I made some tea and drew up the heavy high-backed chairs to the table, and we sat side by side in the premature twilight, close enough to touch, while she nibbled at a few biscuits and I smoked cigarettes to keep her company.

Then she pushed her cup aside and set to aimlessly scrape with her butter-knife at the hardened drippings of candle-wax that littered the table. The wiring was liable to be faulty when it was damp and the bulbs had blown, so I was lighting the place with candles I found in the dresser, when I was at home in these long crepuscular days.

I watched her trawling fingers, the long-boned fingers that give an impression when she plies a knife and fork of self-absorption and over-refinement, the nails kept perilously long and tapered and painted with white varnish. Later, in Deauville, I would sit and watch while she devoted herself to the grooming of her nails. I saw how much they were a source of pride to her. Her forehead was knitted in a meditative frown as she scraped with the knife and rolled the gleanings of grey candle-wax into tidy little mountain ranges. I was afraid of saying the wrong thing, of breaking the complicitous expectant mood her remark about not telling Pierce had set up between us, of bearing in upon her the gloomy ennui of the lodge and the tedium of my company. I was leaving her

131

to her thoughts, and waiting for her to take the lead. Etti always had the upper hand with me.

Missy, nestling by her knee, set up her usual whingeing for attention. I was, I suppose, overwrought and febrile as I increasingly was in these weeks; anyway I was suddenly filled with resentment towards her. The blatantly importunate way she was gazing up at Etti, and her ragged and pathetic appearance – she could look particularly pathetic in the wet weather – made me mad with exasperation. Also, absorbed in my own affairs, I had neglected to bathe her. She was a bedraggled-looking wretch. Now she was whining to be taken on to Etti's lap.

'Get away,' I shouted. 'Get away outa here.'

There was nothing particularly odd about this, it's how they commonly in Fansha reprimand a cat or a dog poking around where it shouldn't. The pitch of my anger however was a surprise even to myself. My teeth were grinding with temper and my voice came out rough and criminally threatening as if I were ready and willing to wring the freak's scrawny little neck to a thread.

Once or twice before I had shouted in anger at the poor creature, but never with such brutality as this. Emitting a shrill moan of protest, she slithered across the floor and buried herself under the couch. Etti let the butter-knife drop with a clatter on to the table. With apparent dispassion she scrutinised my mutinous face, as we listened to the raucous intakes of breath coming from under the couch, the panicky hyperventilation as Missy snorted like a horse after an exhausting run.

I knew I should go to her and console her as best I could. But I did not. I was spent, as if some bridge had been crossed or some line, stretched and straining too long, was released. I should go to Missy, my shame told me. But the sympathetic impulse was absent in me. Etti would go, I knew sullenly, and she would soothe her. What could Missy ever do, no matter

132

how I might ill-treat her, except agree to be soothed? And then, Etti would leave us alone to our misery. But Etti did not go to Missy. She stayed where she was, her dark luminous eyes fastened on me.

'You know, Marty, I think you're jealous,' she remarked after a short while. Her voice was cool, even careless. But her eyes shone with the glow of revelation and made a lie of her coolness.

'She's hard to manage,' I pleaded. 'She gets fractious in the rain.

'Did I tell you that I've decided her father must have been a Greek or something?' I lurched on, managing a crooked grin. 'She belongs to a land of sun-bleached stone and high desert mountains. A dry parched terrain, where maybe a few olive-trees are growing wild. But even the olives . . .'

Etti interrupted my tortured attempt to extricate myself.

'You needn't be jealous, Marty.' Etti resumed her raking of the crumbs of candle-wax, methodically making them into hills and poking them apart again. 'There's no reason for you to be jealous of a poor half-human creature like that.'

'Is that so? And who should I be jealous of?' It might have been a jest but my voice was strangled. I was grasping her arm. I felt it soft and slender under the crisp shirt.

She turned her head away. But her body rested unresisting and malleable against mine.

Was I wrong in what I did? The question was of no import-ance then, so can it be now? I did not care then. And all I care to remember now is how I held her and the burning rush of liberation as I placed my lips to her cool damp forehead, to her cheek, and at last to the line of her warm mouth, my face lapped by the smooth curtain of her hair.

'What are we going to do?' My voice, I knew, was urgent, over-demanding.

'Oh Marty. I don't know.'

She withdrew from my clasp. Why did I pressure her like this?

'I must go,' she announced.

There were the click-clacks of her boots in the passage. They faded and were gone.

But after this there was a new calm and lightness inhabiting the house and, in my head, the sensation of a burden lifting and a new season starting.

27

THE RAIN CEASED. The cut fields lay palely brown under a still and hazy sky with green shoots sprouting up among the stalks, riddling them into an untidy patchwork. In the pastures it was the season of quiescence and repleteness, and the sheep lay about in bundles in the lush grass, perfectly contented in their mindlessness. Already, the light was changing, and the crows had set up their harsh caw-caws.

Impassively, I took note of how Missy was wearing now a wounded and watchful look in her eye, reflected too in her heavy gait as she tottered to and fro in her private suffering from the yard to the house. Some spark in her was failing, I told myself. I did not know how it might be rekindled. In fact, it is more truthful to say that I was not in a mood to try.

I was not, at least, severe with her, I was never explicitly cruel. I fed her regularly with the food she had always agreed to eat, treated her when I thought of it to chocolate, bathed her when I had the time. Never succumbed again to a fit of temper with her.

But her response was as muted as my attentions were perfunctory. I had little heart anymore for the retailing of stories to her or the recitation of rhymes or the singing of our songs. In any case, her wary uncandid manner did not invite them. The very way she looked at me conveyed a spirit of morose retreat that I found as repellent as perhaps she was finding me.

I had come to see her destiny as hopeless and beyond my resolution. What was it to be? That botched life lived out day after dreary day as a prelude only to something worse, like a refugee who passes his days in a sinister waiting-room, barred and inhospitable. Waiting for some great event, its character unknown, that might release her and that it was up to me to bring about.

At this time, I was seeing her as an oppressive, accusatory and needy presence in the house. Her predicament left me in a state of discomfort and resentment. It was a responsibility I wanted to evade. I had my own great event, concrete and gloriously terrible to wait on. Self-absorbed, impatient of Missy's insoluble existence, I was floating free and light as a festive balloon.

When Etti came, we would stand at a distance from each other and talk about ordinary things. But that was all right, a break as it were between the acts. She told me about Pierce's hay fever and Andrea's antics with her fruit diet and acted out with hysterical giggles the carry-on of her comical riding-instructor. Flirtatiously she would ask my advice as to whether she should have her hair cut, whether I thought dresses suited her best or pants. I entertained her with tales of the goings-on in Toby's, told her about such a one and such a one, whoever it was who happened to be there the night before, happy to vent my grudges against this fellow or that. Mimicked Young Delaney's conversation, making him out to be as laughable and ludicrous as I could. Missy was not herself these days, I would say as an aside, and Etti would murmur gentle nothings to her as you would to an ailing child.

But always immanent in the distance between us was a babbling ether of tender confidence as if, somewhere far away from Fansha and its coils, we were secretly sipping champagne together.

28

IN MY STATE of impatient expectancy, I was restless, unable to remain for any length of time in the house. Leaving Missy to stew in her chosen juice of moroseness and accusing hostility, I went whirling around the countryside morning noon and night on the Norton, wrapped in my new-found irrational exuberance as in a protective garment. Carrying on essentially like an over-sexed knight who goes off jousting hither and thither wearing his armour of missionary joy while his lady waits on him in her tower. And longing, I obscurely hoped, for his return.

By way of association with Etti's enthusiasm for horses, half expecting to find her there, to hear her name announced as a competitor over the Tannoy and to watch proprietorially but unseen in the crowd as she flew over the jumps, I biked off to the gymkhana at Holycross. Ambled among the hawkers, queued up behind horsy children in their hard hats for a hamburger, watched the performing monkey, ran into Andrea and JJ Quinlan going about arm in arm. Later on, in the squash of farmers in the beer tent I drank too much and roared up the roads of Fansha in the early hours, setting all the dogs wild.

Another day, when it was sombre and close, I was drawn to the forestry several miles away, forcing my way like a clumsy hunter through the thick growths of nettles and odd unappealing forest weeds with their bulbous buds and dull alien leaves. Deep among the trees and the dark ivy and bramble, there was a heavy pungent smell as if the air was over-rich or alien too in some way and midges swarmed up around my head out of the moisture-laden greenery. For a long while I stayed there sprawled under the dappled dancing leaves, my head in a swoon of crazy thoughts, while beams of fitful sunlight beat in upon me among the trunks.

I came stumbling out of the trees, over-heated and hardly knowing where the hell I was. And was set upon with rampant hospitality by a family from the city on holiday in a cottage all on its own on the edge of the plantation. They were so isolated there and eager for local colour that I suppose they'd have made friends with the devil himself as long as he turned up in cut-off wellingtons. They sat me down in a deck-chair at the log table on the mown patch of scutch-grass and brought me tea and a plate heaped with thick slabs of cake. There was a grand specimen of a Great Dane who sat attentively by my side and wolfed down the cake I fed him. They were harmless city types who in turn regarded the countryfolk as harmless and fascinating, so I fascinated them with long silences and country remarks to the best of my ability. Then they took me round by the road in their car to where I had left the Norton. I saw in the *Tipperary Star* a couple of weeks later that the Great Dane was shot for chasing after sheep. That night, I crashed a buffet dance in Hayes's Hotel, a GAA fund-raiser for a rival club to Fansha's and, still crazy, picked a girl up and took her home all the way to Golden on the back of the Norton.

Pierce was becoming uneasy at my absences. He was leaving me notes. Coming in at some unholy hour of the night or early morning I would find a neatly folded note pushed under the door. 'Called around 7. Hope you're okay.' 'I have a man who's very keen to talk to you. A Local Historian. Get in touch.' 'I called to enquire would you be interested in a pup

138

from Hayes's bitch, the Retreiver.' Pierce was always a bad speller. At the end, in smaller more bashful writing, there would always be 'Love P.'

This new inclination of mine, careering around the place, disturbed my brother. Pierce took little pleasure in my company, indeed I suspect he would really have preferred to avoid me, even to be able to forget about me. But he was afflicted with a fraternal obligation to keep an eye on me. I suppose he saw himself in loco parentis. I paid no attention to these notes but went my own way and never went near him.

There was another morning when, feeling land-locked and fidgety, I had a sudden desire to see the ocean. I shut up the house and headed out on the empty mountainy road that winds through the remote townlets of Rearcross and Newport to County Limerick and the coast. Crouched low over the bike, the panorama framed in my goggles, farmers saluted me from cars and tractors as I sped past, rangy mountainy animals eyed me from across the low stunted ditches and the yellow furze blazing on the hills. The roar of the Norton gave me an illusion of omnipotence and great speed. I was high as a kite. Pretended to myself I was the lead in a road movie, and the mountains and the animals and the people were walk-ons, placed there for me to race by in my starring role, a maverick hero with the world and all the women in it at his feet.

From Fansha to the ocean-shores of County Clare, it's a long way. When I dropped down into the flat spare fields of North Limerick where bevies of crows fussed over tresses of hay, pecking at the stubble, I was exhilarated and starving with a hunger I had not known for a long time past. Landed at last then into the sea-light, the light that hurts the midlander's eye, into a town strung with coloured festival flags, where the ocean fell tired and whispering on to a silvery beach strewn with sea-wrack and white-skinned bathers.

My face was hot and inflamed with windburn. The air tasted of salt. In the seafood bar in the pink hotel I dined on what they were passing off as chowder but I could tell was salty package soup with a couple of rude chunks of salty fish in it. What they described as a seafood pancake had only a few crusts of elderly smoked mackerel for a filling. This too tasted mainly of salt. But I ate with gusto. That was the taste of the ocean and that was fine.

The tide was out and the sea a long way off. I walked blindly across the sand into the sun for what seemed like hours. When I reached it the water was icy at first. Then it was suddenly warm as a saline bath. I swam far out into the milky west leaving the herd of bobbing heads behind, into the yellow heat of the sun, into the glinting mystery of the ocean. It was this I had come all that way for. All around in the slow warm wash of the sea, I felt the presence of Etti. Nearer to me there somehow than at home, as if the long mountain roads I had traversed had led us like a circular route ever closer. An illusion bestowed by solitude and by the sea to a lover.

And finally turning slowly back towards the shore, I was joltingly reminded of Missy, could not help seeing how the grey bleariness of the sea under the sudden shade of a passing cloud had the hue of Missy's eyes; of her eyes, her once-bright eyes since her stubborn retreat into melancholy. I was quickly able however to relegate this discomfiting thought to the veiled corners of my mind.

When I came up from the beach it was evening. The long sun was slanted and weakening over the town and over all the houses looking the same way blindly out to the ocean. The groups of sunbathers too had come in off the beach. I rambled up and down the main street among the dense and motley crowd. Holiday-makers wandering from one bucket and spade shop to the next, paler-faced locals emerging sceptical and blinking into the evening light, self-conscious farming families in their Sunday wear – these I picked out at once as my kith and kin – and the browner sleeker ones who were tourists. Everyone, white, pink or brown, licking the obligatory toppling ice-cream cone, the children dropping theirs on to the dusty pavement and calling in dismay for more. I bought myself one from a stall. There was faded bunting hung along the main street and loudspeakers strung on corner buildings. I had landed into the thick of the annual festival. That evening was its shining, teeming moment. I followed the crowd towards the small town square.

There was a dais hung with striped canvas and carnival fairy-lights, and local dignitaries seated on chairs borrowed from the parish hall. One after the other, they made politicking speeches from loud-hailers, the words booming meaninglessly over my head. Then the results of a beauty contest were announced. Three well-made sleekly corn-fed-looking girls mounted the platform to be rewarded in reverse order of merit with a gaudy tiara each and a hearty round of applause.

I was happy standing there, finishing up my ice-cream cone and watching everything. The western faces around me, broader and wilder than our foxy features in Tipp, the giggling girls and the beefy dignitaries; I was freed from the tedium of running into anyone acquainted with me and washed clean of wariness by the sea.

The Beauties of the Burren were assisted in their descent from the dais and another round of clapping was dying away. A girl next to me in the crowd spoke to me.

'Are you enjoying your holidays?' she demanded shyly.

In spite of her shyness she had a gamey way about her, and fair frizzy hair matting in the salty damp of the air. Carried along on a wave of riposte, I followed her across to the bar

141

of the hotel where I had dined earlier. Outside in the evening breeze off the sea, it was growing cold. I was glad to be sequestered in the darkening warm room out of the wind with a pint in my hand and the girl laughing in her Clare accent at my side. She led me over to some brothers of hers, big excited young fellows home from America in bright T-shirts who looked at me in the same gamey way.

'What part of the country are you from?' they demanded. 'What are you drinking?'

Not waiting to hear my reply but moving on to another enthusiastic handshake and another shout of 'What are you drinking?' This was a relief to me, that I was not called on to give any account of myself. The whole bar filled with similar set-ups, all shouting and laughing and mingling in a general frenzy. 'Great crack,' the brothers hollered, 'great crack.'

Later again in the night, I was kissing the girl in the porch of a blue-painted terraced house and she, making play at pushing me away, was pulling her fingers through her tangled hair and considering me with coltish curiosity.

'Are you staying in a B & B?' she asked me.

'I'm not,' I said.

'In the hotel?' she enquired, impressed.

On a whim, I told her yes, I was staying in the hotel. It suited my omniscient mood to make up untruths, to be the mystery man with his motor-bike helmet hanging over the gatepost from some remote part of Ireland seducing a girl in the dark that he picked up in a seaside resort.

She gave me her mouth again. Her thin dress seemed to melt away under my touch. I drew her down into the shade of the tall hedge and we had sex, quick and urgent, her skin hot and salty under mine on the cool grass.

You could hear the waves of the sea fall slow and

languorous on to the shore near at hand. I began to wonder then where I had left the Norton.

'Will you be around tomorrow?' she asked.

'I will,' I said.

29

I DO NOT REMEMBER what her name was, that girl in Clare. And I hardly remember what she looked like, only that she reminded me of Caroline. Maybe because of the smattering of freckles and that independent thing in her. And it is Caroline's face that I see when I think now of that blue house by the sea and the salty taste of the girl's skin.

I have reached, I reckon, that point in one's life when there is nothing new under the sun. And everyone you meet is an emanation of another, a ghost from the past when we saw each other fresh and sensational for the first time. No one was insignificant in that other time. Not the cheerful ginger-haired fellow I no more than nodded to crossing Front Square. Nor the sad girl from Sallynoggin weeping into her coffee in the Buttery over her exam results.

They were the first. That we see them no longer is perhaps better. Somewhere they are living their mythical lives. Now I do not remember the face of a girl I made love to only a few months ago. Because it was really a phantom I was kissing, a revenant Caroline I was screwing.

Why Caroline? Why not Etti? I can't say. Except maybe it was the simple shallow thing in me, the clean wave-washed thing in me from the old times that was kissing Caroline.

30

THE BIKE'S PETROL-GAUGE was alarmingly low on the last stretch under the bleak land-locked dawn sky with the humps of the mountains darkly massed around me. I was nearly done in by the time I puttered in the gate to the lodge.

The note awaiting me under the door had a querulous tone in it. I read it out aloud to myself by the grey light from the window.

'I promised the Ffrenches you'd bring them over the spreader tomorrow. Get in touch. P.' His customary 'Love' was absent.

Missy was mute and still under the couch, one leg awkwardly protruding. Sleeping. A few dismal scraps in her dish. But she had consumed enough to keep her from death's door anyway. A brave old thing.

Contrite suddenly about my carry-on, I stretched out on the couch under an old winter coat from the back of the door, to keep her company for what remained of the night. To find me there when she woke up would, I felt, appease her. After a fruitless attempt at sleep, I got up and took a fair few Solpadeines to ease the restlessness in my head. I slept then until nearly midday.

When I awoke, Missy was sitting up on the rug, with an expression of passing harsh judgement on me from a safe distance. I felt okay, apart from the remains of the headache which was not what you could call severe, and the chastened mood a hangover produces. A spin out to Ffrenches' would be enough travelling for me that day, I decided. And put me on the right side of Pierce into the bargain.

Missy's eyes had their wounded and wan expression as if her private thoughts were bleak. But she stayed close by my side as I washed a plate for her at the sink. We breakfasted together. I gave her a good brush and tickled her ears and made a bit of chat. Then I ironed a clean shirt. Part of my ritual of preparation before going up to the house. Missy seemed reasonably contented or at least resigned when I was leaving, as if she accepted her solitude as the new order of things.

Above in the yard Pierce was on his hunkers, tinkering with a bit of machinery. His large hands pulling intricate bits of it out with the quick expert movements that could make me feel inexplicably hostile. I glanced involuntarily over at the house. It had an empty look to it. Etti was probably not in.

'The dead arose and appeared to many,' Pierce remarked.

He did not look up. It was hard to say whether his frown was one of concentration or of displeasure.

'Thanks for your daily communications,' I countered.

'You should let me know when you're going to be away,' he said.

He was anxious about me. I was touched, though I didn't show it.

'Would you be free today for a spot of work by any chance? Of course now, if you were tied up with anything, I wouldn't dream of keeping you from it.'

Pierce in a rare moment of irony.

'You mentioned something about the Ffrenches',' I said.

'They were wanting the spreader.'

'I can go up with it if you like,' I said.

'Were you on the tear?' he asked.

'Just gallivanting.'

'Gallivanting. I see.' Smiling now, he squinted up at me.

146

'Maybe I'll have a bite of lunch before I go,' I suggested.

I had just eaten breakfast. But I had a strong impulse to go into the house on the off-chance of seeing Etti.

The frown returned.

'If you want. But I told them you'd be up with it before midday.'

'Sure I'll hit the road straight away so,' I said quickly.

Pierce put down his tools, wiped his hands on a rag and walked with me up to the upper yard where the spreader was all ready and hooked up to the tractor.

'Is there enough diesel in her?' I asked, for want of something to say.

'Plenty,' he said. 'I filled her myself.'

Chugging off, I waved. Softened, he waved back. Pierce was easy to soften. He had no talent for conflict.

31

MAYBE IT WAS out of some obscure sense of restitution. To the Clare girl, to Etti, to Missy. Anyway, when I reached what we call the Loop, where the track from the upper yard crosses the avenue that runs down to my place, I came to a halt. Then, instead of continuing along the wider farm-track to come out on the road farther up I took the avenue.

I ran into the lodge and scooped up Missy in my arms. Upending the wicker laundry basket I grabbed a cushion from the couch and threw it down inside and pushed Missy down on top of it. Without a travel-basket she might prove hard to manage. She would have to perch in front of the steering-wheel on my lap.

She struggled desperately to get out of the basket. 'Off on a little spin, Missy,' I wheedled. I clapped the lid shut and fastened it securely. Ignoring the fact that she was terrified of strange noises and especially of traffic, I wedged the basket into the small space behind my seat on the tractor. She had been too much alone lately, I told myself, my presence alone would calm her. And I remembered myself as a small boy, delighted at being thrown into the back seat for the spin whenever Robert was going into town or off to see a farmer on some business or even just up to the Cross for a few messages.

As we set off, I called out expressions of encouragement and reassurance to her. But it was impossible for her to hear anything I said, or for me to hear any response she might make over the racket of the tractor. After a short while, I didn't bother any more.

The sky was on the move, with a brisk wind lifting the heavy foliage of high summer. Over from the west the wind was blowing, like a wave across the land, ruffling the birches and thorn-bushes of the coast and the fine weighty trees of the midlands, whistling its vaguely troubling tune from hill to hill. I thought of the girl over in Clare, maybe hanging around the hotel all day on the watchout for me. She was a funny, sexy girl.

My satisfaction at the thought of her was mixed with some regret. She had been very taken with me. But in a few days my image would be fading from her mind and some more reliable and simple chap than myself would come breezing into town to catch her up with a better promise. I was almost glad now I hadn't run into Etti when I was up above with Pierce. The deferred expectation of seeing her was enough to pitch me into a state of mild exaltation.

I hummed a few bars of a song and wondered what the Ffrenches wanted the spreader for. They have their land set down to the last acre, though it's said they're so harmless they get next to nothing for it. Giles, I decided, must have got one of his fits of industry that would soon peter out in a failure of energy or nerve. He would tinker around with the spreader for a day or two and, a long time after, it would come back to us with vital bits missing.

Giles and Dickie and Malachy Ffrench. Thin waif-like fellows in their thirties, but going on nineteen, awkward with the diffidence and indolence of adolescents. When I run into any of the Ffrenches up at Toby's, we dutifully stand each other a round and drink up in a strangled attempt at bonhomie as they haven't a word to say for themselves. More the type to flop at the long bockety table in their basement kitchen

149

with a bottle of whiskey than to hang out in the pub. Giles is the best of them, cuteness-wise. Though he has recently succumbed to the family penchant for marrying out and has brought home a girl, Ully, from Germany. Up at the Cross she is known to one and all, with no apparent sign of mischievousness, as Woolly.

The Ffrenches marry fey foreign girls they meet on their travels abroad. Who take too long to break in to the rugged ways of Fansha and fetch up, according to local wisdom, marooned and despairing on the farm at Kyle. And any acclimatisation they painfully acquire is lost in the next generation as the latest young bride arrives with unfailing monotony from the Continent.

Kyle is a run-down pile of a once-grand mansion at the end of a long, overgrown avenue up Reakle direction. I had been last up there some time before Christmas when we make our ritual calls to neighbours like the Delaneys and the Ffrenches with a presentation bottle of whiskey. Under the supervision of Woolly, the German ingénue, the three lads were out decking with remarkable ineptitude the big fir on the front lawn with coloured lights. That's the kind of thing they spend their fits of enthusiasm on.

The Hawkinses have had an old fellow-feeling with the Ffrenches since the time when they were both the leading families in Fansha, a stature reflected in their possession of pews next to each other in the front row of the gallery in the chapel. The new church has made all that stuff redundant. But Pierce was a great stickler for carrying on the old tradition of the presentation of a Yuletide bottle.

Just as Kyle rose into view around the curve of the avenue, my elbow brushed the wicker of the basket and I pulled up, suddenly reminded of Missy.

How would I explain the basket with Missy in it to the

150

Ffrenches? One of them could be depended on to poke his head into it out of curiosity.

In the local gallery of oddities, the Ffrenches were perhaps still marginally ahead of me. In my head, I could hear Dickie's or Giles's voice now with an edge of superiority and advantage in it: 'By the Lord Harry, Marty, that's a weird-looking beast . . .'

Interspersed with the big old leafy chestnuts along the avenue that the crows clamour in from morning to night are the stumps of trees the Ffrenches have felled in lean times down the years. Beyond them is a narrow field that had scarlet poppies now weaving above the high grasses, their smell carried on the air pungent and aromatic. It would have made a good strip of hay if the Ffrenches had got round to saving it.

I climbed off the tractor and tugged the basket from its place and carried it into the shade behind the thickest trunk where the earth was brown and dry and sweet-smelling. It would be well hidden there from the casual view of anyone coming along the avenue. Fearing Missy's protests might be insuperable, I did not release the lid to explain to her my purpose. I would not be long away and she would be cool and undisturbed there, I told myself, under the shade of the tree. Then I drove on towards the house.

32

AT ONE TIME, the Ffrenches used to breed Dalmatians. Another time again they had pigs and last year Malachy invested a fair bit of money in bees for a honey-making enterprise. Then his enthusiasm waned. There was nothing they could get to pay.

Kyle gave the impression of having been discreetly deserted. There was no one pottering about the place. No dog came tumbling out of a ditch to lunge at the tractor and yelp a greeting, only the crows perched on the roof cackling raucously as they took off for the trees. Little to suggest habitation except a few yawning curtained windows and the creeping dereliction kept barely at bay by signs such as an axe lying against a wall and an abandoned tub of whitewash. I chugged around to the back and found the gateway into the yard blocked with a heap of cut timber. Chopped in a fit of valour by one of the Ffrenches – who had then concluded, lassitude overtaking him, that the effort of carrying it the last few yards to the woodshed was simply not to be borne, and chucked it. Lurching back around to the front sweep, I parked the tractor on the unweeded gravel.

On the steps up to the front door, a plastic flower-pot with a struggling geranium in it was languishing, like a thing a child would plant and then forget. By this time, Madame Ffrench was tugging open the door with some difficulty to greet my arrival. She was wearing a fawn-coloured man's cardigan buttoned up to the neck. Kyle is known to be damp.

Belgian by birth and wistful affiliation, Madame Ffrench used to enjoy a bit of renown in Fansha for her exotic quality of chicness. As a foreigner, she was magnanimously excused for this. Her sequestration in Kyle however, and a long widowhood and the passage of the years have knocked it out of her. A gaunt woman nowadays with tired wispy hair tied up in a chignon, that has the dowdy look of an old-fashioned countrywoman's bun.

Her welcome was warm but forlorn and limply hand-wringing. She was deeply upset, I knew, at the sight of the tractor and spreader parked on her forecourt. But she submitted to yet another vagary of Kyle with a defeated grace.

'Boys,' she called out in a tone of almost convincing delight as she ushered me through the hall, 'it's Marty. Marty is here.'

In her low fag-ridden voice, she pronounces 'Marty' pleasingly with a low burr in the r.

'Marty who?' called back one of the lads from below in the basement region. I couldn't tell which of them it was. Then there was an exclamation.

'Fuck. It's Hawkins.'

It was plain that the burst of desire for the spreader had already dissipated. In my own mind I resolved that I was not going to drag it back to Foilmore with me again. The Ffrenches had requested it and the Ffrenches would have it.

At the top of the rickety stairs Giles appeared with the same vaguely hapless bearing of his mother. Never was a family so out-bred as the Ffrenches. But they have the washed-up quality of people who have been in-breeding for generations.

'Marty. You brought the yoke,' he announced heartily. Affecting gratitude.

'Pierce sent me over with it. A matter of urgency, he said.'

'And now we're at the painting.'

153

Apologetically, Giles laughed. I interpreted this as a statement that the enthusiasm for the spreader had passed.

'Well. It's here anyway.'

I gestured towards the forecourt. Giles crossed to the window and examined the spreader with a keenness he did not often display. Hoping perhaps to find some flaw in the delivery that might make it unacceptable.

Giles was followed up the stairs by Woolly. Woolly is famed at the Cross – and one's welcome at the Cross is assured once one is famous for something – for her heavy consumption of analgesics. Mrs Keogh delights in relating, in the significant murmur she uses when she gossips about one customer to another, how she goes straight to the toiletry shelf when she spies Woolly's approach and has a selection, aspirin, Panadols, Hedex, Phensic, effervescent and tablet form, arranged in readiness on the counter for Woolly to study with knitted brow at her leisure. Mrs Keogh seems to approve of this fetish. It is symbolic I suppose of their mutual troubled womanhood even if Woolly is foreign and unforthcoming, gossip-wise.

Woolly gave me a weak smile from under her stringy fringe and took a long voracious sip from the mug of tea she was clasping tightly in her hands as if she was deriving much-needed life and sustenance from it. She was wrapped in an unappetising assortment of dun-coloured cardigans and had the pallor and the blinking wide-eyed gaze of someone not long up out of bed.

'Afternoon, Ully dear,' said Madame Ffrench in a surprised tone of greeting, adding substance to this impression.

Woolly took another long sip, eyeing us wordlessly. Then she turned and drifted back down the stairs again. In the silence, her sandals slapped with an apathetic shuffle on the linoleum-covered steps. Madame Ffrench emitted a sigh.

'Come into the library, Marty,' she invited, summoning for

herself the part of chatelaine, a part she has little chance to practise at Kyle.

A few tall glass-enclosed bookcases with elderly books in them justify the room's appellation.

Through the long window loomed the tractor and its shackle. I saw that Missy's basket would have been clearly visible. I was glad I had jettisoned it.

'This will all have to go, of course,' announced Madame Ffrench grandly, gesturing towards the mahogany hunting-table laden with a clutter of paper and files. 'Before the guests arrive.'

'You're having visitors?' I enquired.

'Guests. Yes. Paying guests, Marty,' she said happily with a complicit smile.

'If we can get them,' corrected Giles, who was padding in our wake like a faithful dog. He wore an excited expression of barely concealed pride. But the Ffrench lads would never want to be found guilty of counting their chickens before they're hatched.

'You'll have a drink with us, Marty. To the guesthouse.'

Madame Ffrench threw open a walnut cabinet, badly scratched. But the cabinet was bare. Except for a single gin bottle, plainly empty but which she shook in hopes and then held squinting up to the light.

'Nothing to drink, Giles?' she demanded sharply.

'No,' he answered. 'Looks like there isn't.'

'Go to the kitchen and find something.'

With barely disguised reluctance, Giles padded off. I was mildly surprised he did not seize with alacrity, in Ffrench and indeed Fansha fashion, the chance to join in a drink.

'Yes, we're opening up as a guesthouse,' continued Madame Ffrench buoyantly. I could see that her hands, clasped protectively over her flat bosom, were trembling.

'Of course, Marty, only to give us all something to do. Ully has kindly offered to do the cooking. And the boys are full of plans . . .'

Her voice trailing off as if my bemused lack of faith in the project communicated itself to her. She looked in the direction of the door and made a clicking noise with her teeth.

'So that's why you wanted the spreader,' I said, determined to press them into relieving me of it.

'Did Giles ask for the spreader? I have no idea why he asked for a spreader.'

With a distracted air, she went to the door. I went after her.

'Giles,' she called. 'Are you bringing that drink for Marty.'

We met Giles at the top of the kitchen steps.

'We're out of drink,' he said. 'Ully is going to bring up some tea.'

'Thanks,' I protested, 'but I won't wait for tea. I just brought round the spreader. Pierce said . . .'

'How is Pierce?' Madame remembered her manners.

'And that nice girl of his?'

Not waiting for a reply, but murmuring vaguely as though thinking aloud.

'Dickie will have something. I'm sure Dickie has a bottle secreted somewhere.'

She reached out to take my hand.

'Dickie is repainting the red room for the guests,' she told me coquettishly. 'Come on up and say hello to Dickie, Marty.'

Giles was dismissed. With a dignified sweep as if marshalling a swirl of skirts about her, she began to mount the cocoa-coloured marbled stairs to the upper floor. I thought with a pang of conscience of the wicker basket abandoned in the shadows behind the tree. Yet I tagged along behind her in her relentless search for alcoholic refreshment. My curiosity at this new aspect of Madame Ffrench's eccentricity, so determinedly hospitable and thirsty, irresistible.

Dropping my hand, she fairly raced ahead of me up the stairs. I came out on to the landing just in time to see her heading briskly down the dismal length of corridor to the left. Diffidently following, I nearly blundered straight into a clothes-horse hung with blankets and men's cottons to dry. Artfully positioned under the long skylight in the roof to catch any stray rays of sunlight, its feet resting on the leather covers of slender ancient-looking volumes to arrest its tendency to list. There was a time once when I would have stopped in my tracks and got on my knees on the dusty floor to pore excitedly over the books, toppling the washing and not giving a monkey's. All that stuff is behind me. My curiosity now extends only to the domestic and affective. Led by the sound of raised voices, I found my way to the red room.

Dickie, his face flushed, his hair luridly speckled with red paint, was decanting emulsion from one container into another. An enormous revolutionary stride was being taken at Kyle in this act of redecoration, even if the red room would continue to be red. A great deal of painting is done annually in Fansha. But it was something the Ffrenches never went in for.

Dickie, I could see, had not obliged. At his side his mother was hovering ineffectually, wringing her hands anew. She had taken to the sup, poor old thing, I saw, and the boys would not humour her. I would, in their place. We might as well try to be happy one way as another.

'God bless the work, Dickie,' I said loudly to announce my presence.

Framed in the window was the black cypress tree standing up on the edge of the lawn. Beyond it the rough pasture straggled towards the dark hump of the wood. The view and the vacancy outside looked funereal and ineffably lonely. The white waves

157

of the sea, the great buildings of cities and their ceaselessly moving crowds, the tops of mountains, the delusory backdrop of the world, all far away, and dematerialising as I looked, into thin air. This was what poor Madame Ffrench, marooned at Kyle, saw. Woolly too perhaps. You could understand the longing for some drug to induce dream or oblivion.

Dickie looked up from his cans.

'You brought the spreader,' he said.

'So it was you who wanted it.' I was relieved. Dickie would sort me out.

'No. I didn't ask for a spreader,' he stated heavily. 'Did Giles mention a spreader? Was it Giles wanted it, Mother?'

His mother rolled her eyes.

'Giles!' she exclaimed in a tone expressing derision and contempt.

Clutching her cardigan about her, she rocked to and fro on her feet in a fervour of thirst. With studied but admirable sternness, Dickie ignored her, stepped between us with his brush and pail, and with a lunge started on a fresh patch of wall.

Madame Ffrench turned to a last and desperate tactic. Grasping my arm she returned us both to the corridor. Placing a finger on her lips to signal an imminent confidence, she drew me into the dank haven of a high under-used-looking bathroom.

'Marty, dear,' she murmured. 'I know you will do me a small favour.'

Rifling furtively inside her cardigan, she pulled out a tenner.

'Bring me a Jemmy, will you, Marty, like a good boy. Leave it for me by the gate-post. Under the stone that fell off the pillar. There's a nice little hidey-hole there.'

Her laugh was bravely girlish. I tried to wave aside the tenner but she thrust it into the breast-pocket of my shirt.

'Please, Marty. I shall be very grateful.'

She pressed her finger to the jagged line of her mouth and made her eyes wide and staring, to remind me it would be our little secret. Assuming her old Belgian gamine coquetry, learned in a more coquettish time.

33

I LET MYSELF OUT and unhitched the spreader and dumped it where it was by the front steps. Madame Ffrench had more to be anxious about, I decided, than any eyesore of a contraption. I wondered who else she inveigled into fetching her supply. The drop by the gate-pillar was obviously in regular use. Ully probably. The two of them busy concocting cocktails of Jemmys and headache-pills together when the lads' backs were turned.

Backing the tractor up, I glanced towards the house. Outlined dimly in an upper window Madame stood, importunately waving and signing some mute plea to me. I was a fellow, I said to myself, that the needy and the abandoned seek out. Though I was surely the last fellow you could rely on to deliver. I suppose I was a last recourse.

Arriving up at the place where I had left Missy, I could not make out the basket nestling in its place in the shadows behind the tree. And I was stupidly pleased because this seemed to indicate that someone coming along the avenue could not have seen it either. Pulling up, I walked with stealth across the grass, so as not to alarm her at my approach. When I rounded the trunk I saw that the basket was not there. Pacing around in mounting fear, I found it a short distance away, half-hidden in a grassy hollow, upended on its side. The lid was flapping open on the ground, and Missy was gone.

There was a smell of sick. I saw that she had been retching and had thrown up the toast I had been glad to see her get down around noon. She had been wretched. My thoughtlessness appalled me. As a child I had been myself prone to carsickness. I should have foreseen that the diesel fumes of the tractor would be twice as sick-making.

In the grass, feathers were lying. I imagined a bird, dead and ripped to pieces. But the feathers were from the stuffing that had spilled out of the cushion when her scrabbling feet had torn it apart in her terror and despair, rocking the basket until it fell and rolled over and over, and the hasp was released.

Missy had been through some bad times. But she had never been held captive, alone and sick, in the darkness and claustrophobia of a cramped wicker basket. She had to come to Foilmore for that, I told myself bitterly. What in God's name had been in her mind as she struggled in panic to be free?

And now, as if she were nothing more than a mindless clucking hen, a fox on the prowl had carried her off. This was the first of my fears. All around was the rough field, bordered at the far end by tangles of thorn-bushes and a straggle of higher untended saplings. If by some miracle she were still alive, she would be cowering in the long grass, out of sight. Missy had little taste for exploration. She would not have the courage nor the necessary buoyancy to go far.

Traversing the field methodically as I often did at Foilmore, looking for a stillborn lamb or one dropped by a heedless ewe, I searched for the small pale hump of her. Assuring myself as a means of encouragement and solace that she would stand out starkly among the red flames of the poppies. Calling 'Missy, Missy.' 'Come to me, Missy,' I called, 'come to Marty.' Softly, reassuringly, hopefully. After all, the Ffrenches kept no fowl or lambs or anything to interest a fox, there was unlikely to be a fox, I told myself.

But other fears quickly assailed me with their gruesome images, all the hazards of the wild. The black crow screeching in the tree-top had plucked out her eyes. Wandering on to the

161

road, she had been run over like a rabbit by some passing vehicle. She had fallen into a ditch and with the onset of night the fox or a rambling mongrel or the Great Dane from the cottage by the plantation would get her. Like a fool I was flailing around in the long lank grass, losing my method and incapable of seeing anything clearly. I would not find her even if I passed close by and she would die heartsick and lonely in this stranger's field.

I returned to the upturned basket and made an effort to be calm and to think coolly. There was a perceptible dimming of the sky already. The scarlet poppies had lost their midday glow and loomed like hostile wraiths above the lank straggle of the meadow, their heads hanging as if with the burden of a tragic secret knowledge. At the far end of the field beneath the trees, a bluish mist was shrouding the undergrowth and there was a faint but penetrating chill with that ominous intimation of autumn in it, which can set in as soon as mid-summer has passed.

From the direction of Kyle there was silence and no sign of any movement. I was grateful for that. At least I would not have to deal with the Ffrenches. They would all be inside at their usual routine, moping around with tepid cups of tea and scribbling short-lived plans with battered Biros into note-books. The air looked smoky. A fog was rising. Missy would catch a chill, pneumonia. Pneumonia could surely be fatal to infants, especially to an undernourished infant wretched with betrayal. I closed my eyes to shut out the terrible emptiness of the field.

Then, slumped by the basket, I had a flash of inspiration. I could call Etti. She would help me, she could be at Kyle in no time in the jeep. She could bring Pierce's powerful torch and, though night might be falling, Missy's bright eyes would shine out in the darkness. And in any case, to Etti's call Missy would emerge gladly from her refuge in the fastness of the field when she would not come to mine.

Hope flooded through me. There was a telephone box at Reakle half a mile up the road, and half that again if I went through the fields. Galvanised into action, I tore through the poppy-field and across the ditches and came out on the road with the telephone box only a hundred yards off.

It was Etti who answered. I got straight to the point.

'Where's Pierce? Did he take the jeep?'

'No. He's down at Clegg mending fences.'

'Etti, listen to me. Get into the jeep now and come up to Kyle. She's gone missing, I can't find her. I'll meet you halfway down the avenue.'

'Okay,' Etti said. Imparting perfect, immediate trust in me and her willingness to postpone comprehension. I had put the receiver down and then I remembered and had to call her again.

'I was just leaving, Marty.'

'I know. But call into Toby on the way and bring a bottle of Jameson with you.'

'How much? A naggin?'

'The full bottle.'

'Okay.'

I knew she would leave at once. It was only when I was tearing through the last ditch into the poppy-field that I remembered I had forgotten to tell her to bring Pierce's torch.

My vigil now by the basket was tranquil and quiescent. When I heard the approach of the jeep, the noise of its engine seemed subdued and stealthy as if Etti shared my knowledge of the necessity for secrecy. She drove in off the avenue and parked it among the trees. She was wearing red calf-high wellingtons with bare legs and a short skirt, like an old-style but playful farm-girl. Somehow with Etti, things were always

163

charged with a sublime playfulness. My heart was beating fast. She looked out across the field.

'It can't be too hard to find her.'

I believed her. I took her hand.

'We'll find her,' I said, 'now you're here.'

Hand in hand, we walked the field. Up and down, then left to right, Etti's slender soft hand in mine. Etti was calling to Missy now, cajoling, pleading, humming her songs. I left it to her. Missy could be stubborn as a mule where I was concerned.

'Missy pet, little lambkins. Come to Etti. Don't be hiding, Missy. Marty didn't mean it, pet, Marty loves you . . . Missy knows Marty loves her, Etti knows it, come, Missy, and we'll take you home, home to Foilmore, Missy my pet . . .'

But there was no reply. No answering rustle in the grass, no blundering into view of the pale questing head, no mewls of protest and of need. The greyness of evening was enveloping the field, the rising mist damp and chill. It was all fruitless, the only pale and hopeful but illusory thing the clusters of oxeye daisies looming white and mocking as desert mirages.

But I did not feel mocked. I was deeply grateful. To walk with Etti alone in the dusk of the evening among the scents and flowers of the fields, our hands entwined and the trees a roof above us, this was all I could have asked for. This I had miraculously orchestrated. The search for Missy was only an excuse, a conspiracy on which for once the gods of love and luck had smiled and plotted with me. Etti of course could not have known anything of this, how my heart was full with happiness as I led her by the hand hither and thither through the blood-red poppies of the scented fields of Kyle.

At last she stopped and removed her hand from my clasp. We were standing together in the middle of the field. Her face as she looked up at me was pale and featureless as a moon, apart from her eyes shining in the shadows.

'Marty,' she said hesitantly. 'It's possible that, well . . . Maybe we're not going to find her.'

I looked away from her.

'I'm sorry,' she said, her voice low and full of feeling for my sorrow. 'But Marty . . .' She was clearly reluctant but felt it had to be said. 'Maybe it's for the best.'

She reached up and brushed my cheek with her fingers.

'It will take a while. But with time I'm sure you will be able to accept that it was for the best.'

I caught her hand and placed it in my hair and bent down and kissed her on her upturned mouth. And her eyes were shaded and her lips soft and yielding and our bodies pressed close, warm and fevered in the damp chill of the field.

34

'M ARTY? IS THAT you, Marty?'
With a sharp intake of breath, Etti stepped away from me. Some fellow was standing there, only a few feet distant from us. It took me a moment or two in the gloom to recognise him as Malachy Ffrench. In the last burst of light slanting through the trees, his face showed up the dark glow of sunburn and his pale-coloured eyes were gleaming. With glee at what he had seen, I thought, furious. Marty and the brother's wife, necking in the field at Kyle. What a story to relate at the Cross.

'Good evening, Mrs Hawkins,' said Malachy, nothing more than politeness perceptible in his tone.

Wordlessly, Etti nodded.

In his arms he was holding a bundle that looked, as if I were seeing her for the first time, all flaccid skin and brittle bone. I could not read Missy's expression. Her head was buried in Malachy's shoulder as if she could not even bring herself to look at me.

'Did I give you a fright, Marty? You're as white as a ghost.'

'Not at all,' I said. 'I'm fine.'

'Were you up at the house?' Malachy asked.

He seemed in no hurry to hand Missy over.

'I was. I brought over the spreader,' I said.

Malachy nodded. But I could see he had no interest in the spreader either.

'What do ye want it for anyway?' I demanded brutally. I

166

was trembling and, thinking he wouldn't have an answer, I wanted to put him at a disadvantage.

'We're opening up as a B & B,' he replied in some surprise. 'Did they not tell you?'

What the hell could a spreader have to do with a B & B? But I couldn't be bothered enquiring. I wanted only for him to hand Missy over and to get Etti and herself away from Kyle.

'Is that herself you have there?' I asked, as nonchalantly as I could.

'Who?' he asked, startled, looking around him.

'The lamb. I was looking for her.'

He looked down at the thing in his arms.

'Is she yours?'

'She is.'

'By the Lord Harry, Marty. She's a weird-looking cratur.'

'She was bottle-reared,' I said defensively. 'You know yourself.'

'We had one like that once,' he said. 'But it died.'

'We were frightened she was dead,' gabbled Etti.

'I was up in the polo field,' Malachy was saying, 'and I heard something crying. I could have sworn it was a child crying. I turned around and there was this thing following me along like a dog.'

'I'd say it's a dog she thinks she is all right,' I said with a forced laugh.

He looked down at Missy in his arms.

'She's asleep,' he said, lowering his voice.

'I'd better take her home.' I reached out for her.

'I'll take her,' said Etti, stepping forward, her arms outstretched.

Carefully, he handed her over to Etti. And any curiosity he had about her appeared to evaporate.

'What do you think of the B & B?' he asked eagerly. 'Would you say 'twill be a goer?'

'I'd say it will,' I said. 'It's all leisure activities now. That's the way we'll all be going yet.'

His eyes gleamed as he nodded seriously in agreement. An orangey striped silk scarf with greasy streaks on it was knotted around his throat. It looked attached to him as if he had been wearing it day and night for a good while.

'It's the tail end of the season,' he said. 'We'll be only testing the waters.'

Malachy is generally regarded as the Ffrench with his head most consistently in the clouds. I was glad it was he and not either of his brothers who found Missy.

'It gets dark early enough these evenings,' said Malachy.

'It does,' I agreed.

'Night so, Marty,' Malachy said.

And with the suggestion of a bow, 'Goodnight, Mrs Hawkins.'

With a wave of his hand he went off up the field in the direction of the house.

Etti was silent and walked at some distance apart from me. Without a word we stumbled, as if newly awoken from a luxurious sleep, across the lumpy grass to the jeep. She reached in to find the Jameson and gave it to me as if whatever I wanted it for was of no interest to her. Missy was acting as if I were simply not there. Tenderly Etti placed her on the passenger seat. Then she drove off. I got back on the tractor. By the time I was turning out on to the road, the tail-lights of the jeep had disappeared. I had to climb off the tractor again then, remembering that I had to leave the whiskey in the place under the stone for Madame Ffrench to find.

As I drove home to Foilmore, I was trembling with a jumble of emotions so that I had to keep a tight grip on the steering-wheel to hold my hands steady. Desire, guilt, love, anger and exaltation. And when these subsided a little, I examined the tangle of my feelings in that time, when I was searching in the field and imagined Missy dead. My fears had been genuine enough. But mixed in with them there had been an undeniable glimmer of relief at the lifting of a burden. I had looked out over the hazy poppy-field and had seen her lying there at the far end of it, invisible, serene, the ordeal of her life resolved. For a short while, she would lie there, a small hummock of white amidst the red, unflinching under the heat of the midday sun and the discomfort of the rain, still and at rest before she dissolved into the dark bed of the forgiving earth.

It would have been an unforeseen blessing, her successful disappearance. Though I had fled at once from its reality. Being well acquainted with the carcases of mauled sheep, blood oozing on to the wet grass, the eyes plucked out, the tongue lolling and twisted. Too ghastly to be able to nourish any illusions about her fate.

It's for the best, Etti had said. There's an end to it, she was saying. And I was not stricken though I led her to believe I was. I had accepted quite coolly what she meant. That the field might be Missy's grave was as nothing to me if it could be mine and Etti's bed.

35

ONCE AUGUST WAS in and the days were shortening, Fansha exploded into activity as if, like the insects, we were joined together in a last frenetic dance. On cue as they always do, the visitors appeared and the whole place switched into its customary holiday mode. Every category of relative, sons, sisters, daughters, cousins, nieces and nephews descended on the area in droves, from home and abroad, from the coastal cities, from England, America, and the industrial cities of Europe, with their entourages in tow – smooth-skinned children, sleek spouses, boyfriends, girlfriends.

In highly polished cars bearing foreign registrations, bashful aunties, boisterous uncles and old lads on sticks were ferried around to a refurbished abbey here, a new lounge-bar there. The roads choking up with all this unaccustomed traffic strung out patiently in line behind ambling tractors pulling tottering loads of hay and trailers heaped with fertiliser bags of turf from the bog. For those few weeks in Fansha every day was nearly as bad for traffic as the day of a big hurling-match in Thurles. This was the regular refrain of complaint to be heard up at the Cross anyway.

All day strangers drifted in and out of Toby's. Most of them were unknown to me but all the same oddly familiar in feature or gait so I could with a bit of mild reflection as I supped my pint put one of our local names to a face. Manufacturing a simulacrum of their summer lives elsewhere, they carried Toby's tables and stools out to the front yard into the hazy sunshine and set up a fashion for drinking by the roadside. Toby was grumpy but forbearing.

'They turn back into little children the minute they get home. Sure we have to humour them I suppose,' he told myself and Young Delaney in a tone of benign resignation as the two of us stood, a carefully calculated distance between us, in the kindly gloom at the bar out of the flux of the rearrangments.

'Children with pocketfuls of cash. What could you say to that, Toby?' cackled Young Delaney.

The sun large and generous in the late afternoon. Then a mattress of cloud effacing it and the visitors shivering, their browner faces suddenly fading. I finished up and went over to Keogh's for a few messages.

'Doesn't Veronica look lovely, Cissy. The spit of Sinead,' Mrs Keogh was exclaiming to Mrs Quinlan in a blatantly false tone of admiration.

Veronica, the youngest of the Quinlan girls, had arrived back from a stint as an au-pair in Berlin in a phase of metamorphic alienation. What was left of her shorn hair dyed a matt shade of ebony-black, a handful of rings inserted in one ear and two more in her nose.

'I don't know who she's like,' murmured Mrs Quinlan. I could see that with her declining influence an air of bemused passivity was settling over her like a protective cloak.

'Isn't it great to have her home? For a while anyway,' gushed Keogh. Her small eyes eager with malice-tinged commiseration. As though Veronica had been restored to us from a sojourn on the moon by some whimsical aliens. The younger Quinlans were acquiring an unpredicted reputation for wildness.

'Maybe you should try it, Mrs Keogh,' put in Andrea, behind us in the queue, at her most hearty. 'Saves a fortune on hairdressers.'

171

As I was picking out a few tomatoes, Cissy Quinlan came over to give me the time of day. She makes a point of being kind to me, to compensate perhaps for her relief at Caroline's timely defection.

'Any plans for your holidays, Marty? Ah, but I suppose Pierce couldn't spare you . . .' Empathic, Cissy would be presuming I needed a break. My monotonous life. Something like her own, conducted backstage, diffidently, observing the comings and goings . . .

'Caroline should be home any day now. She'd love to see you, I know that, Marty . . .'

Her voice fading. Embarrassed, fearing she was conveying the wrong impression. So, heartily, to put her out of her misery, I enquired about Caroline's dentist. When was the big day?

A date in March was set, she wasn't sure, was it the twelfth? A Saturday anyway to ensure a good turnout. He was in Frankfurt for the year, learning more about orthodontics. They were over and back, the two of them. But Caroline wasn't too keen on Frankfurt. Not easygoing, the Germans. Not like ourselves.

'Tell her to give me a call,' I suggested. 'For old times' sake.'

'I will,' she said. Relieved, happy. It pleased me to be able to make Cissy Quinlan happy.

36

A ND WE TOO had a visitor. As he usually did in August, Fintan turned up. My old pal from Trinity. Fintan came down to see us in Fansha about twice a year, for his weekend in the country. The August visit was the first stop on his annual peregrination across Europe. With a backpack and a strong pair of walking-boots to trek between remote villages in countries like Hungary and Czechoslovakia.

Fintan. Fintan, our nemesis. Our chorus for the tragedy. Positioned for his role since the late October day we first shuffled through fallen leaves together as junior freshmen across Front Square to the Buttery after a lecture.

Pierce dropped in that afternoon. He wouldn't stay, he said, he was on his way up to the upper fields to select the ewes for early lambing.

'It's fierce close,' he remarked. Fansha speak, which I interpreted as a wish to keep me at a distance. Naturally, in the circumstances, at the time I was glad to go along with that. I have time enough to regret it now. The fair lock of hair over his splendid brow was dark with sweat. I was to go into town, he said. Fintan was inside waiting for me to pick him up.

'Fintan,' I exclaimed in surprise. With the way my head was churning recently, I had forgotten about Fintan and the likelihood of his arrival.

'The same man,' said Pierce.

Fintan had come in on the afternoon train from Dublin and had rung up Pierce from Rodge Butler's.

'Have you a clean pair of sheets handy?' enquired Pierce, considerate as always.

'I have,' I told him.

'You could have some from above if you need them.'

He offered then to let me have the jeep if I wanted it.

I was sorry I told him I had the sheets. On the pretext of looking for sheets, I could have gone up to the house. Etti would be there. I was momentarily dizzy with an image of our two heads close together as we rummaged side by side in the linen cupboard.

'I'll take the Norton,' I said. 'Fintan is fond of the Norton.'

'Suit yourself,' said Pierce.

On his way out he halted, catching sight of Missy in her refuge under the couch. The set of her long head had been downcast all morning, her ears cold and shrinking from my touch. She wasn't on top form at this time. She had never really returned to form after the unfortunate episode at Kyle. I was making renewed efforts in my attentions towards her but her responses were muted. Her sense of pride, I guessed, had been grievously wounded as well as her trust.

'Still with us, I see,' he remarked. 'You're keeping her going anyway.'

'I am,' I said. 'She's coming along fine. In fact, I'm thinking of putting her in for a prize at the Show.'

Pierce made that forced laugh of his. 'You're a funny fellow, Marty.

'Bring Fintan up to see us,' he offered then. 'We'll have a few drinks.'

'He might not be wanting to stay that long,' I countered.

But I followed him out to the gate.

'You know Fintan,' I muttered, sorry for my ungraciousness. Sullen, and rueful after. That was the manner I could not help adopting with my brother.

37

I WAS RASH TO turn down the offer of the jeep. It would have been the handier form of transport. When I landed into the crepuscular gloom of Rodge Butler's and put my head inside the snug – a man of determined habit, Fintan always takes up residence in the snug – the first thing I saw apart from my old pal was a great swollen purplish-blue rucksack sitting up on the seat beside him. It was of a size and bulk the Norton was not intended for. Fintan himself neither. His body, always chunky, had filled out. He looked heavy on his feet. A man now, undeniably. I wonder what note he was taking of different but no less fateful changes in me.

He was on his fourth pint by this time, the filmy glasses he was finished with lined up in front of him like trophies of his prowess at leisure activities. Leaping to his feet as soon as he saw me, he swept me into his compulsory mood of bonhomie.

'Here he is. The lad himself. Rodge. Bring us another.'

Old buddies, this is how Fintan likes to regard himself and Rodge. Whether Rodge in fact remembers Fintan from one visit to the next I wouldn't be too sure. With old customers and new, Rodge has the same severe ungiving manner of implied disapproval when he serves up a drink. Like a man who observes in his purveyance of the demon drop salutary lessons in human frailty and wantonness and proclivity to spectacular decline. Compared to Rodge Butler, taciturn Toby is a sunny Jim.

On the run in to Rodge's, I had been somewhat grudging

in my welcome for Fintan. My head too full and impatient with my concerns to spare him his quota of time and attention. I was glad all the same though to see his big flushed homely face. It was clear he had not been spending too much of his time lately in the library. If I had known how things were going to turn out, would I have ordered him to finish up his pint and run him straight back to the station to catch the next train out? Hard to say. I am the wrong-way kid.

To convey my welcome, I gave him a playful puck in the ribs. His face had developed persistent lines, I noted, that gave him a grave and serious look and, around the temples, his dark hair, cut like a boy's, was dusted with grey. He was cultivating a stubble which had nearly as many grey hairs in it as black. Altogether, he was looking newly distinguished in a homespun kind of way. The hardworking academic at play.

'Up Tipp,' he grinned.

'Up the blow-ins,' I returned.

An old joke we have. The son of an itinerant bank man, Fintan has no equivalent to what he regards with envy as my rootedness in the rich loam of Tipperary. From here, there and everywhere, is Fintan. First saw the light of day in some little town in County Louth whose name he claims to forget and from which he was soon removed to another little nameless town in County Monaghan. Up and off again then to some other one-horse town in a new county every couple of years after that. He has seen the length and breadth of Ireland, has Fintan. But complains of understanding nothing of any of it. So has adopted Fansha as his native place, the locus for his insertion into country mores.

'I'm just settling in for the evening,' he said.

'And no better place, Fintan. You always had a talent for finding out the crack.'

This was a joke. Except for Fintan and his backpack, the

pub was empty. And Rodge himself, plodding up and down behind the counter, his shoulders bowed as if all the troubles of the world were visited upon him.

A rootless city fellow, Fintan persists in a romantic belief that Rodge Butler's, reeking of stale beer and lavatorial whiffs from the Gents', is the epitome of the country pub. And that the lounge-bars fully established everywhere now, in all their mock-panelled plush and comfort, are an aberration, a mutation that will die out in a generation for lack of viability. On the contrary, of course.

Anyway, the dreary smells, the cigarette advertisements from the Fifties, the tick-tock clock with its dingy dial, the Babycham deer on the mahogany counter, the lamps under their yellow glass shades illuminating the dust that hangs in the silent air, the snugs partioned off like confession-boxes bathed in ecclesiastical gloom – Fintan loves it all. And when Rodge goes, go it will with him. That day can't be so far off.

I have a kind of remote residual affection for Rodge's. However, I suppose I am no longer capable of fixation on finite things. I see in them all but dust and ashes. In comparison to me, Fintan is innocent and blinkered and vital as a child.

I could see he was not too comfortable on the narrow horsehair banquette. He kept shifting position and restlessly throwing his legs this way and that, like an over-active boy at mass. But he would never let on. That could suggest capitulation to the comfort of the lounge-bar.

'I succumbed to the fit of wanderlust,' he said.

'How long are you staying?' I asked.

'I'm free as the breeze,' he declared. 'Except for your man.' He gave the rucksack a punch.

'You should have warned me to bring the tractor and trailer. I only have the bike,' I said.

'Are you still roaring around Tipp on the Norton?' He

beamed. 'I was afraid you'd have come down in the world and be reduced to a Carina or something.'

'We don't all have fine jobs in Trinity College,' I said.

He glanced at me with momentary pity and seemed about to make some expostulation. Then he thought better of it.

During our second pint, there was a bit of a hiatus in the well-worn groove of our repartee. I sank fugitively into my familiar thoughts, heedless of Fintan already as if my guest had been with me for days and had thoroughly outstayed his welcome. He punched the solid gable end of the rucksack, summoning me to attention.

In an offhand and breezy manner he told me that he had been offered the Lectureship. This was what he had wanted and worked for ever since I first knew him, steadily making his way up the ladder through Assistantships and all the rest of it. It was what I had once wanted. And worked for. It had been long enough in coming, but Fintan had made it. I felt an unreasonable twinge of jealousy.

'Good man,' I said, obliged by our long association to encourage him in his undertakings.

He tried to conceal his pride with diffidence.

'You think it's a good move?'

'Sure it is, Fintan.'

He's a subtle enough fellow, Fintan, and he was careful not to make it too plain. But he had always been mad keen to be safely established in the Department. As I had been once upon a time. For him it had not been a walkover, as it had been shaping up to be for me. But I had been thrown off the pace.

'We'll have another,' I said stoutly. 'Let's celebrate.'

'Here's to you, Rodge,' he shouted up the bar. 'The first stop on my grand tour.'

We had a chaser to drink to that. His gaiety was infectious.

'And now, Matt the lad. Tell me, what are you up to?' he asked. Though he didn't wait for an answer. Not that I had

179

one, for his consumption anyway. He wouldn't, any more than I would myself, expect me to be up to much.

'How are you getting on with the fleecy flocks? How's Pierce?'

My friend Fintan joined fervently in the general esteem for my brother.

'And herself? Goretti.' He enunciated her name with a drawling, vaguely mocking tone that annoyed me, and he made a little knowing grin.

We were in the habit once, Fintan and I, of making a joke of Etti. That was in the early days, after she and Pierce were first married, when I was young and callow and a dab hand at hiding the facts even from myself. Fintan had been down to Fansha a fair few times. But he had not noticed that I had changed. I had moved on, out into the solitary spaces of the heart.

I was suddenly depressed. I wanted to get drunk. It was the only way I would be able to handle Fintan.

'Let's get plastered,' I said.

He had no objection. He thought it was on his account and his cause for celebration. To accompany the intake of drink, we rehearsed the old topics. For a start-off, discussed the issues of the day. The failings of various government policies, the latest impasse in the North, the causes of wars and famines farther off, I gamely attempting shows of erudition I could not quite bring off and Fintan flashily and cynically compensatory. Magnanimously he explained to me the mysteries of CD Rom. I advised him as to Tipp's chances in the Final. For enthusiasm about the hurling prowess of his adopted county, there is hardly a one to match Fintan in Fansha. We were in full and mirthful agreement as usual that yokeldom was rapidly claiming me for its own.

He went on to retail the gossip of the last year. What my former colleagues and acquaintances of the library and the pub, and, in a few cases, of the bed, were up to. Career-wise and affair-wise and money-wise, which in the comestibles of conversation was always to Fintan the heat and sweetness of the digestif. Names and faces I had forgotten ushered out of the past for my amusement, posturing, picturesque, comical, their small tragedies and farcical ambitions and foolish gaffes laid open to my gaze under Fintan's sharp and urban wit.

In the old days, I had never failed to be amused. That night in Rodge's, they floated dimly into view, sad insubstantial figures, newly worthy of human sympathy. Like characters in a novel whose hidden frailties have been skilfully exposed to our bountiful understanding and pity. To Fintan, they were still the ridiculous cast of an operetta, posturing with false hair and falsetto protestations.

When he knew me, my heart was small and empty and hard. Now it was swollen and tender and my mind as busy with its private spectacle as a neon-lit city boulevard. I was obsessed. And my obsession was more unspeakable and deserving of shame than any of the harmless scandals that Fintan raked up with glee to entertain me.

It was growing dark. Rodge turned the lights on in the empty regions of the bar. The cream-painted walls leaped into their stained and dingy distinctness.

With deep concentration, Rodge was reading the evening paper. Little fear now of any new arrivals to break into his peace, with their demands for drink. The old boys don't like to grapple with the long climb up the railway hill to Rodge Butler's any more. Especially now that Rodge has come to regard his customers as nuisances and interlopers, serving them up their drink with censorious and reluctant sighs.

Fintan nestled in against the rucksack as if glad of the support. I could sense him watching me for a while, as if trying to read some news from my face.

'Well, tell me. Who's the girl?' he asked. He had decided to be serious, to be kind, to summon up a display of his old concern for me.

'What girl?'

I blustered, my face hot. 'There's no girl. Apart from the usual.'

I was determined not to let him know my business. Fintan belonged to the past.

He laughed. 'The usual. You were always the man for the usual. You'll never change, Marty.'

I suppose he liked to think that about me.

'What do you make of that murder, Rodge?' I called out. There was a murder over in Limerick that, for want of anything major, was making the headlines.

'You wouldn't know what to make of it,' called back Rodge.

'I'd say it was the brother.'

'You could be right,' agreed Rodge.

'Did you ever think of joining the police force?' put in Fintan. 'They could use an ace detective.'

'Could they use the Norton?' I rejoined.

Fintan smiled. But he seemed absent. He settled in against the rucksack.

'I'm in love, Marty,' he said.

'In love? That's a quare one,' I said, 'for you.'

'You're wrong, Marty,' Rodge called down to me. 'It says here the brother is ruled out.'

'That's only what they're saying,' I called back. 'They play a long game.'

'This is serious,' Fintan said.

'No harm in that,' I bantered.

'I've proposed to her.' His voice was low and diffident.

I was surprised. Though Fintan claimed to be in a continual condition of expectation, he had never been in love. Now he was talking marriage. He had the job he wanted and now he had the girl. She was called Maeve. I remember little else that he told me about her. She was something in Public Relations.

'Legs up to here?' I suggested, though I was sorry for my compulsive ungenerous try at being flip. Fintan was a leg-man.

He nodded. 'The legs are divine, Marty. But it's the soul I love.'

Compared to Fintan's easy unproblematic situation, my own seemed impossibly bleak.

'There's a pair of us in it,' I blurted.

He looked at me with a ready receptiveness.

Was it competitiveness? Or the old intimacy between us breaking out? Probably a case mainly of having had too much to drink.

Anyway, my heart declared itself. With a perilous and exuberant sense of legitimisation, I heard myself name her, my love, Etti. Fumblingly, I outlined the developments of the last months. Airing absurd hopes and possibilities I was hardly aware I nourished.

To my confession Fintan listened with the calm, under-standing, priest-like manner he adopts when he is the recipient of scandalous gossip, designed to elicit information and divert caution. But I was confident he would not gossip about me. This was a tacit clause of our old pals' contract. And there was the mutual recognition that my story, wretched as it was, was a payoff for his and therefore sacred.

The more I talked the more wildly hopeful I became of some kind of blissful future for me. What form this might take was unclear to me but my ruthless conviction of its inevitability must have appalled Fintan. As I talked I became convinced that Etti was consumed with the same ruthless ardour for me. My reserve was cast to the winds. I left Missy, however, and her role in bringing Etti to me, out of the reckoning. Fearful maybe that this crazy tale of a house-pet, half human, half sheep, would make even Fintan seriously question my sense of reality, if not my sanity. Astonished even myself by my declamations. And was immediately plunged, as I at last exhausted them, into despair from a realisation, once voiced, of their hopelessness.

Like the wise confessor who has divined paternally one's secret thoughts and actions, Fintan told me that actually he had always known, or at least had a fair idea.

'Even at the funeral,' he said. 'I was watching. And ever since. You couldn't keep your eyes off her.'

'Come off it, Fintan.'

I made my protestations, loudly. But of course he was right. In those days he knew me better than I knew myself. The little there was to know.

He did attempt, old pal that he is, to be understanding. That he was grieved and unable to offer me any encouragement, however, I could tell. He saw it as an infatuation. It was impossible, it was pointless – so how could he, as a reasonable man, see it in any other light? It was just a further sign that Marty was going from bad to worse. Don't be an eejit, man, was what he wanted to say. Forget it. What future could there be in it?

It was Pierce he was thinking of, it was Pierce he was concerned for, I knew that. Not the fulfilment of my delinquent desires, nor Etti's. Like anyone who ever came in contact with the man, Fintan had a deep admiration for Pierce. Anyway, his allegiance to the status quo was prudent and strong.

In rapid retreat from contention, we had another pint to drown my sorrows and another attempt at a comradely bout of Up Tipp.

Rodge came limping down the bar.

'Will ye finish up there now, lads.'

'Just one for the road, Rodge,' I wheedled.

184

'That charm of yours won't work on me,' growled Rodge.

He went back up with his heavy tread and turned the lights off with a slow click. In the gloom, the faded tobacco boxes on the shelves were gleaming with a dull lustre. The talk had excited me. I was nostalgic already for the wild hopes it had induced. I wanted to stay on and drink some more and somehow retrieve them.

'We're entitled to drinking-up time,' I shouted up to Rodge.

''Tis old time I keep here,' said Rodge.

Fintan was delighted with this quaint remark. But he saw I was in danger of being truculent. He knows that side of me well from the old days.

'Right you are,' I said. I drained my glass and I stood up. That surprised him. He stepped out after me into the night. Rodge firmly shut the door and barred it behind us.

'Maybe you should give Pierce a call,' he suggested, nervously appraising myself and the Norton.

'Up on the bike with you,' I ordered.

The town had closed up for the night. Down the railway hill we lurched, past the turf accountants and the grocers' shops with their keepers immured behind their silent wine-dark wooden shutters, into the lighted pool of the Square. The air was heavy and close, demanding something bracing, violent, some action.

I was laughing hysterically. There was nobody about except a few kids loitering around Supermac's. I felt high as a kite and loutish and eager to alarm the whole place with some noisy hot-blooded outrage of youth.

'Where's the crack?' I demanded. They looked at us with mild curiosity.

'Ye've no crack in ye,' I bellowed contemptuously.

'Keep a grip on that bag now,' I roared out to Fintan, as I weaved around the parked cars, smoky and ethereal under the hazy moonlight.

185

'Straight on now, Marty,' Fintan said, quiet, in command as he always was when faced with my abandon, as I swerved towards Crazy Prices. Quietly, firmly, he directed me out the Fansha road. I would have done the ton if the Norton was up to it. Labouring under the load like Dinny Kilbride's old Cortina in low gear, she could hardly rise above the thirty.

Missy was there to greet me when I fumbled open the door. I had no wish to greet her. She may have been saved knowing this because at the sight of Fintan staggering in behind me under the rucksack she made a dash for her refuge under the couch.

'What in God's name is that?' demanded Fintan.

I chanced a dog.

'Only the aul dog,' I said.

Why did I say that? He would have all morning and probably a few mornings to inspect her. I was in a nervous state, vulnerable with over-exposure and a sense of self-betrayal. I had told him too much. We go back a long way, Fintan and me. But I have developed a habit of reserve that is nervous-making to relinquish. It does not do a fellow any good to be too frank in Fansha.

'The dog?' He raised his eyebrows. Fintan's sceptical look.

Then he forgot about it. He rooted in the rucksack and pulled out a bottle of whiskey.

'Good man.' I slapped two glasses on the table.

'Only a nightcap now,' said Fintan.

'Go 'way with your nightcap. This love business doesn't suit you.'

I poured us out large measures.

'It could suit you,' he said, considering me.

'Could it now?'

'Cultivates the soul.'

I thought about that. It was in my old soulless days I knew

186

Fintan. Soulless and heartless and capably functioning. Fintan saw the new embryonic soul in me.

We chinked our glasses, nearly knocking splinters out of them, and drank to our loves.

I called the first toast. 'To Maeve.'

'To Etti,' said Fintan valiantly, calling the second. He was hesitant enough. I am surprised however that it didn't stick in his throat.

'You're the first to know,' he told me. 'About the engagement.'

'Sure she'll have half of Dublin told by now,' I slagged him. 'You know the women.'

'Ah. But Maeve,' he said gravely, 'is not like other women.'

Then he bid me goodnight and bumped his monstrous purple pack behind him up the stairs to his room. Fintan was always able to hold his drink better than I could.

When all was quiet upstairs, I coaxed Missy out from her refuge and lifted her on to my lap murmuring maudlin nothings to her until she dropped off to sleep. Finally I went up to bed myself. And lay awake until first light when the wardrobe loomed into ghostly view, old incoherent memories of Fintan and myself dredged up from the past chasing each other in my head, my thoughts lurid with anxieties about the hard road down which I was separately travelling. And vaguely grateful for the new perilous sensation of being slightly less alone.

38

I LONGED FOR A reprieve from these careening dislocated thoughts, the oblivion of calm undreaming sleep that I imagined Fintan in his room across the landing had no trouble in achieving. But when sleep did find me at last, I dreamed of Etti. She was coming to meet me down the long field and I was waiting for her under the chestnut. She was coming towards me slowly but steadily, always distant and indistinct but always coming closer I was certain, as I stood in the shade of the tree, impatiently waiting. And then when she must surely have reached me, who appeared but Young Delaney, his back turned to me, a monstrous figure blocking out the light. He did not look like himself, he was a great looming shadow only, but I was in no doubt that it was he. He walked up to meet her as if by entitlement and she stretched out her hand to him and he took it and they moved off away from me together into the darkness of the forest. Except for this detail the dream was quite realistic. In that spot there is in reality no forest. But in the dream the trees seemed impressively strong and rooted there in their rightful place. I called out for my brother. 'Pierce,' I called violently, 'Pierce . . .'

I sat up in the bed racked with anger and outrage. The room was flooded with the gross light of a fat voluptuous harvest sun. I had not pulled the curtains and my eyes flinched from the light and my head was heavy with a fearsome headache. I heard noises from below in the kitchen and remembered Fintan.

39

HE WAS CRACKING eggs into the pan.
'You had a nightmare,' he informed me.
'Did I?'
'You were calling out to Pierce.'
I sat down at the table. He put a mug of tea and a strip of Solpadeine in front of me.
'Should I feed the dog?' he asked.
'Where is she?'
'Under the couch.'
'I'll feed her. She's afraid of anyone strange.'
Fintan was wearing an elegant grey silk robe. His legs were white with a mesh of dark hair on them.
'Nice robe,' I remarked. 'Maybe too je ne sais quoi though for a Professor. Was it Maeve gave it to you? The Trinity wife, you know, is a special breed. Are you sure she's bred for the job, Fintan?'
He peeled two tablets out of the foil and proffered them to me in the palm of his hand.
'You'd make a lovely nurse,' I said.
'Give it up, Marty.'
'Sorry.'
Trying to regain what I saw as the dignity I had lost the night before, I was compelled to put on a show of crassness. Fintan saw through me and left me to stew in my own juice. He retired to the yard and spent the morning sitting out in a deck-chair under the shade of the lilac-bush reading a thriller

189

he had brought with him. Fintan has a great knack for making himself at home.

The billet in Trinity would suit him, I thought dispassionately, regarding him through the open door. One time it would have suited me. Outside my bolthole in Fansha, there is no slot in the wide world to suit me now.

I offered Missy her breakfast. She displayed little interest in eating it. I could not find it in me to coax her. I stretched out on the couch and absently spoke my maudlin nonsense to her and tiredly ran my fingers through her coat in an attempt to render her less eccentric in appearance. Obstinately demanding some more attentive form of communication, she hung her dejected head to one side and her large eyes as she gazed at me were filled with misery.

'Why don't you try talking for a change?' I said to her. 'You're getting to be the age for it.' She made a low moan and turned her head away.

Washed-out and fragile, I observed her without emotion as someone like Fintan must and was both filled with pity for her and repelled. I put her aside and went upstairs and got myself washed and dressed.

By lunchtime I was in recovery and suitably chastened. I made us a bite of lunch. Eggs again, scrambled this time.

Fintan, mopping up his plate with appetite, discoursed on my life as he saw it. He was sorry if he sounded harsh or unsympathetic, he told me, but I was clearly in need of a bit of plain talking, man to man. I was living an existence, he went on, which, though it might be regarded as agreeable enough, was disturbingly empty. It was not exercising my brain on any meaningful level. It was conducive to unwholesome brooding and unrealistic flights of the imagination.

'Listen, Marty,' he said, 'why don't you come with me?'

'Where?'

'Anywhere you like. Europe. Wherever you want to go. I've

190

a date to meet up with Maeve in Munich in the first week of September. Until then I'm free. It would clear the head. Give you a new perspective on things. You need to get away, Marty.'

'Maybe I will,' I agreed. Though I had no intention of it. It was generous of him to want to rescue me from the perils of stagnation and rural idiocy, I told Fintan. But I didn't tell him how he was unnerving me, upsetting my fragile equilibrium. He was too much the voice of reason. He was intruding on my habit of thinking. I wanted him to be off. I was fond of Fintan but I wanted him to be off.

This, however, was not destined to be. Fintan had the look of someone settling in for a while. The stage was set, the tragedy ready to commence.

'I hear your former inamorata is engaged,' he remarked.

'Who's that?'

'Caroline.'

'I know,' I said. 'He's a dentist.'

He finished up his tea.

'I don't want to keep you from your work,' he said.

This was a bit of a dig. He knows I'm basically expendable around the place.

'Maybe we should go and give Pierce a hand,' he suggested. 'Might take your mind off things.'

'Let's do that,' I agreed.

Fintan went upstairs to put on his boots for the fields, the flashily sensible designer boots he treks around Eastern Europe in. Divining my squeamishness and detachment, Missy kept out of sight. I warmed up some milk and left it in to her.

Pierce was in the lower fields selecting the lambs to be drafted for the mart. By early evening, we had them sectioned off.

40

'COME UP TO the house and have a drink,' invited Pierce.
My impulse was to refuse. I had little confidence in
my ability to handle the urbane sociability the occasion would
require. To sit there and watch Fintan make knowing eyes at
Etti, seeking to get information out of her and passing his
urbane judgements on us all.

'Love to,' said Fintan.

He would. Bask in the presence of the fair and noble Pierce.
Get the lie of the land.

Etti came forward to shake Fintan's hand. She gave me a
kind of bashful smile. A rosiness suffused her pale face. She
has a tendency to blush unexpectedly. I felt a rush of warmth
for her, as if my whole body flushed in sympathy. And after
a short while I found that I was deeply happy to be there,
quiet on a small upright chair in a shadowy corner, in a
pretence of mild and restful boredom while my College chum
was monopolised by my country kin with their country
manners.

Pierce was pouring the drinks. G and Ts for himself and
Fintan, vodka for Etti, Jameson for me.

'Ah, the cocktail hour,' Fintan said. 'So this is the hard life
of the farmer we layabouts hear about above in Dublin.'

Etti sat at the table by the window, giggling a little too
loudly at smart alecky remarks like this of Fintan's. I did not
often get the opportunity to observe her in a social setting.
She seemed to me to be shy as a gangly child, which she

192

was attempting to disguise with an essay in bravado. She was wearing a murkily glowing flowered dress, sleeveless, her arms white slender columns, folding, unfolding, her hands gripping her glass as a small child grips her glass of lemonade for fear of letting it fall.

Something was making Pierce jumpy. When the rest of us were still only making a dent in our second drinks, he was already up mixing himself another.

Fintan, taking everything in, was in his element. My apparent detachment would not deceive him. He was enjoying himself thoroughly, but I would be hauled up for a lecture from him later, I was thinking. Etti went and joined him on the couch. Her dark head lay against the soft cushions, her eager face turned to him, receptive to his every word.

Fintan was telling them about his Lectureship. It was with the usual offhandedness but you could tell he was basking in his success. They were appropriately impressed.

'A Professorship next, eh, Fintan?' said Pierce.

'Ah now, I've a few hurdles to jump yet.'

But he would jump them. His career was on a steady upward curve.

'Would you like to be a Professor, Marty?' asked Etti with apparent artlessness.

'Ah, now. There's a difference. Fintan has the qualifications to stand to him.'

I recited this in Pierce's slow Tipperary enunciation, cruelly dragging out the syllables. Qual-if-i-caa-tions.

Pierce stood up and went to the long window. Uneasy, as if he were the master of our fate, our eyes followed him, watched him look out across the sweep of tufty lawn where the evening light was falling away behind the trees. Then he turned and swung his empty glass in our direction.

'Anyone hungry?'

'There's a whole spring lamb in the freezer,' said Etti.

193

'Jointed,' I explained to Fintan. 'Cut up. Chops basically.'

'Don't you get tired of lamb?' asked Fintan. 'Not that I'm tired of it,' he added hastily.

'We do,' giggled Etti. 'That's why there's a lamb in the freezer.'

Pierce poured himself another drink.

'We have to celebrate this man's promotion,' he announced. 'We'll dine out.'

Forty minutes later we were seated at the bar in Ti Max. Started on the hock and ordering a wiener schnitzel apiece.

41

To travel on whim to the foothills of the Slieve Blooms for a bite of supper in Ti Max was not a regular habit of ours. But Pierce was liable to make a noble gesture like this when it could be least expected. Normally, it was a practice he reserved for anniversaries. His and Etti's. Festive occasions, like New Year or my birthday. In this too he resembles Robert. The faint disapproval at wanton expenditure on food and drink that you can partake of in your own house at a fraction of the price.

I was touched at this token of hospitality towards me and my friend. Or maybe his purpose was to please Etti. Touched but wary, which made me defensive and, in my manner, ungrateful.

Etti was idly, dreamily, clasping and unclasping her bag. Like a child who liked to listen to the metallic click the clasps made and was repeating it over and over.

'For God's sake, Etti.'

To Fintan or anyone else this expostulation of Pierce's would have sounded mild. To me, knowing my brother, it was explosive. Pierce removed the bag from Etti's reach. Etti raised her eyebrows and smiled. Slightly apologetic but mostly playful. It granted to me however a flush of triumph. My triumph over Pierce, illogical and obscure. I was wary, but exultant.

To be out and about with Etti was in itself something. To imagine for a moment what it would be like to be here, alone, just the two of us – the very thought made my blood race. Even with Fintan and Pierce tagging along, I was finding the outing to Max's intoxicating. It seemed to represent a fortuitous step in the direction of something exalted and inexorable.

Her mercurial whimsical laughter spilled across the pale-green table-cloth, her eyes shining. She sat opposite me. The table between us seemed unnecessarily wide. I wanted to be closer to her. I moved the epergne of leaves and blackish pansies which was obstructing my view.

She got up to go to the Ladies'. My eyes followed her progress across the room. As she disappeared from view I slumped bereft in my chair as if she were gone for good. Causing Fintan, seated beside me, to give me a furtive admonitory puck. A couple of fellows then making their way to their table stopped to display the bonhomie endemic in Ti Max, rescuing Pierce and myself from our fraternal sullenness.

'How are ye doing, lads?'

'Prices can't be too bad, what?'

Greetings from all sides. For Pierce, the broad and candid smile of mutual understanding. For me, the reserved or faltering smile that does not quite reach the eyes. As if uncertain of quite who I was, of my place in the scheme of things. Easy categorisation counts for a lot.

'Nice evening.'

'Out for a bite?'

Hearty summer-time meaningless stuff, replete with well-being.

Bobby Loftus the vet was at an adjacent table with a tall well-turned-out girl.

'A Ryan Cormac,' Pierce confirmed. 'From Tubber.'

Fintan was inordinately gratified to be inserted like this into the local scene.

Murt, the garage man from The Rake. With a harem of

dark-eyed cheerful ladies in peacock colours and a couple of their consorts.

'They'd be the wife's sisters. The Fennellys. There's a fair lot of them in it.'

Next up, two trim middle-aged ladies, with the healthy weather-beaten look they get from brisk mornings out on the golf-course.

'Ex-teacher in the convent and the widow of a bank manager. He used to be in the AIB,' murmured Pierce, giving them a friendly wave. 'Died young. Fond of the sauce.'

'Do you know everyone, Pierce?' enquired Fintan with inordinate admiration.

'Nearly everyone, I suppose you could say.'

I am at a loss myself to know how Pierce had such a wide acquaintance. Mine is more or less confined to Fansha. But then I'm not a conversible type of fellow, not like Pierce. Even Max himself, rotund and jolly in his mild Teutonic way, came over to pay his respects, to unfold our rose-pink napkins and wish us bon appetit as if Pierce were a weekly patron of the house. I suppose a good restaurateur picks up on this kind of thing. The men to know.

I was relieved to see that the hint of oddness in his demeanour that my brother had projected earlier, a suggestion of some inner tension or disturbance, seemed to have dissipated. To all appearances, he was back on form.

'Fansha is out in force,' I exclaimed, spying JJ and Andrea nestling side by side on a banquette in a dim corner.

JJ's gaze was fixed on Andrea with consummate devotion. They were both oblivious to all acquaintance such as myself or Pierce. Here, I saw, was my chance to show off to Fintan my knowledge of the parish.

With something of my old style of the raconteur, I outlined to Fintan the mystical quality of their relationship. Their appearance in Ti Max not a source of scandal or even tasty comment, due to it being universally recognised that what they share is of a noble quality, far removed from the earthly domain of carnality or romance. That in the public mind JJ's discourse with Andrea is imbued with the quality of prayer as to a minor divinity, a ministering angel. An act of piety in which the community has decided to participate. Nobody passes any remarks.

Raising in Fintan delighted and appreciative laughter at the charming rural innocence he decided to accept it represented.

'You never lost it, Marty,' Pierce said. Considering me with a complex look I could not read.

Fintan was kneading his eyes with laughter. Pierce ordered more wine. And I watched Etti make her way back to me through the rows of tables.

As she came, casting vague smiles and distant hellos as the bulky occupants shifted in their chairs to make way for her. Their greetings I could see deficient in the requisite degree of heartiness, hers in the essential cheer of clubbiness. Transparently conveying to them that she did not remember their names or their positions in the local schemes of things. This they would not forgive her.

I saw how Etti and myself were both in the same category of the vaguely suspect, the not-belonging. My knowledge of her, my confidence, made me slightly dizzy.

After the schnitzels, we were offered raspberries from Max's own canes. 'Heaped in buttery shortcrust nests and glazed with a syrup of raspberry liqueur,' I read out fulsomely from the menu. My reading was not however evocative enough to tempt Pierce. He went straight to the brandy.

I didn't eat a whole lot of it. But I enjoyed that dinner. The dishes in Ti Max with their colourful sauces had a heightened taste like a revelation of how food could be, like the culmination of a hot and perfect summer somewhere, somewhere sublime and simple where the earth smells of dry aromatic herbs. I was intensely high. High on wine, sure, but high above all on Etti. I saw Fintan take note. His look, as he watched me, was reproving. 'Steady on there,' he murmured to me at one point, 'steady on.'

Pierce ignored his coffee and ordered another brandy, a double. He tossed that off and signed to the waiter for the same again. His index finger as he wiggled it over his glass had a drunken droop. He was not himself. My alarm, uneasily mixed with a feeling of triumph, returned.

And at the prospect of having to go out into the night, which seemed to me to wear a bleak and hostile aspect, I was suddenly lowered. It was as if I was granted a warning or an intimation of what was to happen and how my life was to be. I didn't want to leave Ti Max, I wanted the night to go on. I had an infantile longing for us to remain there indefinitely, safe in our familial circle around that candle-lit rosy table while the night outside sank into its weighty blanket of dark; never to go back to the furtive lives we daily and separately endured. My lugubrious ludicrous life passed with only a lachrymose mutated lamb for company . . .

I heard myself emit a bitter guffaw of a laugh. It seemed to me that they looked at me without curiosity or surprise and looked away again. That's what Marty has come to, I could see them thinking. That's just Marty.

'Will we make it back to the Cross in time for a glass?' asked Fintan.

Fintan's nostalgia for the bucolic rural life he never knew was deeply involved with the Cross and the characters to be found there.

'Hardly,' I said.

'Course we'll make it,' said Pierce, draining his glass and getting heavily to his feet. Oddly shambling and oversized in his crumpled linen summer jacket, fumbling in his pocket for his Visa card, he headed for the desk.

'Pierce is pissed,' I announced.

'He's not used to drinking,' protested Etti defensively.

This pained me, the proprietorial wifely thing in her. Would she defend me, I was driven to ask myself, would she excuse me?

We stood in silence at the jeep while Pierce rooted in his clothing for his keys. I could sense Etti's and Fintan's apprehensiveness. But they said nothing. At last he found them and made to climb into the driver's seat. His movements were heavy and befuddled.

I stepped forward. 'Why don't I drive?' I said.

'I'm driving,' insisted Pierce. His voice was woolly and thick with drink.

'Come on, sweetie. Let Marty drive.'

There was a tender and intimate note in Etti's voice that smote me to the heart.

'That bastard.'

Sharp and clear, Pierce spat the word out. As if with all his heart he meant it.

'That bastard won't be driving anywhere.' Thick and slurred again now, his voice.

Fintan turned to look at me. His expression was shocked and alarmed. In my chest my heart was suddenly beating violently like a war-drum. I wanted to hit Pierce.

Calmly Etti reached out and extracted the keys from Pierce's clasp.

'I'll drive,' she said.

'Hang on a minute. Why did he call me a bastard?' I demanded.

I went up to him and confronted him. His eyes looked huge and swollen and they slid away from my face and down in an abject way towards the ground. Nobody said a word.

Mutely, Pierce turned away from me. Head bowed, he shambled off in the direction of a ragged line of trees at the edge of the carpark. His gait submissive like that of a truculent bear who has been frightened off with pitchforks and threatening shouts. I felt a sudden though unwilling sorrow for him. At least that much can be said for me.

'He just wants a pee,' Fintan said, his relief obvious.

Sure enough, Pierce was weaving a slightly uncertain path towards the broad-girthed trunk of the nearest tree. We stayed by the jeep and watched with silent intensity his every step. Attaining his port of call, he leant against the tree, motionless for a moment, as if concentrating on raising himself out of his drunkenness to do the necessary. In the darkness, the chestnut's heavily burdened branches luridly lit by a nearby lamp hung down around him like peering faces.

His hands raised in an abandoned supplicatory gesture, he clasped the tree-trunk above his head as if for support, and rested his head against the bark. Intently, we watched his pale bulky shape outlined on the black cylinder of the trunk, and intently listened to the guttural noises he had begun to make. It was some time before we realised that he was weeping.

This weeping of Pierce's, low and strangled at first, became louder, with a note of unstoppability in it. I had not heard my brother sob since he was about ten. At our parents' funeral, he confined himself to a pink swollen face in the morning and silent tears that he mopped away with a large cotton handkerchief from Robert's drawer. The two of us at our parents' funeral put on an appropriately manly show, as if vying with each other in manliness.

In this deep racking crying now, this painful and uninhibited release of untold woe, I could hear the unmistakable note of Pierce's crying when he was a boy. In those days his sobs once they started used to go on and on. Most of the time, after he had cut his knee or I had broken some toy of his, he would accept the injury with equanimity. But sometimes without warning the floodgates opened. There was a blue tractor he loved and whose spring I overwound. He cried for hours. There were other things too I was careless with and broke.

He won't be able to stop crying, I thought, we won't be able to put a stop to it. I could feel the old irritation mount in me mixed with the contrition that I used to have to endure when I had caused him to cry. Only I knew how unstoppable Pierce was when he cried.

I heard the crunch of a footstep beside me on the gravel. It was Fintan making a tentative movement towards Pierce. I saw Etti reach out to hold him back.

'I'll go,' she whispered.

I was inflamed with a sudden unexpected resentment. Why should Etti go? What did she know about Pierce and his woes? I was to be shut out, relegated to the role of the uninvolved and the powerless. When anyone could tell this was only between my brother and me. My legs were limp. The ground seemed to be unsteady beneath me. When I leant back against the jeep and lit a cigarette, my hands were trembling.

Etti was patting Pierce's shoulder like you would pat the neck of a nervous horse. Attempting to quiet him. Murmuring things to him that I couldn't hear. With a jerk, Pierce turned his head away as if to shake her off. Unabated, his racking sobs continued.

Again she reached out and patted his shoulder and nuzzled her head in her wheedling, soothing, determined way into his side in the attempt to prise him from his clasp of the tree. You could have thought the tree was her rival for his affections. I found this comical, for some reason. Roughly, impatiently, Pierce reared up, so that she had to release her hold. Helpless, no more tricks left in the bag, Etti stood away from him. She was at a loss as to what to do.

I ground the butt of the cigarette into the gravel and crossed the carpark and walked up to Pierce. His broad back was turned to me, pulsing with sobs. I went round and faced him. Opposite me stood Etti. I suppose Fintan must have been interested, though appalled, to note how we formed the apexes of a ragged-cornered triangle.

'Pierce,' I murmured.

He lifted his head and looked at me. His expression was anguished, abject and angry, all mixed in. Of old, I knew that look.

'You can hit me if you like,' I said. 'Though I should warn you that if you do I may have to hit you back.'

Without a moment's hesitation, he lunged at me and threw a punch that landed full on my nose. A childish rage over-whelmed me. I threw one back and missed. It made ineffective contact somewhere on his forearm. He had moved with an unlikely smartness out of the way. I tasted the salty savour of blood on my upper lip.

Pierce wasn't crying any more. At intervals a brief tremu-lous sob racked him but I recognised that as the tail-end of his outburst. It was dark, but his eyes caught the light from the lamp under the trees and shone like two small fiery beacons in the blur of his face. I wondered would the light blind him and would I do better next time and be able to knock him down for once and for all?

Fists raised we confronted each other. I was making quick dancing movements, punching the air, urging him on. He wasn't taking the bait. I felt nimble on my feet now and decided to go in for the attack. When I did, he caught my two clenched fists in his in mid-air and held them down firmly by my side.

'You can't drive now anyway, Marty,' he said. 'You're bleeding.'

He released me. At the same time, he dropped his guard. I could tell the fight had gone out of him. If I went for him

203

I would have a good chance of plastering him to the ground. And yet, I let my hands lie at rest where he had placed them.

'I was just thinking about your tractor,' I said. 'Remember? The blue one you had that I broke.'

He gave me a wry smile.

'That was a long time ago,' he said.

'I'm sorry anyway,' I told him.

Bursts of laughter and loud voices spilled into the carpark. There was a pool of light by the restaurant doors which Max had opened to encourage an exodus. They were straggling out of Ti Max, all the groups of diners. Pierce's crowd, jolly and complacent.

'We'll go home, Marty,' Pierce said. 'We'll get no good out of fighting.'

He took my arm and we walked like that back to the jeep.

Etti was already seated at the steering-wheel, Fintan next to her. Pierce and myself sat without speaking side by side in the back, as we used to, squabbling and feuding, when we were ten. That was in another time. The moon had appeared out of the clouds. It hung next to me on the other side, low in the sky, its curious face big and ghostly and as if it were passing cold judgements on me.

When we arrived at the Cross the ditches were chock-a-block with parked cars. Toby's was obviously still jumping anyway. Etti brought the jeep to a stop and Fintan got out.

'Goodnight,' I said to my brother. 'Goodnight now, Pierce.'

He clasped my hand for a moment and then, with a playful puck on the shoulder, let me out of the jeep. I did not look at him because I was too busy looking at Etti, watching for a sign.

'Goodnight, Marty. Be good,' was all she said in her flippant Fansha way, and she shifted the gear-stick into first and drove off.

I did not want to go into the noise and tat and treachery

of Toby's, I did not want to leave them. I wanted to be carried on to Foilmore and to go to my old room and sleep chastely like a boy in our chaste triangle, equal-sided and isosceles angled. This wish was subterranean in me but I see now this was how it was. It was not possible, however, it never would be possible. This too was how it was.

42

'WHAT A NIGHT,' said Fintan. 'Now for a quiet pint.'
He was clearly relieved at how it had turned out. I saw though how with some part of him he had relished the whole quasi-fratricidal affair.

We arrived in to Toby's at that time of the night when they were all in full flight, their heads loosened with a load of drink. In my strange, lost and sober condition, coming in from the cool pallor of the night, the place looked like bedlam. Bellows of laughter from one corner, snatches of country and western songs starting up in another, the air a fog of cigarette smoke, and strange women with tanned robust flesh and day-glo outfits screeching with laughter.

'Now, lads. Keep it down, keep it down,' Toby would plead in a regular mantra as he scurried hither and thither behind the bar. With the number of females present there was a heavy demand for shorts and mixers. Toby is happier when he is left to his morose meditations pulling long meticulously judged pints.

Fintan, though the atmosphere could hardly have been his idea of a rural idyll, rubbed his hands in enthusiastic antici-pation. Apprised of my wish for a pint, he strode up to the bar where I desultorily watched him engage the old fellows in convivial banter. Laddy Minch sidled up to me.

'You're in late tonight,' he said.

'We were dining out. At Ti Max,' I told him.

'Ah. You have a visitor.'

Alert, that. Laddy knows the form.

Fintan returned. I drew him aside.

'What do you think?' I demanded.

'What do I think of what?'

'Etti.'

He took a long swallow from the Budweiser he was drinking eccentrically from the neck.

'She's a looker all right,' he said finally, wiping his mouth with the back of his hand. 'But she's not too bright, is she, Marty? Not your class, I'd have thought.'

'Would you ever get a glass for yourself,' I said. 'They'll only say you're ignorant to be drinking like that out of a bottle.'

I turned back to Laddy.

We talked about this and that. The weather, Harte's greyhound that won the race, the state of the roads. Fintan displaying a keen interest in country matters, brightly asking intelligent questions, drawing Laddy out. I left him to it.

I was thinking about Etti. It was no news to me that she was not exactly Mensa standard, brain-wise. What Fintan was really saying was, put the brakes on, Marty. I am not going to go along with you in this. The girl is not for you.

'You're a fine figure of a fellow,' I heard Laddy say. 'What do you do with yourself in the city?'

Poor old Laddy. Taking a shine to a handsome man while he himself hardly knows why. Does he imagine we all go around admiring each other's physiques in his harmless way? I cocked an ear to hear how Fintan would handle him. He didn't seem at all put out. His left foot was jigging compulsively to the rhythm of the ragged chorus in the corner. A sign maybe of being rattled. And maybe not. I heard him embark on the story of his Lectureship. To which Laddy bent his ear to listen with grave and flattering attention.

A light hand grazed my back. I turned.

207

'Good evening, Young Hawkins,' said Caroline Quinlan.

It was a long time since I had laid eyes on Caroline. For a moment I was not sure this fine thing was indeed my old girl. The wan studenty look was discarded. She resembled a woman of the world, sleek, sophisticated, slender. Everything about her looked newly polished, the rich colour of her hair, her skin, the brown jungle-print slinky dress. Not a type of female we see a lot of at the Cross. Out of the low-slung dress, her small breasts sprang and the long slope of her shoulders. Her body looked new. Not a body that was anymore familiar to me.

'Well. You're a sight for sore eyes,' I said.

Caroline made a slight grimace. This remark she would interpret as a symptom of my deterioration consequent to being stuck in the sticks. She was eyeing Fintan and Laddy over the rim of her glass. Even her eyes looked polished, their greeny colour intense as if she were seeing more piercingly through them.

'Is that Fintan I see?' she asked.

'The very man,' I said.

'He's changed.'

'Improved, would you say?'

'I wouldn't, actually.'

Caroline never was too fond of Fintan.

'None of us are getting any younger.' She sighed.

'But some of us are getting even better-looking,' I proffered.

At this, she smiled. Confident that I meant it. We had always at least been honest with each other.

'Just what I was going to say myself as a matter of fact,' she returned with a charming gallantry.

I was indeed very charmed with this remark.

'You're blushing, Marty,' she teased me.

This was no lie. I knew my face was burning. I don't believe

Caroline had ever caused me to blush, not like that, bashfully, like a boy after a compliment.

But inside, out of the sight of those piercing eyes, I was cold. Cold with sudden desire, and with the knowledge of what was happening between us, of what Caroline seemed to want to happen. And at the same time my nerves were unsheathed, my conscience and my feelings wandering and confused. After the evening I had passed, I was lost, wide open, ready to clutch desperately at any warm and receptive and forgiving thing, anything from the past.

But also it was something about Caroline herself, something newly achieved that I was driven to discover. I had the sensation of not knowing her at all. Once she had been mine and I hers, in my fashion. She was asking of me now to be – and she had to be, I felt with a sense of urgency – repossessed. She had grown up. She was conspiring to present her grown-upness to me.

We must have made some conversation but I have little memory of what about. I remember her eyes as she examined me provocatively over the rim of her glass. And, fearing to unsettle the fragile balance of our understanding, that I assiduously avoided any reference to the dentist.

Fintan was deep in conversation with Laddy.

'It's so stuffy in here,' said Caroline. She made a grimace.

In my own mind, I made a quick decision. Fintan could find his own way home.

'Have you wheels?' I asked.

She nodded.

Her car was red, with a Dublin registration. A Micra or something, the kind of natty little car women are encouraged to drive. She drove with an expert recklessness, using bursts of throttle and smart braking, appropriate to traffic lights and nippy parking. She had become someone I recognised, with a jolt of attraction, but who I did not know.

43

IN THE EARLY morning, a thin yellow bolt of sunlight was falling on the bed, on the brown flowered slip of a dress in a wrinkle at its foot. The lemon-coloured early light diffused through the heavy foliage of the tree outside the window threw a dark lacy shawl over her bare skin. I had forgotten to draw the curtains. She was half-lying across my chest, languid, burnished, oddly innocent, wearing a slight womanly worried frown. She seemed to be asleep.

I had not slept. When I closed my eyes, I had immediately and involuntarily thought of Etti. The temptation to pursue this image had induced a guilt that made me snap into wake-fulness. I suppose, in my favour, I can claim at least to be essentially faithful.

In my head, I replayed the jumbled pictures of the row with Pierce, trying without much success to make sense of it. Who had come out the victor, who had lost face – that was what was concerning me. I was finding it difficult to come to a definitive conclusion in my favour. Then I fell to thinking, with more weariness than guilt, of the freak below in the kitchen, how she had cowered under the couch at our arrival so that Caroline had not been aware of her at all. She would die of hunger, the way the two of us were going.

I was wondering now, the thoughts going round and round in my head, what Caroline expected of me. Did she expect something of me? I hoped, nervously, that she saw me as only a stray patch for her to sow some last wild oats in before she took the plunge. I wondered would that be Fintan's reading of the encounter? Or would he go for my conscience and twist the knife in? I hadn't heard Fintan come in. I lay as patiently as I could waiting for Caroline to wake up.

At last she stirred and turned her head to look at me. Her eyes were quiet and childish, a revenant of the eyes I used to know, that I had left behind in another life.

'It's morning,' she murmured with a note of surprise.

I longed to be solicitous, to be capable of giving her whatever it was she might want. And at the same time I wanted her to go.

'I should go home,' she said. 'My mother will have a fit.'

'She would not approve,' I agreed with uncalled-for promptness. 'When you consider the circumstances.'

'What circumstances?' she asked sleepily.

'The circumstance of your engagement,' I said.

She made that face of hers, expressing distaste.

'Oh. That circumstance,' she said.

She sat up and searched for her dress.

It was going to be manageable, I thought with gratitude. She would ask nothing of me. Her departure would be clean and honest and undemanding.

'What time is it?'

'Nearly six.'

'She gets up at seven.'

Slowly she pulled on the dress and hitched her knickers up under it. Then, instead of making a move to go, she sat on the bed as if lost in thought, her back bowed.

'Marty?' she asked softly after what seemed like a long while.

'Yes?' My vague exasperation hard to keep at bay.

'Do you get fed-up?'

'Why should I?'

'Well . . . Fansha. You know.'

211

'Occasionally,' I replied. 'But I guess I'm a basically self-sufficient guy.'

She found her sandals and, raising her feet in turn on to the bed, slowly fastened the straps around her ankles.

'We haven't really talked, Marty, have we?' There was a sad note in her voice.

Guilt nibbled at me again. We used to be friends once, that was what she was implying. Once we had what might be regarded as a successful and intimate relationship. And now here I was, reduced to using her like a casual pick-up in a bar. But my secret life was churning and absurd and sacred. Fintan had got too much of it out of me. I almost hated him for it.

'How do you feel about this marriage of yours?' I felt bound to ask. Dutifully, while averting the focus from myself.

Vis-à-vis the fiancé, Caroline's emotions were perhaps as turgid and unsayable as mine. But whatever they were, my manner hardly invited confidence.

'Oh, Marty, I don't know,' she murmured at last.

Then frankly she looked me full in the face.

'Worried,' she said. 'Scared.' Willing me to enquire further. I didn't bite.

'They say that's normal,' I said. Evasively, flippantly. 'It's a normal phase. Everyone goes through that when they're engaged.'

She was examining her nails.

'So they do say.'

I drew the sheet up to cover my shoulders and turned my head away as if to compose myself for sleep.

'Let's talk soon,' I said.

As dismissals go, it was barely even polite.

From the bed, I waved. 'See you later.' I threw that out as a sop.

She gave me a twisted wounded smile, with a tinge of

Quinlan hauteur in it. Caroline had always been haughty. I heard her steps creak on the stairs. Then, with a shaming sense of relief, I listened to the engine of her car start up and its diminishing hum on the road into silence.

I know now that, though seeming to call out for me to save her, she had thrown me a lifeline as I drowned. I refused it. As the gods had sent her, a final offering, the gods left me now to my fate.

We never did have that talk. Soon, I was far, far away. Far from Caroline or any other instruments of salvation.

44

I FELL INTO A light and troubled sleep. On finally going downstairs sometime around noon, I found Fintan, safe and sound and seated in the kitchen, a mug of steaming tea clasped in his two hands. He was observing Missy with a keen curiosity. She was stretched at an awkward angle on the floor, lapping with a kind of tired persistence out of a bowl of milk with some porridge oats floating in it.

'Did you warm the milk?' I enquired.

'I didn't think of that,' he said. 'Sorry.'

The door and window were wide open to the freshness of the day and the place was tidied and aromatic with the nostalgic smell of furniture polish.

'The new man himself,' I said. 'Where did you find the polish?'

'Under the stairs. The tin is an antique, by the look of it.'

''Twould be old all right,' I agreed.

'What is it anyway?' He gestured towards Missy. 'This thing here.'

'A monster. I suppose that's what she is. Small-sized certainly as monsters go. But a monster all the same.'

'You can say that again.'

'She's partial to music,' I said. 'And stories. Why don't you tell her a story?'

At this point, I couldn't give a damn about Missy or Fintan or whatever he might think of me. If he had pushed it, I would have given him the rundown on her, past, present

214

and future. It would keep him off more uncomfortable or compromising topics anyway. But he didn't push it. Maybe he figured he'd be better off discussing the two of us with Pierce later on. Get the sensible story from the sensible man.

'You were getting on famously with Laddy,' I remarked. 'Did you give him the secret sign?'

'Would you ever stuff it, Marty?' He was furious. 'Would you ever shut the fuck up?'

'Sorry,' I said.

He turned the radio on, very loud. Some jangle blared out. I was aware of an imminent pain in my head. I reached out and turned it down.

'The news won't be on for a while,' I offered placatingly.

'I wouldn't hold my breath for the news,' he said. 'I got the news already.'

'Oh,' I said. 'What's the forecast?'

'It's to keep up,' he responded though he was still sullen.

That touched me, his use of the country locution.

'They'll be at the hay today,' I told him. 'Bringing in the bales. You could give them a hand with that.'

I knew he'd be happy as a sandboy helping with the hay. Sure enough he perked up.

'I'm handy with a pitchfork,' he said modestly.

'I know you are.'

He looked at me with a mixture of suspicion and contempt. He wouldn't trust anything I might say now for a while.

'Why don't you go on up above and see what they're doing,' I suggested, though I was afraid he might take that up too the wrong way.

'What will you do?' he asked.

'I'll be up later on.'

He drank off his tea, tucked his shirt into his belt in a businesslike manner and left me.

215

'See you later,' I called to his departing back.

In recognition of my salutation, he raised his hand in the air. The next time I talked to Fintan after that was on the telephone that night in Deauville.

45

I WAS THINKING OF going back up to bed for a lie-down when I heard a step in the hall. The first thought that jumped guiltily into my head was that it was Caroline, back to blaze in righteous feminist fury at me with those new eyes of hers. My conscience flinched in anticipation. But Missy, recognising that step before I did, made a sudden dash for the door in a show of welcome. This, if I was ever in doubt, was how I always used to know when it was Etti coming.

I was struck at once by how white-faced she was, a different quality to her usual pallor. Her eyes had a glittering shine in them. She had come, I assumed, to give me a lecture on my behaviour towards my brother. I had an acute and generalised sense of guilt that day. She was slightly breathless as if she had run at full belt down the avenue. I pulled out a chair for her at the table. She picked Missy up on to her lap and Missy lay in against her with a sigh of happiness.

'It's warm,' Etti said.

'It's going to keep up.' My voice came out pitched low and strangled. 'According to the forecast anyway.'

'We shouldn't complain,' she said. She raised her head from Missy's and gave me a knowing smile.

I began to say how sorry I was. About the way the night in Ti Max had turned out and my carry-on. There was little in the way of an excuse I could find for myself. The words came out lame and unconvincing and soon trailed off. I could see however with some bemusement that this subject did not seem to hold a great deal of interest for her.

'I have a plan, Marty,' she said suddenly.

My heart leaped.

'What kind of a plan?'

My scepticism was an affectation. At her words my thoughts had immediately jumped at the notions that of late were always working in my head, crazy unformed plans for Etti and me.

'A plan for Missy. We have to do something, Marty.'

'There's nothing we can do. Have her put down. That's the best we could do for her.'

My disappointment made me sullen and cruel.

'We could take her away. To a kinder place. We could take her to France.'

The words 'we' and 'France' had been combined in one sentence. A mad elation began to take hold of me.

'To France? Where now exactly in France were you thinking of?'

My hands were shaking. I placed them out of sight behind my head and tilted my chair in a show of detachment.

'Look. We could take her there.'

She picked up a glossy magazine she had brought with her from the clutter on the table and put it into my hands. It was a copy of *Hello!* or some similar production, I suppose; I didn't bother to look because Etti had already folded it open at the pages she wanted me to see. On the left-hand side there was a full-page soft-focus picture in glowing Provençal Technicolor. That famous gap-toothed smile and the sun-dried straw-coloured hair and the trademark dark sun-glasses – Ms Brigitte Bardot, clutching a lamb which nestled happily against her sun-kissed maternal bosom. Not unlike the way Missy was nestling now in Etti's arms.

Slowly, attempting to think rationally, I turned to the

opposite page and scanned the text. I knew vaguely that this former sex-kitten was a fervid lover of animals. The article described the extensive animal sanctuary she had assembled at her home in the South of France and the varied species she tended there in blissful surroundings. Ms Bardot's esteem for animals was perhaps as great as that for humans, the writer asserted with uncritical approval. Ms Bardot firmly believed they possessed the yearnings of the emotions and of the soul just as we do and treated them accordingly.

It was a gushing and celebrity-fawning piece and, to Etti, deeply impressive. 'You see, Marty,' she burst out, 'Brigitte Bardot would take her on. I'm sure she would. That lamb there is one she rescued from the slaughter-house. Missy could be happy, Marty, we could explain about her. Brigitte would believe it and she would love Missy and understand her . . .'

Etti spoke pleadingly, urgently, as if she had to persuade me of the rightness of her arguments before I could call a halt to them. I had no intention of calling a halt. Her plan, preposterous but to me entirely persuasive, was that we should take Missy to this benign refuge and place her in the care of this motherly, nurturing, glamorous creature. The same Brigitte had I suspected however a jaundiced view of humanity. Would the adulterated animal that was Missy find a place in her affections? But I had no intention of expressing my doubts to Etti.

'When were you thinking of going?' My voice was hoarse and thick with excitement and fear.

'We could go now.'

I was unable to say anything, whether for or against. She gained confidence.

'I packed some things in case we might be able to go now.'

'What about Fintan?' I did say then, though feebly. 'I can't leave Fintan on his own when he's only just arrived.'

219

I knew quite well I was going to leave Fintan, and without a qualm.

'But Marty. That's the very reason why the best thing is to go now. Fintan will be company for Pierce. We'll only be away a few days. It will only take a couple of days. Won't it?'

She was suddenly doubtful. She had never been to France. 'Have you told Pierce?'

She hesitated, looking down at Missy, before she answered.

'We can phone him once we get on the road. I don't think we should tell him yet. You can be sure he wouldn't let me go if I told him.'

I wondered what was going on between Etti and Pierce. I wondered what had gone on between them the night before when they drove on alone to their marriage bed. But I did not dare to ask. I did not dare risk any fractures in the plan, in the delicate net of subterfuge she had so audaciously spun.

Defiantly, Etti tossed her head. Daring me to oppose her with any wimpish talk of wifely duties. She knew what she was after, she had her own agenda. I saw that.

46

S HE HAD HIJACKED the jeep. It was parked up at the Loop, a small suitcase flung on the back seat. Already, it had a fugitive look about it, like a transport for refugees.

I threw some stuff for myself into a bag while Etti made a bed for Missy in the rear of the jeep from straw she found in the outhouse and the old brown Crombie coat Missy was so fond of. I carried Missy up then and settled her on it. She was quite serene and happy, in Etti's company she was happy.

I took my credit cards, pristine and unused, from the drawer in the bedroom. I pulled out the basket Missy had travelled over to Kyle in, from behind the door where I had thrown it that evening. As if I was only going up to the Cross for a few messages I left the door on the latch, and I walked up to the jeep and threw the stuff into the back seat and I climbed into the passenger seat beside Etti.

The boat for France was leaving Rosslare in Wexford at about five. Etti had come supplied with this information from some holiday brochures Andrea had given her that were lying round since earlier in the year. If we drove hard and didn't stop, we could make it in time to board.

We drove without speaking. My chest was churning with a tumult of emotions. I found it hard to light a cigarette because my hands were trembling. And yet I have to say that my head was cold and clear and sure about the inevitability, if not the rightness, of what we were up to.

Swerving through the Cross at speed, we met Young

Delaney in his Escort. He waved. We overtook bald-headed Veronica Quinlan pedalling fast somewhere on her bicycle. Old Maddy Forbes, out clipping her hedge, waved cursorily at the familiar noise of the jeep.

By nightfall the news of our flight would be the talk of Fansha. Hinting at inside knowledge, they would be telling each other how Pierce and myself had been at loggerheads since day one, glee mixed with sorrow that the simmering pot had boiled over at last. Wondering what the hell Etti could be up to, they would greedily seize on the worst scenario. Only Pierce, once it was all explained to him, would perceive the nobility of our actions. Pierce would work away as usual through the day and drink steadily with Fintan into the night and wait patiently for our return.

I went through all this in my head, coldly and with detachment. There was no time to stop. Passing through towns and villages, crowded with cars and tractors, the streets appeared strangely silent and ephemeral as if in the dark interior of the jeep we were in a small and private cinema where the sound of the picture had been turned off. Pink, green, yellow painted houses baking in the heat, over-bright, over-sweet, a man in a cap and a woman in a blue dress talking, mouths opening and closing as we rocketed past, not speaking, on our way towards the olive bush and the mountain-top. Sunlight and shadows, the darkest foliage, the fiercest green, so dense, so shiny, so hot, racing on as if the slavering wolves of the world were yapping alongside in the trees.

Would they come after us? I was tortured for a good while with that fear. Saw Pierce leap into Ned Murnane's police car and the two of them flying along behind us in hot pursuit. Lights flashing, siren blazing, the citizens of the little towns stopping to watch, to offer information.

'A jeep? They went that way, Officer. Going like the clappers. But you'll catch them up, no problem.'

222

I peered back through the rear window. On the long ribbon of road stretching back the way we had come, there was no bright siren flashing in the sun, no vehicle remotely following this description. The ambling summer traffic even, we had left far behind. We had the road to ourselves.

'She'll be dying with the thirst,' Etti said, coming out of her silence as we came into Inishtiogue. 'We'll have to stop to buy some water.'

She pulled up on the slope of the main street and I ran into a shop at full belt and brought back a magnum of Tipperary water.

'Sparkling,' said Etti doubtfully, examining the label. 'Will she drink sparkling water?'

But Missy lapped it up. I filled her bowl again. Etti and I took ravenous swigs from the bottle, passing it back and forth. I reached out once and wiped her wet mouth gently with my fingers. I could not help myself. I knew it was up to me, now that we had embarked on this outrage, to be calm, in control. Biting into her lower lip she looked away, troubled and unsure. But what she needed maybe was reassurance. After that we were easier with one another. Missy didn't seem to mind the fizz. By the time we set off again, she was asleep.

47

SOMETIME BEFORE FIVE we breasted a hill and saw below us at its bottom a shimmering milky sea and a big white ferry waiting. Into the yawning mouth at the stern, a line of cars, small as toys, were crawling forward one by one, as into an ark. I had a joyous sensation of escape, of an imminent war and borders which had urgently to be crossed, and that we had made it.

'It's a ship,' breathed Etti.

A little fever of excitement was taking hold of her. It was infectious. We had put a lot of road and a long dazzling afternoon between ourselves and Fansha. Now that we were here, facing the white ship and the open water, we were suddenly festive and excited like a young pair at the commencement of their holidays.

We were last in the queue. In case there was some regulation about bringing pets on holiday abroad that could mess things up, we hastily pushed Missy, struggling vainly, into the basket and shut the lid tight and artfully draped the Crombie over it. It looked like a picnic hamper. Taking a hamper for picnicking in France seemed an exuberant and innocent gesture. I was wistful for it to be a hamper and for everything to be simple and innocent and as it might appear to the unsuspecting world.

'We're booked up,' announced the clerk.

He was an officious red-faced fellow with a moustache.

'You can't just turn up like this, you know.'

He took evident pleasure in conveying this information to us in his flat Wexford voice.

'Sure at this time of the year we're always booked up weeks in advance.'

The thought that we might not get on to the ship had not crossed our minds.

'Could you not fit us on?' I pleaded.

'We could of course. As long as you find some character willing to put you up on his roof-rack.'

The fellow laughed at his mean little joke. Limp with dejection and fatigue, Etti slumped over the steering-wheel.

'Will you move off now, please. You're causing an obstruction,' said the clerk.

'We're not obstructing anyone,' I told him sullenly.

'You will be in a minute,' he said.

The long cavern of the car-deck was open and beckoning. I had a sudden crazy impulse to drive on, knocking him aside. If I was behind the wheel, I would have. Etti started up the engine.

'Go for it,' I told her, my teeth clenched with anger.

'Oh, Marty,' she said forlornly. And, backing away from our escape hatch, she pulled up a short distance away.

'What now?' she asked.

'One to go,' called one of his colleagues to the fellow with the moustache. 'A Volvo.'

He looked at his watch and then up the hill in the direction we had come, shading his eyes like a general looking for the cloud of dust that heralds the arrival of his troops.

'We could go to the hotel,' I suggested. 'Maybe there'll be a berth for us tomorrow.' It was the last thing I wanted to do. Etti gave me a sad, infinitely weary look and made no reply.

In the silence between us, I heard faintly the shrill notes of a telephone. Bitterly I watched as the mustachioed fellow picked up the phone in his kiosk, turning his back to us as he talked into it, as if he suspected us of trying to eavesdrop on him. With bitterness, I watched him as he put it down and the officious way he straightened his cap on his head and his slow ponderous gait as he came out from behind his glass partition and walked over towards us.

He rested his elbow on the roof of the car and he bent down to peer in at us.

'You were thinking of travelling today, were you?' he commented.

'We were bedad,' I replied, attempting to match his sarcasm.

'You're in luck so,' he said. 'We have a cancellation. This last vehicle we were waiting for, they're broken down outside Wexford town. New clutch required, apparently. They won't be travelling. Not today anyway.'

Whose hand was this, the hand of fortune or of malign fate? During the long night in the bleak limbo of the hotel, wouldn't either or both of us have had a failure of will? Or would we have found ourselves back in Fansha even before the fall of darkness, as if after a jaunt to the beach, no damage done?

Had I known what was to come, would I have turned away from the clerk and his tidings of joy? I would not like to have to answer that question, even if I could. As easy to wonder why she or I were ever born.

48

ETTI AND I TRAVELLED together as Mr and Mrs Hawkins. Which, ironically, was no lie though neither was it the truth. In the comfortable little cabin prepared for the Volvo family and assigned now to us, we sat on our separate berths, in our masquerade as man and wife, and stared, limp with exhaustion and the tremors of receding terror, at the chugging opacity of the sea and the flat land of Wexford contracting into the sea-haze behind us.

How easily it could fade away. How insignificant it all could so easily and quickly be, I thought with a furtive surge of triumph. Ireland and Pierce and Fansha and Young Delaney and the whole lot of them.

'We never rang Pierce,' breathed Etti. Her face was stricken.

'Maybe we could ring from here.'

I said that to console her but I regretted it as soon as the words were out of my mouth. Visions of speed launches rushed into my head, harbour police in shiny black malevolent capes in hot pursuit, the ship's propellers churning in the wrong direction . . .

'From the ship?'

'Why not? We could ask.'

She began to rummage in her bag.

'We'll do it from France,' she said. 'The minute we arrive.'

I was hugely relieved. Etti too wanted to be safe, out of reach on the other side where we could not be overtaken.

I released Missy from the basket and prepared a couch for

227

her under my bunk. She could explore the cabin as she liked. It was not the kind of ship where an obsequious but keen-eyed steward was liable to come knocking for admittance bearing fresh towels or room service. She seemed pleased with her new situation and curious, going back and forth in the small cabin from Etti to me to be patted and climbing in her clumsy way on to the berths to look out at the milky-blue sea.

I realised that happiness had suddenly overtaken me. I was simply and adventurously happy, like a young man going casually away on a trip with his beloved. And suddenly, too, I was starving. But it did not seem a good idea to leave Missy alone while we went to dine, when she had just been released from her captivity and was restlessly padding about.

We could give her a sleeping-pill, Etti suggested.

'Where would we get a sleeping-pill?'

'I have pills.'

Until then I did not know that Etti had a sleeper habit.

I went up to the self-service café and got a carton of milk and a packet of biscuits. With her nail-scissors, Etti cut a green capsule in half and emptied out the granules on to the bedside table. We mixed about half of the contents into Missy's supper of milk and crumbled biscuits and cajoled her into swallowing a good portion of it. Then I sat and waited for her to settle down and watched Etti pencil in her eyes and mouth and brush her hair.

When she was in the bathroom, I was assailed with a new fear. That the dose of sedative might be too heavy and Missy would die in her sleep. But it was not, to my shame, the fear of Missy's loss that most appalled me but the scenario that opened then before my eyes. Etti would cry for a short while. Then we would take Missy up on deck before dawn when everyone was sleeping and the boat was quiet and, in the light of the moon, drop her over the side into the cold silvery sea.

228

Her slight stiffening body would make only an inconsequential splash as it hit the water and the ship would draw inexorably on in its cold and stately advance away from her.

But what really affected me was that there would be no reason then to drive to Provence in search of Brigitte Bardot. In fact, there would be no reason even to disembark. Etti, grieving and remorseful, would wish to stay on board until the ship turned around, wanting only to be returned to Rosslare and thence to Foilmore as quickly and efficiently as sailing-times allowed.

I went and crouched on the floor beside Missy. With watchful apprehension I waited on each rise and fall of her chest. She seemed to be breathing normally and I was reassured. But I saw then that each moment of this time I had so miraculously and improbably achieved to be alone with Etti was fragile and precious.

Once again we sat opposite each other at a restaurant table. No more fancy a one than the evening before, but this time of an ineffable luxury because it was the first night we ate alone together, Etti and I. Having eaten nothing all day, I was starving. I don't remember what we ate, however. Perhaps I was unable to eat anything.

What I do remember is an inundation of rosiness. A buffet spread with pink joints of salmon and our table by the window looking out on the purpling water and the rosé wine Etti ordered. I remember how, opposite me, her face loomed, fresh as a flower belying our mad dash south. And the absent way she poured the wine so it made pink stains on the cloth as she told me about her life as a girl in town. A tale of childish events and adolescent torments of no great importance to her or anyone else any more, I suppose. But important to me because it was to me she was recounting them with a hesitant intensity as if I was the first she had ever confided them to.

229

'Do you think I'm dim, Marty?' she asked. Waving aside without heed my protests and denials.

'I was stupid at school. I was no good at school. I got that from my father. It was all I got from him. I turned out a great disappointment to my mother. Poor thing. She's a sharp lady, my mother. And she found herself living with a collection of dimwits. My brother is as bad as myself.'

At this I laughed. She gave me a bright smile in return.

'Still, I was clever enough for Pierce,' she remarked.

What did she mean by that? Was it a comment on Pierce's lack of sharpness? Or on her own compensatory qualities?

In our family, I enjoyed a reputation as the clever, the quick one. But later on I came to see Pierce's solid adult intelligence to be the valued kind and my brand of cleverness as not worth tuppence. Which was also Fansha's more or less explicit view of the two of us.

Briefly now I saw the enigma of Etti's nature revealed to me for the first time in the harsh light of her own self-judgement. It was true, she was not clever. Not like Caroline, who could probe my pitiful soul with those eyes of hers and protest with righteous contempt at what she saw there. But this was what was so hopelessly appealing to me about Etti, the unknowability of the childish but keenly sentient, the mystery of a mind filled with shadowy impenetrable spaces. It was what gave me this sense of childlike shallow happiness. My love for her, and I knew it was love, was subversive, the kind that would be regarded by all reasonable men as a vice, against nature, cruel even, and to be enjoyed infrequently, and then furtively.

I can see all this now. But that night in the crowded restaurant with no one taking a blind bit of notice of us or we of them, under the rosy light of the fringed lamps with France moving towards us in the night and the consciousness of our successful flight settling a luxurious generosity of time and space about me, I felt it only as a flitting moment of unease before joy rushed in and chased it out.

Later, as we lay in our separate berths, I reached out to take Etti's hand. She had taken her sleeping-pill and her response was slack and disconnected. Then I followed her into the innocent oblivion of sleep.

49

WE AWOKE LATE and found Missy had been sick in the night. She seemed a little confused and not herself. Etti sent me off to the restaurant to breakfast alone. When I returned, bringing some milky cereal in a bowl for Missy from the self-service café, Etti in turn went for her breakfast. She stayed away for what seemed an unbearably long time. I gazed at the map of France posted on the wall of the cabin and worked out from it an extremely circuitous route to Provence. How were we to track down Brigitte Bardot, I wondered. Eventually, we would have to fetch up there, whichever way we went. How would she receive us? Would she too turn away in distaste from Missy? Or would she see in her a new and exciting cause célèbre? From the corridors, I could hear the homely Irish voices calling and laughing to each other. I heard them as a prying chorus, oppressive and threatening.

Later on there was the sedation again of Missy to see her quiet and untroublesome through the day. Then the scramble to the car-deck and the anxiety of the long queue for disembarkation in the discomfort of dust and heat and shouts and the noxious-smelling fumes of the vessel. But the shouted orders and instructions were in French and came from matelot types, foreign fellows wrinkled and brown from a blazing Continental sun. And that soothed me, the near-certainty that we were safe at last in our escape.

For a long time we were crawling into the blinding

afternoon sun, tail-gate to tail-gate in a line of cars with their obscurely threatening Irish registrations. '94 Ds. '96 KEs. At last the open motorway stretched away to Paris and the south. And at what looked like it would be the last roundabout for a while, I veered on impulse left, towards the east.

And almost at once we were alone. On a long straight ribbon of a Route Nationale, alone except for foreign cars with blonde golden-skinned madames at the wheel, the sun at our backs, the cool verdure and flaxen hectares of Normandy's cornfields about us, and the cars of our compatriots left behind in the race to the south.

Etti made no objection. She trusted me. Abroad in the vastness of a foreign country, she was placing herself and our mission in my hands.

'We can double back further on,' I said, to reassure her. 'We're taking a less busy route. Where there will be less traffic.'

This I still fully intended to do. She nodded in agreement and gazed out the open window, her hair flying in the warm breeze.

'It's not how I imagined it,' she announced critically once, turning to me. 'Not for Missy. But it is very nice, Marty.'

The land was lush, grassy, pastoral, like Tipperary on the best of days.

'She does hate the green stuff,' I agreed. 'But never mind. We'll be in the dusty south soon enough.'

'In the sanctuary. With Brigitte Bardot,' said Etti firmly. As if she feared I might waver in our intention, but warning me that she would not.

The heat of the day was abating. I saw a sign for the town called Honfleur. I had been in these parts years before for a day or two on a student jaunt and remembered that it was pretty and typique. Where, as they say, on mange bien. Why should Etti not have a look at Honfleur? I was on a high of happiness, of illusion.

We drove into a small sea-town of tall grey slated houses arranged in a square around the harbour, ancient, trim, bourgeois and touristic. I felt the old seductive pull of history, liberated from its rigour and detail and mundanity. Honfleur made me think of Napoleon for some reason, and his wilful march across Europe. I surged with a sense of power, of Napoleonic imperium.

'Cocktail-time,' I announced gaily, drawing to a stop under the trees by the limpid water.

She turned to look at me with that stricken look of hers.

'That's what Fintan said,' she murmured. Too late I remembered the gathering in Etti's house and Etti in her dress and Fintan's joke about farmers and the cocktail hour. What was it, only two days before? But it came to me out of the dim past as if weeks or months had intervened. I had a crazy sense that since that distant time in a remote place another life had begun.

'We have to ring Pierce,' she said.

I could have kicked myself.

'We'll do it now,' I said. Breezily, as if this telephone call was the easiest thing in the world, a trifle.

She temporised. 'Well. After our cocktail,' she suggested. 'The cocktails will give us courage.'

We joined the file of chic weekender types on their desultory promenade along the pier, and for the time being we put Pierce and the telephone call out of our minds. Perhaps we already knew we could not simply telephone; could not say, we are in France, we are taking Missy to Brigitte Bardot. We would have to say, yes, together we have run away, we are mad or bad or both, we are beyond the pale of your forgiveness. But Pierce, forgive us, we do not know what we are doing. Of course we did not want to face that.

At a café terrasse we chose white-cushioned chairs under a blue and white striped awning. Etti lay back against the faded blue canvas antimacassar, eyes clamped tight to shut out the glare of the evening sun. Her mouth, I noticed, had a set and worried look when she was in repose as if her dreaming thoughts were dimmed with shadows.

I wanted to stop her from thinking, I wanted to keep melancholy at bay, I wanted to induce in her something of the insouciance and ruthlessness of the holiday girls who flung themselves down on the café chairs with their pastel golfing sweaters draped over their sinewy gymnastic shoulders, bestowing the bise bise on stray acquaintances. I ordered a bottle of champagne to be brought to the table. I knew Etti was childishly keen on champagne.

This impulse, I suppose, set the tone for our subsequent delinquency. From then on, we were always a little drunk, living on champagne and coloured cocktails and kirs and anything euphorically sparkling we could see. Play-food we dined on, finger-food, heaps of crustaceans served on beds of ice, frites, sugary bourbon biscuits. When a pang of conscience or imminent restiveness threatened to imperil our strenuously thoughtless idyll, I would order another bottle, instantly, in my cold-blooded watchfulness. I could be drunk enough on Etti's presence. I had little confidence however in mine having the same effect on her.

When it was growing dark, we bought ice-cream at a kiosk and returned to the jeep and fed it to Missy with her sleeping-powder stirred into it. I went off then to look for beds for the night. I asked about rooms in the place where we had dined and in the hotel adjacent to it and in another and finally in a pension at the end of the pier looking out on the sea. But it was the height of the season. There were no beds to be had in Honfleur. This somehow did not bother me at all.

The moon was up, hanging large and white over the

glimmering water. In the balmy night air I watched for a long time the slow lazy wash of the waves on the narrow shore of moonlit pebbles and the groups of people wandering in and out of bars, their faces blurred, their white garments illuminated to incandescence by the mauve neon halters they laughingly bought from the halter-hawkers. There by the soft velvety water and the tinkling boats gently rocking, I felt myself at last to be one with the callous sweetness of the world, ruthless and happy, and Fansha and everybody in it drifting away from me into the meaningless past.

When I returned to the jeep, I found Etti stretched out on the floor, wrapped in some old coats belonging to Pierce or maybe Raffles, thrown in the back and forgotten. And Missy nestling alongside, small and luminously white in the moonlight, her front feet flung carelessly out, against Etti's chest. They were already deep in sleep.

Quietly, I lay down beside Etti, feverishly caught between a fear of disturbing her and a longing for her to drowsily turn to me. I remember wondering whether in the circumstances I would get any sleep at all and if I should take a sleeper myself to ward off the familiar host of terrors that might assail me in the dark. Idly, I watched the reflections of moonlit water that palely dappled the interior of the jeep. And must have been too comfortable, too voluptuously tired to go scrabbling for the pill-box. When I awoke, day was already well established and the Continental racket of scooters was filling the streets of Honfleur.

They were both anxious. Missy up to her old tricks, wan and disinclined to eat, her eyes filmy with dejection, Etti nervous and newly anxious about getting her settled in her new Provençal home. That was, after all, why we were here. And certainly she was nervous and anxious too about the other problem, the telephone call, though it remained tacit between us, neither of us having any heart for it. And, maybe

236

she too, as much as I, was reluctant to leave Honfleur where we had found a fleeting rest together, even if it was delusory, between our separate pasts and separate futures. It was at Honfleur that we breathed voluptuously the heady air of escape, of duty relinquished, which, though we only inchoately recognised it, we were loth to give up.

'I know exactly how to get to Provence,' I told Etti to reassure her. 'I've been looking at the map.'

Trustingly, she nodded. She didn't ask but as far as I was concerned Provence was a long way off. We'd be on the road for a long time yet and there was nothing I could think of beyond planning for that.

We were not long left Honfleur when we passed an arrowed road sign. I took note that it said Deauville. But Deauville meant nothing to me, apart from its status as a seaside resort with a certain cachet. Etti, however, her face newly bright and alert, turned swiftly to look back the way we had come.

She grabbed my arm. 'Deauville,' she said. 'Marty. We've just passed the sign for Deauville. That's where the racing is.'

'It's out of our way,' I objected, stupidly intent on Provence and the most circuitous route to the south.

But then I was filled with the desire to indulge and please her; and with the furtive realisation that Deauville could provide a further delay. I made a perilous but smart U-turn.

'We'll take a look at the place,' I said. 'Why not? Check it out for lunch.'

We were a bad influence, each on the other. But she could always bring out whatever ounce of gallantry was in me, could Etti.

'Isn't it a bit early for lunch?' she protested. But she smiled and I knew she was pleased.

50

At my first sight of it, I did not take to Deauville. I saw a town of the nouveau-Normand style of architecture, mocked-up beams and aspirant mini-châteaux, thick with honking bevies of the latest BMWs. Over-chic, over-brash and hysterically bourgeois, stuffy and glittering and pretentious. But what I also saw before very long was its heartless anonymity and narcissism. That if you had money to throw around, which I could make a good show of doing with my assortment of relatively virginal credit cards, it would leave you alone.

Behind the tinkling fountains and the hot August blooms of the public gardens in the square, I spotted the tall splendid façade of the Hotel Normandy. I saw at once that it represented the old Edwardian glory-days, the discretion of elegant, vaguely louche hotel-life, and that Etti would like it. Leading her by the arm, I ordered a table in the restaurant for lunch. We were advised to wait and take an aperitif. We were suddenly in holiday mood again. Semi-delirious with it, we sat on a long sofa in the cool vastness of the salon, sipping champagne kirs and observing the passage of spoiled patrons to and fro.

At least I watched Etti observe them. Our clothes were crumpled, we were tired and in need of a wash. But this gave us a rakish look that seemed to consort with the place. In any case, a studied absence of interest in their fellow Normandy-ens seemed to be the dominant manner of the hotel.

'We should have brought Missy in to lunch,' Etti remarked.
'Why?'

'Look,' she said. 'The dogs.'

The salon, I saw, was crawling with dogs. Spoilt dogs, pettish dogs, big and small, black poodles and white, dressed in tartan coats or glossy with an excess of vitamins, carried like fractious infants in their owners' arms or hanging incuriously about, as bored as their Madame and Monsieur.

Pity for Missy, subsisting like a neglected child on irregular ice-creams, gave me a brief pang. She was all alone again in the jeep under the noonday sun, though I had taken care to park it in the shade of a small tree. Also we figured that its closed-in sides should keep her from the worst of the heat. We took care to reassure each other in any case that she liked the heat.

'Poor old Missy. We couldn't bring her in here. Not without a new hairdo,' giggled Etti.

A hotel that was dog, pet-friendly. This new perspective on the Normandy sowed the germ of an idea in my mind.

Etti gripped my wrist.

'Did you see him?'

'What? Who?'

'Steve Cauthen. With a girl. He must be staying here.'

I was only vaguely aware that Steve Cauthen was a jockey of some repute.

'Are you going to go all horse-mad on me now?'

I affected tedium, though her excitement and willingness to be impressed was joyful to me.

'I might be. Let's see what's running today.'

She perused a race-card she had picked up from the low table, her forehead creased in concentration.

'The Prix Morny,' she concluded. 'For two-year-olds.'

'We can go if you like,' I suggested.

A shadow of doubt crossed her face. It was speedily

replaced with a smile of pleasure. Ruefully, she bit her lower lip.

'We have to see the Morny,' she agreed with resolution. 'We can't miss the Morny, now we're here.'

51

THE WAITER CAME to take away the plates after our fruits de mer. I enquired whether dogs were allowed also in the rooms of the Normandy.

'But of course, M'sieur,' he said. 'The dogs of our clientele are welcome everywhere in the Normandy.'

'Their horses aussi?' giggled Etti.

We were well embarked on our career of effervescence for the day, a mood shot through with a poignancy, both terrible and sweet because it was so fragile, so open to siege on all sides from enemies real and imaginary that must somehow be kept at bay. For the moment, luck and cunning were on my side. But innocence and right, I was convinced, would triumph in the end. Pierce had taught me that.

Etti's horse won the Prix Morny. I can see him now, Rattrape, the jockey Guignard in the saddle in his acid-yellow cap and his yellow blouse billowing behind him in the light hot breeze. Coming with a noise of thunder up on the stand-side of a fellow in red, effortlessly, unbeatably galloping for the post, huge, apparently enormous, a giant horse dwarfing the puny cohorts behind him.

Allez Guignard, Allez Guignard, roared the crowd like a giant wave of the sea as he came through, a swift looming brilliance obscuring the sky. Though we could not make out, not yet, what it was they were saying. And were calling wildly together, go on Rattrape, go on Rattrape. The only uninitiates in the crowd, naïvely shouting out the name of the horse.

My interest in horse-racing, awakened in Deauville by Etti's enthusiasm, was short-lived but intense. We won other races on the lawns of Deauville that afternoon and on the afternoons that followed. But it is only the names of Guignard and Rattrape and Morny that I remember, strung out like thorny pearls on the memorial wreath of my lost joy.

To shield her eyes from the unaccustomed glare of the French sun, Etti was wearing shades. I could not read their expression but I sensed the illusion of autonomy and power her win gave her. I felt it myself. And I recognised it as another weapon for me to use.

At the close of the day's racing, as long shadows haunted the grass and we joined the procession to the gates, already Etti had the card for the next day's races in her hand. She was already expectant. Left to herself, however, she would conscientiously turn aside from Deauville and be well on the road to Provence when they were run. It was I who caused her to falter. As a valiant but overstretched horse falters at a jump and is lost.

Until it was safely secured, I did not let her know that I had taken a room at the Normandy. It had seemed impossible. But once more, my devilish luck held out. I left Etti at the jeep, occupied with attempting to soothe Missy in whom the day's solitude had induced a serious state of nervousness and distrust. I told her I was going in search of cigarettes. Instead, I hurried over to the hotel and enquired at the desk with as much coolness as I could muster whether there was a double room available for a night or two.

No. I was told. Not now at the height of the season. It was after all the season of the racing, M'sieur. So sorry but absolutely not.

I went and stood in the foyer, dejected and tired, gazing unseeing across the gardens and wondering what to do. Unable to come to any decision I was making my way slowly towards the steps when I felt a tap on my shoulder. The desk-clerk and another dark-suited smoothie were beaming graciously upon me

'M'sieur? You are in luck,' said my fellow. 'My colleague tells me that Monsieur and Madame Blanchard are checking out this evening. Something urgent in Paris. They have to return . . . Alors, M'sieur, if you wish to have the room . . . It will be ready' – he consulted his watch – 'at seven o'clock.' And he bowed and gestured with a magnanimously welcoming flourish in the direction of the desk.

The old story, a reprise of our miraculous wafting at Rosslare on to the boat. Fate grants no reprieve. Laughing, I followed him.

'You are a lucky man, M'sieur,' repeated the fellow as I gave him a card and my details. Conveying with a knowing smile and a twinkling eye his calm French empathy with my manly ardour.

'We have a dog,' I told him.

'Your dog will be very welcome, M'sieur.'

On my way back to the jeep, I stopped in the shade of an awning to rest and mop my face, which, on leaving the Normandy, had broken out into a nervous sweat. Happening to glance in the window of the shop under whose cocoa-striped awning I was standing, I saw a fetching array of dog-stuff. Leather leads, harnesses, feeding-bowls, brushes, coats. All kinds of luxurious paraphernalia for dogs. It was a dog boutique, called La Chiotte.

Madame was helpful but disapproving of my haste.

'Normally we like to measure the animal, M'sieur. Our coats are most elegant and comfortable when they are custom-made to fit.'

I imagined what an insult it would be to her ideas of canine elegance were she asked to measure Missy. Unfortunately there was no time, I told her, for a tailored outfit. I wanted something at once as a wedding anniversary gift for my wife. Yes, my wife, it was our first anniversary in fact, adored her little dog, I told Madame. A poodle. A white poodle, white as snow, and smart as a whip.

Mollified, Madame helped me to pick out a harness in soft green leather that I thought Missy, unused to a lead, might be amenable to wearing. Then a coat made of cocoa-coloured linen, light but capacious, affording maximum coverage. Both items were discreetly etched in embroidery with the words La Chiotte. They were incredibly expensive. La Chiotte was, Madame proudly and reprovingly intimated, the equivalent of Dior in the canine world.

Etti chewed her lips with worry and doubt when I told her that we had a room in the Normandy, awaiting our arrival. But I could see the light of pleasure in her eyes.

'We do need a good night's sleep,' she agreed at length. 'And the room will have a telephone. We can ring Pierce from the room.'

The facility of a private telephone seemed to lend a veneer of responsibility and virtue to the decision. Etti cooed with admiration over the things I had bought for Missy at La Chiotte. Then she set about dressing her in her new attire.

'They'll be wondering why she's wearing such a big coat in the middle of summer,' she said critically, surveying her work. 'And it makes her look even thinner. Her bones stick out through it.'

'We can say she's convalescent,' I said.

'Can you say it in French?' laughed Etti. She was excited as a child again.

She carried Missy in her arms through the foyer in the Normandy and up the stairs to the second floor, behind the porter who carried our bags. I tipped the fellow generously, as if it were necessary to buy his confidence; and then we were alone with the telephone. I had half hoped that my

244

crazy luck might hold out and there would be no telephone, that the anachronisms of the Normandy might extend to a rule of no new-fangled intrusive instruments to disrupt the playfulness of guests in their rooms. But there it was, looking at us. And once again, we resorted to delaying tactics. The usual things. Baths. Resting on our beds. Careful perusal of hotel literature. Organising room service. Champagne for us. For Missy ice-cream and lait chaud.

'Dinner?' I suggested casually at last when Etti was dressed and had finished drying her hair. I was half hoping she had managed for the time being to put the telephone call out of her mind.

'We have to ring, Marty.'

Her tone was heavy and upbraiding. She came and sat on my bed next to the phone.

'Yes. Let's do that. Let's ring,' I agreed with a show of casualness.

She picked up the receiver. Held it for a minute close to her ear. It was a pale-green telephone to match the decor. She put it down again.

'Shouldn't you do it, Marty?'

'No. You do.'

'Why?'

'It's you he'll be wanting to hear from. You know that.'

She sighed. 'I suppose you're right.'

Her fingers were poised over the buttons.

'The code first,' I said gently. The code for Ireland had remained obstinately fixed in my head since the day before when I looked it up.

'I don't know the code.' She replaced the receiver.

'Zero zero three five three,' I told her firmly.

Slowly she took up the receiver again and dialled. It rang for what seemed a long time.

245

'He's not there,' she said. I heard the hope and relief in her voice.

Just as I was about to reach for her hand and take for her the decision to hang up, I heard a high-pitched distant voice reply.

'Hello?' Etti said. Her voice was trembling with nervousness.

'Oh. Is that Fintan? Hello, Fintan. Is Pierce there? This is Etti.'

Tensely, she had clamped the receiver close to her ear so I could hear nothing from the other end. Only Etti's nervous, secretive, apologetic words, spoken with a transparent haste to have the conversation over and done with.

'You don't know when he'll be back? We're in France actually. I know, Fintan. I'm sorry. But he's not to worry. I'm fine. We're in Deauville at the moment. But we're leaving tomorrow, well, probably tomorrow . . . Look, I'll call again. Tell him I rang and he's not to worry . . .'

She turned to look at me, her hand over the mouthpiece.

'It's Fintan. He wants to talk to you.'

I panicked.

'Say I'm in the shower.'

'He's in the shower, Fintan. Fintan? Fintan?'

There was the slow click as she replaced the receiver.

'He hung up.'

'It doesn't matter,' I told her. 'Don't mind Fintan. You know what Fintan is like. The main thing is you rang. The minute he comes in, Pierce will know that you're all right, that you rang. That's the main thing.'

'I should have explained to him. About Missy.'

'You did fine. Fintan wouldn't understand anything about Missy. You can explain to Pierce.'

She began to sob.

'I'll explain to Pierce,' I comforted her. 'It's all my fault anyway. Pierce will see that it's my fault.'

'No. It's my fault.'

I could not bear to see Etti cry. Not when it bleakly exposed to view the illicitness of our days of happiness. To comfort her, to dispel the memory of Pierce, I pulled her to me and covered her tear-streaked face with caresses. When I fumbled with the buttons that lay under my hands, she turned her flushed face away, heated and damp from my touch and her crying. But she stretched, quiescent and unprotesting, to meet me when I reached inside her open dress.

It was almost night when I was aware once more of the room and the novelty of its gilded furniture gleaming here and there in the dusk. A slanting band of heavy gold from the waning sun was creeping low down the farther wall. Against my chest, Etti's dark head lay peaceably in sleep. My stupid life, aimless and despairing, appeared to me at that moment as rich and achieved, hazed in fulness. I held Etti in my arms and when I awoke, hours later, the room was lit with the brightness of morning.

52

IN DEAUVILLE, WE lived like the idle rich, though more fortunate and happy than they, because it was all new to us. The Continental quality of the sun we were unused to, the perilous headiness of our forbidden love. Every afternoon we were to be seen on the green lawns of the racetrack, Etti beautiful in the new dresses I picked out for her in the smart boutiques. Under the shade of the candy-striped umbrellas where we reserved our table daily for lunch, the waiters beamed fondly on us, perhaps recognising in us the fated lovers to whom the French are always partial. Etti named for me the famous trainers and owners at their tables and the jockeys who came swaggering up to them to pay their respects.

Once, a bottle of champagne was sent over to us at our table. We never did find out who it was from. We accepted it as our due. To be petted, admired, made much of. Looking back, it seems to me that we won on all the races, we were always calling the winner home, delirious with triumph. But I suppose that is unlikely to be true.

In the evenings, when we returned to our room, Missy would be waking from her drugged sleep. We would take her out then for her evening promenade, wrapped up in her chocolate linen coat, carrying her in our arms to protect her from the curious or contemptuous gaze of the other prom-enaders with their boisterous barking dogs. Barefoot, we walked on the warm sun-bleached planches by the beach, until we had left them all behind, the coloured beach umbrellas furled and turned to black against the waning sun for company, standing like watchful but benign sentinels at attention all the way to Trouville.

Far along the beach towards Trouville, when the last of the sun-worshippers were departing and we were more or less alone, we would put Missy down and remove her expensive coat from La Chiotte. And she would set off, lurching bravely and eagerly across the soft sand with her staggering gait towards the brisk white rollers of the sea.

And while Etti waited for us at a beach café, lingering over some long cool coloured drink, I would go to fetch Missy, meeting the silent beach attendants gathering up the white chairs in the bluish light. And Etti's tinkling laugh as I paddled in the warm shallows after Missy would travel across the sands to me. She was different, Etti was then, my French Etti, browner, gay, and reckless.

Later on in the balmy dusk, we would leave Missy to fall again into her sedated sleep in the gilded room on the second floor and we would go out into the streets to dine. On some stylish terrasse, usually the Drakkar, because it was our favourite place, we would take our seats, lost in our illusory world among all the other happy and thoughtless vacanciers, Etti's face glowing opposite me on a plush banquette, her fingers deftly breaking open the shells of delicate sea-creatures, as I had taught her to do.

Sometimes, in search of a nightlife like the other revellers, we stayed in the bars, drinking until it was late. But mostly I remember returning early to our room in the Normandy. To lie in her arms in the tangled sheets, drunk on the brightness of the day we had passed and on each other.

Was this how Etti felt too? I never had any cause, then, to doubt it. But who knows what was going on in her head? I never did know, quite. And I suspect I never wanted to, not then, when the perils of knowledge and confrontation were so great.

53

Occasionally there were moments when I would be forced to confront the shrouded nature of my understanding of her. This had the power to chill me to the bone. Then I would draw the shutters on those icy vistas and face into the sun again.

One afternoon, over lunch on the racecourse we were observing, which was a fairly relentless pastime with us, the conspiratorial carry-on of the rakish gang at another table and the wistful demeanours of their thin, over-dressed, anxious women. They were from Paris, from the Parisian underworld of gangsters, we had long ago decided. We had fallen into the habit of observing them, we had come to know them on the racecourse, they were the inhabitants of our new landscape. To make up stories about them excused us from discussing anything more significant.

There were other people to watch. An English trainer and his entourage, their table laden with champagne buckets. A charming haut bourgeois couple, elderly, their white hair smoothly coiffed, who bestowed on us the indulgent smiles of ancient lovers. But it was the sinister Parisians who fascinated us, who held our attention and our imaginations. We christened them the Paris mafiosi.

'I never could live up to Pierce,' Etti remarked.

With a frown, she considered the Paris mafiosi and sighed.

'Pierce is so good. You don't know what it's like, the burden of living with someone so completely good.'

Though inwardly I flinched to hear uttered my brother's name, I answered with a show of flippancy.

'So you'd prefer to live with a gangster in Montparnasse?'

'Maybe he would suit me better,' she said.

She said it with a sad gravity as if she believed it.

Our sense of guilt at least must have been equal. It was guilt that made us avoid any suggestion of telephoning Pierce again. We had after all spoken to Fintan. Fintan knew our approximate whereabouts. He had passed the message on. This fact comforted us in our private oppressive moments of consciousness of duty abandoned, of scandal, of fraternal and wifely betrayal. These moments were fleeting, easily chased away. Consequences, Fansha, Pierce and all the rest of them could not be allowed to raise their heads. That way reality lay.

There was another time, when the inevitability of our return struck me with an unendurable force. To Etti, valiantly flippant again, though I was sure my desperation and earnestness must show through, I suggested, 'Let's elope.'

Was it whimsical, the response she made?

'You know I can't elope with you, Marty. You have no prospects.'

I remember how cold I felt despite the close oppressive midday heat when she made that statement, a sudden physical sensation of iciness deep in my chest to match her impassive feminine coldness. It was true. Maybe that was why I was convinced she meant it. That, and the cold reality of our situation rearing up.

I had no prospects; my whole existence was a negation of prospects. While the man she was married to, my brother, loomed before her, remote but fixed, planted like an oak in his fields in Fansha, waiting for her to be restored to him, to enclose her in his broad acres, to clasp her to his bosom, large and solid and dependable. We were both in our separate

252

ways depending on Pierce. To be good, to be forgiving and understanding and nobly deceived as only Pierce could be.

And yet, with a part of me, I admired this coldness of hers. For the first time I felt she was worthy of my brother. This was what they shared maybe and what they confided in each other, this mundane rigour and modest ambition and trust in the future.

Did that exchange take place on the day of the storm? No, I do not think so, because after that moment of truth, there was time still left to us for dreaming and forgetfulness. There was time to banish the chill from my heart, to put those thoughts out of my head so that her words represented only a momentary bleakness in the intoxicating golden light of our time in France.

54

It was the day of the thunderstorm that everything changed.

On the racecourse that afternoon, everything was already different and vaguely disturbing. The green lawns dull and flat and unshadowed, the trees above them perfectly still and opaque in their blackness. The light monotone, so that the golden faces of yesterday looked newly pale and tired and the sparkle of their jewelled bits and bobs put on the cheap sad lustre of gilt.

In that grey, over-warm, expectant atmosphere, we wandered mutely to and fro, clammy, and consumed with fatigue suddenly, the childish urgency of betting and winning mislaid somewhere in the greater expectancy of what was brewing. For deliverance, we watched for signs, not the insouciantly cocky demeanour of the jockeys nor the ever-changing electronic codes on the screens, but the lowering dark blanket of portentous sky.

Soon, the greyness became tinged with mauve; and then after another while this was replaced by a greenish phosphorescence in the falling light that had a blatantly ominous quality to it. Still the racing went on, the horses cantering down to the start, the punters milling around the windows of the Pari-Mutuel to lay their bets. But the frenetic voice of the commentator sounded muffled and remote like a reassuringly optimistic voice on the radio when the warplanes are already over the city. And the shouts of encouragement, allez Jarnet, allez Jarnet, to the favourite as his horse galloped, splay-legged and sweating, to the post were subdued and uncertain. As if his run was revealed to them in the same moment as an act of vanity and irrelevance.

The deluge began. Tacit apprehension turned to relieved outbursts of laughter as the crowd raced as one man for shelter under the canopy of the stands, jostling for position on the higher steps out of the rain. In there it was tenuously snug, amid the warm denseness of a thousand damp hushed bodies pressed tightly together under the vast fragility of the white-painted canopy with its new strange hue of under-ripe lime-peel. Thick and viscous as a curtain, the rain beat down, bouncing on the hard abandoned lawns where dark pools of water formed at once as if the earth were welling up from its boiling centre to meet the sky.

The racecourse and the woodland beyond were hidden from view in the tumbling mass of sky pouring down. We might have been the last people in the world observing the Apocalypse. To the right, too long for comfort, an acid-yellow splash of lightning glowed. Full in our faces, a neon-pink fork glinted arrogantly with a fearsome crackle. At each flash of terrible light with its concurrent wave of thunder, a tremulous sigh went up from the crowd, half delight, half fear.

Gradually it eased off. The rumbles faded, rays of washed yellow light splashed the lawns and the rain died into a light quiescent drizzle. A fresh file of horses began their promenade around the paddock. The keener punters set off with sodden newspapers on their heads to stand under the dripping trees and assess their chances. The sun, scrubbed, diluted, slightly wan, took up position again, the lawns began to steam gently, and the rain stopped altogether.

There were still another couple of races to go on the card. But somehow we had lost the stomach for further engagement. My fervour had trickled away into the sands, I was newly

255

troubled by the thought of Missy. She had been all alone during the storm in the gloom of the hotel room, lit with electric flashes and vibrating with the noisy claps of the thunder. She could hardly have continued to sleep through it. She would be frightened to death. I found myself in a state of anxiety and fear that I could not put to flight.

'Missy must have been scared to death,' Etti murmured. She had removed her dark glasses and her anxiety made furrows across her forehead.

There was no need for me to say anything. We left the track at once and took a taxi home to the Normandy.

It was late in the long afternoon. Deauville had an air of having been refreshed by a long cool drink. Its purple slated roofs were shining, the hot colours of the flowers in the public garden new-dyed, the fall of the fountains replenished, the garçons bearing drinks on trays to the terrasses and putting them down with a flourish as we passed, boyish and smiling. The smell of joints roasting for early dinners wafted in through the windows of the taxi. I saw again the ruthless carelessness of the town and our precarious place in it and was pierced with a troubled sense of nostalgia. As if it were already receding into the past and I was seeing it with the inward eye of memory.

I knew the time had come for me to broach with Etti the subject of what we were to do. At the same time, I was terribly frightened by the prospect. Fearful that she would insist that our time was up, that she would tell me she wanted to go back, that she would not agree now to continuing on to Provence as we had intended.

All that, the Brigitte Bardot scheme, seemed such a long time ago. From an absurdly innocent time as if we were children when we had made our plans. If we stayed much longer in Deauville, Etti was surely unlikely to agree to carry on south in search of Brigitte. We have stayed away too long, she would say, we must go back. I was convinced suddenly that this was what she must say.

Each day that we remained here seemed to me to be won from time and from Etti's impassiveness with the lucky gratuitousness of a hundred-to-one gamble. From somewhere I would have to conjure up some argument to counteract hers. There was Missy, of course, to be used as a weapon. What were we to do with Missy? We have pleased ourselves, I would claim, however pompous and self-righteous it might sound, and neglected our charge.

But we are also neglecting Pierce, she would protest. What must I say to gainsay that? To convince her to continue with our folly?

As we entered the hotel room, the telephone was ringing. It was room service, I assumed. No reason not to. Who else in the world had our number in our de luxe hideaway in Deauville? The drowsy little freak scrabbled towards us, making low complaining mewls in greeting.

Ask them to send up the usual, I called out to Etti, as I went through to the bathroom. A glass or two of champagne, I figured, would assist me in my case. I shut the door and ran the water for a bath.

When I turned off the tap I heard Etti call out to me. Marty, Marty, she was calling, in a note high and strange. Maybe she had been calling to me for some time and I had not heard her over the splash of the water.

I opened the bathroom door. She was standing woodenly by the small table, gripping its edge as if she might otherwise fall to the floor. Missy was mewling at her knees, pleading for attention. Etti was paying no attention to her at all. I went to her and took the telephone from her hand.

'It's Fintan,' she whispered. 'He wants to talk to you.'

I noticed that her face was drained of colour.

'What's up?' I demanded, sharply, to hide my fear.

257

She turned away and with the slow laboured movements of an old woman went and sat on the bed. Hello, I said warily into the telephone.

I remember Fintan's voice, oddly close and intimate, hesitant, full of sympathy for all our plights. But there was repressed anger and exasperation in it too. He had spent the day trying to track us down in Deauville, he told me. And then, all afternoon after the Normandy had confirmed our residence, we had been out, out of reach.

'Brace yourself, Marty,' he said. 'I have to tell you some bad news.'

Pierce, he said, had been involved in an accident. On the Norton. Somewhere near Enniscorthy, he had run into the wall of a bridge. He had been on his way to France to fetch us back. Fintan had been able to bring himself to tell Etti only that Pierce was badly hurt. But the truth was in fact worse, much worse.

Killed instantly, the Guards had assured him. If that was any consolation. I would have to break it to Etti.

I didn't want to hear any more. I wanted to put the phone down.

'Wait, Marty,' Fintan said in a warning tone. 'We have to talk about the arrangements.'

Fintan had made the arrangements. The funeral was waiting on our return. He had taken the liberty of booking tickets for us from Paris for the following morning. He could imagine how difficult it would be, in the circumstances, for us to have to do that kind of thing ourselves. We should be at Charles de Gaulle Airport by nine. At the Dublin end, Raffles would be there to pick us up.

Throughout the whole conversation with Fintan, his voice flat with that repressed accusation resounding horribly in my head, I said not a word. Except at the end, when Fintan had finished telling me about the arrangements and asked, with that edge of exasperation again, 'You will be there, won't you? You'll be at the airport?' Doubting even that. And for a moment I did hesitate and I looked across at Etti's hunched form on the bed and then I said, 'Yes, Fintan. We'll be there' Then I must have put the phone down.

I suppose it was my silence that let Etti know for sure. She raised her head from the pillow, her complexion wearing its new consistency and colour of stone and looked past me with that stony face.

'We are going back to a funeral,' she announced to the empty gilded room. 'My husband's funeral.'

55

In a while, after I had considered what to do, I rang for a large cognac and some warm milk and pains au chocolat to be sent up. Etti was huddled on the bed, her face turned from me. The cognac I mutely left for her on the bedside table.

For Missy I prepared a plate of the sweet warm milky mush that she was fond of. I broke open several green capsules, as many as I thought she could endure without throwing up. For the last time, I prepared her supper, mixing the granules of Dalmane into the mush with a silver teaspoon with the Normandy crest on it. And for the last time I intently watched her eat. It must have had not too bitter a taste because she ate it up without too much coaxing. Anyway, she usually had quite a good appetite at supper-time.

I dressed her then in her smart linen coat and carried her downstairs as if for her evening promenade along the planches. Already she was growing sleepy, her head lolling to one side, her tongue protruding through her teeth.

I placed her gently in her basket in the jeep and drove out of Deauville, deep into the countryside. With undue care as if a little drunk, I drove around the small roads of that little bit of Normandy for a long time. Once, I parked in the square of a small pastoral village and drank a glass of red wine at the café, outside at a pavement table. I remember the look of nightmare that village square wore in the gathering dusk. How the old men drinking their evening coffees and

260

calvados seemed to throw knowing and malicious sidelong glances towards me as they would at a man wanted for murder. I knocked back the wine and took refuge in the country lanes again. The gloomy fields around me were no more forgiving but then I did not expect nor ask forgiveness.

When I had judged that Missy was no longer breathing, I climbed over a gate into a field with the small still-warm body in my arms and walked through the long grass to a ragged line of low poplars at its end. A crescent moon was coldly blazing, lighting my way.

I would have liked to bury her deep and safe in the ground but I had no implement with which to dig a hole. I laid her down in a hollow under a tree and covered her over with sheaves of grass, in the hope that she would have disappeared into the earth before some voracious farm dog or bird of prey could find her. This hope, I knew, was vain. Then I drove back to Deauville.

Etti had packed. She was sitting upright in the pink brocade and gilded fastness of the Louis Quatorze style chair, wearing her black cocktail jacket, her small suitcase prim and fastened at her feet. The wardrobe doors were swinging open. I could see still hanging inside the gay flimsy dresses I had chosen for her to wear to the races, left for the housemaid to find.

She made no enquiries as to where I had been or what I had done. She did not speak a word at all to me. I saw that she had excised from her heart all that we had been, all that we had shared. In the grey dawn, we drove south, alone, to Paris.

56

THE LIVID SHADES of things in this autumn fog. Round grey shapes of the grazing sheep, the bare branches bluish above my head, their fingers vanishing into cloud. Moss in clumps on the bark where I rest my head. Winter moss, yellowy-green. Like chartreuse. One of those fiesta drinks, turquoise, pink, citron, I would summon the garçon to bring, for Etti to try under the hot striped awnings of Deauville . . . My hands wintry white already. They were brown then. Etti's were paler. The gold of the pagan tribes of the south.

Raffles was on at me again about the dosing for the fluke. We won't have any trouble with fluke, I told him. We didn't have the weather for it. He looked at me reproachfully, that sideways look he has adopted with me.

'Your brother would dose,' he said.

'Go ahead so,' I told him.

I'm bet to the ropes. That's what Young Delaney would say. Then he'd go up the field and hack at a ditch with his slasher. He'll be calling up any day now with the rent for the fields. Will he don the good suit and tie for me like he did for Pierce? Here under my tree, I wait for him to appear and cut across my vision on his way to Etti. To Etti to whom he is paying assiduous court. I will be informing him when he comes that his tenure is up, he won't be getting the Hawkins fields on hire any more. I'm in charge here now.

He will put up a fight. There's a new determination in Young Delaney, now that he's all alone without his mother.

She never woke up from the knife after having her new hip put in. We were in Deauville at the time. It was the heart, they said, the heart gave out. Her heart was weak. I could have told them that.

Pierce attended the funeral. On our behalf as well as his own. In the right place at the right time, that was always Pierce. He didn't look well, they tell me. He was drinking.

'Pierce was never a drinker. Was he, Marty?' demanded Raffles. Wounded at the revelation of this hidden side to Pierce.

Not too drunken however to pay a call on Philly Garnett that morning as he set out for France to fetch us home. And return to me my half of Foilmore. Chivalrous, magnanimous Pierce.

'Too good for this life,' says Raffles.

This has become the refrain in Toby's. Too good for this life. Laddy gives me a nod and then turns away from me and looks up at the television, his hand shading his eye. His pain and distress at the sight of me is, I reckon, real enough.

What will Young Delaney say when he learns about Etti's baby? Would he be happy and willing to play father to this child of mine?

'Don't say that.' Etti gritted her teeth. 'Don't ever say that again. For all they know, it's Pierce's baby.'

I would prefer if it were Pierce's baby. I am happier with the things of others around me, clean, untainted. But I will never let Young Delaney have it. I will never let him have Etti.

'Put it behind you.' That was Fintan's advice. 'That's the only thing you can do. Go home and look after Etti.'

My white hands tremble in the damp chill of the field. Not a day for my tree, no question. Folly to lie here, on the sweaty leathery grass, wrapped in this grey coat of wet fog. Etti averts her face from me. In every young ewe, I see Missy's ghost. So

263

many ghosts parading the length and breadth of Foilmore. You'll catch your death, murmurs Nancy. Catch your death, Marty, catch your death, murmurs Pierce, noble and tender, out of the low ethereal blanket of the sky.